Love you man!

THE TRIBUNALS

THE TRIBUNALS

DAVID SPIVAK

To my Mom & Dad

CONTENTS

——

CHAPTER 1

———

The air was suffocating. Stale air has a way of making one feel that way. A slow, steady suffocation. Jaym stood in the massive square, two levels underground, where nearly a thousand people had been gathered for hours on end to watch the trial of Thaddeus Stevenson. Jaym's legs trembled—he hadn't stood this long in his life. *It must be hour five at this point.* Even worse, his neck was stiff from craning up at the large screens hanging in the cavernous hall. *How much longer can this go on?*

"Do you regret what you have done?" Chief Justice Connally asked. His voice was shrill as it came out of the speakers. Connally was nearly a mile away, above ground in the Grand Tribunal Hall. The crowd was tense as the camera lens panned to Thaddeus, projecting the events on the large screens in the cavern.

"I do not." Thaddeus answered simply, with a straight face and no emotion. The wrinkled skin around his eyes sagged and his face looked tired. *When did he get so old?*

"You nearly destabilized our entire sustenance system. Singlehandedly, I might add. Food rations and distribution are the lifeblood of our society, and this city's longevity could've been in jeopardy had you not been discovered. As someone who pledged themselves to protecting this city and ensuring the perseverance of its people, how can you not have regret?"

People across New Boston were tuning in to what was one of the most important trials in recent time. Thaddeus Stevenson was revered across the entire city. He was often seen visiting the various city squares, orphanages, and food halls, meeting with people from all levels of society. For years, he had been the Secretary of Sustenance, overseeing the city's vertical farms as well as its food storage and distribution facilities, and managing the ration statutes. Nothing was in abundance in New Boston, especially food. Crops had to be grown in ventilated buildings, as the air was too poisonous outside. Other than a few indoor chicken coops, simple vegetables and grains were the basis of New Boston agriculture. Much of the food was condensed into processed cubes and infused with synthetic nutrients—efficient to consume, no need to cook.

Somehow things had always worked out okay with Thaddeus at the helm. Often, he came through the city's lower levels, where the poor lived and underground markets thrived, bringing loaves of freshly baked bread to hand out to children, the elderly, and those who looked like they were barely hanging on. He would not only meander through the subterranean squares and gathering places, but also through the Furrows: the seemingly endless labyrinth of tunneled streets and alleys that weaved together the city's underground.

Jaym thought back to when he had last seen Thaddeus. It had been a few months back, when the Secretary had visited his old job at one of the city granaries. Jaym had been pushing a wheelbarrow filled with corn to a storage facility when

Thaddeus strode in, accompanied by the foreman. Thaddeus wore a long, dark blue robe that flowed as he walked. The luxurious clothing stood out against the industrial machinery. He smiled as he inspected the workers and process lines. As a member of the city's government, he was clearly wealthy. He lived high up in New Boston's skyscrapers, where sunlight streamed through and the air was almost fresh. But unlike the rest of the aristocrats, he had a kind, gentle demeanor. He didn't seem uncomfortable as he moved about the granary. The rich rarely came down to the city's ground floor, and almost never went below to the lower levels. And on the rare occasion when they did, they would travel with heavily armed guards and police, clearly itching to return to the higher, private levels of the city.

In fact, Thaddeus had been an almost constant presence in the Furrows. Jaym recalled being first struck by the Secretary's opulent presence when he had visited the orphanage Jaym had grown up in. All the children would run to Thaddeus and tug on his flowing robe as he handed out treats and bread. Throughout his childhood and now as a ripe nineteen-year-old, Jaym felt a connection and closeness to the old man.

Jaym was fixated on how Thaddeus remained calm, almost serene. *He had to have known this would happen at some point. He couldn't get away with it forever. Has he been living in fear for all these years?*

In an even tone, Thaddeus responded to the Chief Justice's question. "I do not regret my actions. I tried to increase the rations for many years but was overruled by the Council of Chief Justices—my resolutions were voted down by many of you through the years. The rations are simply not enough for the majority of the city to survive. When I took on my Secretary position, I pledged to do whatever I could to provide effective sustenance to all citizens of New Boston. I believe the actions that I took were in line with that pledge. So again, no, I do not regret my actions, Chief Justice."

The crowd murmured. A few even shouted in support. Jaym looked around, trying to see where the shouting was coming from. For the first time he noticed armed guards around the cavern, all tense and at the ready. The more he looked, the more guards he noticed. *They're clearly prepared for the worst.*

It had become well known over the past few years that Thaddeus was not merely bringing warm bread down to Furrows, but that he had been orchestrating much larger schemes when it came to food smuggling. Though no one spoke of it explicitly, undue arrivals of food throughout the Furrows were surely his doing. In recent years, large amounts of grain would appear in distribution centers, the underground markets would have an influx of canned beans, and on rare occasions, fresh vegetables would appear.

The nine Chief Justices all had grave faces as they sat in a semicircle several feet above everyone else. Like Thaddeus, they wore dark robes, but they did not seem half as worn and tired; rather, they looked of good health and gave off a wise, prudent aura. The camera then began to pan from the Justices' bench to the full Tribunal hall. Jaym wished he wasn't so captivated by the trial. But like everyone else packed into the crowded cavern, he couldn't pull his eyes away from the screen. The Grand Tribunal Hall was massive, with dark mahogany walls climbing several stories high and large, imposing chandeliers hanging along the perimeter. Above the bench, the seal of New Boston hung on the wall, encased in gold: a laurel wreath framing Lady Justice holding up a scale.

The justices all gazed at Thaddeus with stern faces, clearly disapproving of the betrayal from someone among their ranks. "But you also pledged to ensure order and justice was maintained in this city, did you not?" The question came from Chief Justice Gregorius Marks. While no Chief Justice was more important than the others, Marks was the most senior and often regarded as the city's chief executive. He maintained an even face while speaking, looking neither angry nor happy. His tone seemed overly dramatic, as if he were feigning confusion.

Thaddeus opened his mouth to speak but Marks cut him off. "We all wish we had bountiful food. We all wish the air wasn't poisoned and we didn't have to take measures to protect our lungs on a daily basis. We all wish we could live with plenty of space out in the countryside. But we live in this world, in a reality grounded in the need to be conservative. We must consider the needs of the greater whole over ourselves. And you, Thaddeus, threatened the very nature of the stability of our society, sacrificing longevity for short term desires. You showed no concern for the tomorrow, but only for today. That is your gravest crime—not merely the stealing and breaking of the ration system, but your disdain for the fragility of the system's endurance."

The other Chief Justices all nodded in agreement. Marks's words hung in the air, creating a sense of tension and dread. Everyone was waiting for Thaddeus's response. He looked Marks directly in the eye and said, "You and I both know whose longevity the ration system is supporting, Chief Justice."

Marks's face immediately turned sour, to a scowl. He stood and said, "Unless my colleagues have further questions, the Chief Justices will now deliberate and determine the verdict of this Tribunal." Marks swiftly turned and descended into a chamber beyond the bench, followed by the rest of the council.

Jaym could feel himself tensing up. *Sticking by his morals is a surefire way to get himself killed. But Thaddeus isn't stupid, he knows what he's doing.* He looked about the cavern, listening in on the bits of murmuring that had broken out in an effort to distract himself. *I wonder where Beck is. He was supposed to meet me here.* The room was filled to the brim with people. The guards were still present, gripping loaded semiautomatic guns. People talked in generally hushed voices. This was the first time ever that a member of high society had committed so grave an act, and the first time in nearly ten years that the Supreme Tribunal had been called to order.

The Tribunal system was the foundation of New Boston's government, and was the reason credited for the city's survival the past hundred years. In the tumultuous years prior to the city's independence, when the governments of old disintegrated, a council of elders had convened to make important decisions on behalf of the people. This evolved into a complex system of Tribunal Councils, enacting policies and providing arbitration. There were several lower Tribunals for various subjects and crimes, typically presided over by one of the nine Chief Justices. The Supreme Tribunal was only called upon for the highest of crimes. The last time it was called to order, the city nearly broke out in a civil war.

Jaym's eyes drifted to the edge of the room, trying to spot Beck. *Useless.* The cavern had many balconies and levels, and along the outer wall were dozens of large openings to the various tunnels and alleys that spread out to the Furrows and lower city levels. Jaym contemplated how many people could feasibly fit in the hall. *Ten thousand, at the very least. Still with some room to move about.* There were dozens of these caverns dotting the city. Jaym felt a pang of anxiety shoot through his body as he was overcome with a momentary feeling of claustrophobia. He closed his eyes and took a deep breath, allowing the feeling to pass. He rarely felt distressed underground, but it wasn't often the crowds were this thick.

In the early years of New Boston, shortly after the city's founding in 2119, the urban designers had built just as much below ground as they did above. The world was a scary place back then: after rising sea levels began altering geopolitical boundaries, countries opened up their nuclear arsenals and a war the likes of which had never before been seen ensued. New Boston had prepared for the worst, building an underground system capable of housing the city's population, should it be attacked, with cavern-like halls to serve as mass shelters. Other cities did the same. Despite never being bombed, many people chose to live underground in the city's early years out of fear. Thus, the underground thrived, with its sophisticated street-like system connecting the various halls, squares, markets—everything.

Eventually, the world calmed down. While several cities survived, they all remained insular. The nuclear fallout had made the world all but uninhabitable. In the few cities that dotted the land, people could find shelter, food, and protection from the deadly air in the form of daily pills. These cities continued to govern themselves, becoming pseudo-states. While each city's governments remained occasionally in contact with others, inter-city travel ceased. The land between cities was a barren wasteland. The nearest city, New Washington, was hours away.

Inside New Boston, people began moving above ground, living in the city's new skyscrapers that allowed for fresher air and light. But life continued teeming in the lower levels. Once one reached the third and deepest sublevel, things started to get dark: both physically, as less power was allotted to those deepest levels, and in a graver sense. Drugs, brothels, things people didn't want noticed. The majority of New Bostoners avoided going that deep at all costs.

Suddenly, the screen came back to life. The crowd let out a short, exasperated breath, and the entire room vibrated. Jaym's eyes flitted about, anxiously taking stock. He became fixated again on the guards at various points around the hall, who had tensed up as the room buzzed with anticipation. Armed and ready—nervous for a repetition of what happened the last time the Supreme Tribunal was called to order. The crowds fell quiet as the camera focused on the Chief Justices exiting their chamber.

The left side of the screen showed Thaddeus's face: stern and emotionless. The right side focused on the Justices on the bench, ready to announce the verdict. After settling into the central high-backed chair, Chief Justice Marks spoke. "It isn't often the Supreme Tribunal is called to order, so I hope all citizens of New Boston have been closely following these events. We live in a delicate society, one that narrowly escaped the ultimate destruction all those years ago. We should appreciate and honor the system in place to ensure that every citizen of the city can live a full, healthy life. No citizen, not even Secretaries and those in high positions within our government, can challenge our system and way of life. We—as the guardians of the rule of law, the glue that holds this city together—will do everything in our power to protect the system. As we always say, 'Justice is about all of us.'" Marks leaned back, his face rigid as steel.

Chief Justice Connally spoke next. "On the matter of Thaddeus Stevenson, we, the Chief Justices of the Supreme Tribunal, find one count guilty of breaking the ration laws, one count guilty of subversion of the City, and one count guilty of lying to government officials. As such, he is sentenced to death."

Shouts and cries erupted around Jaym. The policemen trained their weapons on the crowd, ready to pounce at any moment. More noise was heard from the Tribunal hall onscreen, as Marks banged his gavel to quiet the crowd. Thaddeus didn't move a muscle—his face was as still as stone. Guards had appeared on either side of his chair and began escorting him away, and the Justices slowly retreated to their chamber again. Minutes later, the screen went dark.

CHAPTER 2

———

Shouts and screams erupted around the room. Jaym looked about quickly, trying to figure out what was happening. Scuffles were breaking out between people and the guards, as the gravity of the sentence set in. The crowd had already begun to disperse, with those nearest the tunnels escaping before the scene could get worse. Overlaying the surging violence, a familiar voice began speaking.

"Thank you for tuning in to today's Tribunal trial. The Tribunal system is the central pillar to ensuring justice and order in our society. Please calmly continue about your day."

The calm, almost serene voice reverberated over the agitated crowd. On the bright screens dotting major intersections, Jaym could see the all-too-familiar face speaking the words, repeating every few minutes. Velma. Her dark brown hair was tied up in a bun, and she wore a blue dress with a broach of the golden seal on her lapel. Velma's face graced the many news screens across the city daily, delivering city news, and other important messages. Some people stopped to watch Velma, but most continued hurrying out of the hall. Though people did seem to be less frenzied after seeing the familiar face. Her voice only made Jaym feel more on edge as he worked his way out of crowds. Try as he might, he couldn't escape her soft smile. It seemed everywhere he turned she looked down at him, with her smooth voice ringing throughout the city.

Jaym allowed himself to be taken in by the flow of people leaving the hall. His mind was racing, trying to make sense of what had just happened. He didn't even know where the crowd was leading him, but he followed unrelentingly. *Thaddeus sentenced to death ... when was the last time a secretary was punished by the government? They never take out one of their own.* Jaym felt a strange, impending dread wrenching in his stomach. Thaddeus's trial had capped a month-long stretch of gloom in the city. Food rations were at an all-time low and the city felt on edge. But as always, life would go on.

Out of the cavern, things were already returning to normal. Merchants laid out their wares and food on rickety stands, haggling with parents as their children ran through the stalls. Beggars played rusty instruments, looking for someone to guiltily give them a coin or two. Sly looking men leaned against the grimy walls, waiting for someone to come and ask about where to find more illicit goods.

"Hey, watch out! You step on anything, you buy it!"

Jaym jumped back from the blanket on the ground, and the random assortment of goods on top of it.

"Sorry, sorry," he said, looking down at the seller's wares. A set of teacups, some dull silverware, chipped china plates, a few old magazines. He kept on his way, stopping at a food cart a few stalls down. Jaym eyed the carts offerings: mostly various dark-colored cubes of processed foods. Higher up on the cart was a small splattering of a few days old fruit, including a basket of apples.

"How much for an apple?" Jaym asked.

"Three bucks."

We all deserve a treat after watching that. "I'll take it." He bit into the fruit, relishing the crunch and juice that followed. He realized he hadn't eaten all day. He had woken up late after a few too many drinks last night and rushed to get to the trial and find Beck. Suddenly a wave of panic came over him. *I didn't take my KIP this morning.* He rushed down the street to the small square in the center. There, reassuringly, was a machine standing along the far wall, just outside the Ration Distribution Center. Jaym went to the KIP dispenser and quickly deposited a coin. He pressed the button vigorously, knowing full well he couldn't speed up the machine's process. A small white pill dropped into the machine's bin, and Jaym gulped it down dry.

He turned and leaned against the wall, letting out a sigh of relief. Every person in New Boston, rich or poor, took a potassium-iodine pill, or KIP, daily. The pill protected against the still radioactive air of New Boston. A few days without taking a KIP, and the body would start to deteriorate, leading to risk of infection, weakened bone strength, and eventually death. After the nuclear wars of 2100, the air across the former United States was completely contaminated. The sophistication of the bombs had resulted in a fall-out period that would go on for centuries, so the world had to learn to live with the tainted, deadly air. KIPs kept the human body resilient. And slowly the world became accustomed to the acrid, harsh taste of the air.

Jaym bit back into the apple. *Careless, Jaym. Getting sick isn't going to help anything.* He found an elevator nearby that would lead him down to the city's lowest level, Sub3, and continued on. He jumped into the metal box, which must've had a dozen people piled in, and was soon descending downwards. A few moments later, the crowds and clamor of the market were gone, and Jaym exited onto a dark, narrow street. The Furrows.

While most people avoided the Furrows, Jaym was grateful as he looked around. To Jaym, the Furrows were home. He grew up running through the maze of streets and alleys, jumping from balconies in the various sized halls and squares that served as the small hubs of the underground. The majority of New Boston's population lived and worked at the ground level of the city, or one to two levels above. But it was sublevel three where Jaym felt the most at home. Jaym took in the musty smell and stopped to glance around. Dim streetlights illuminated the dirty stone streets and mold growing on the damp walls. Graffiti was plastered over a nearby sign. Breathing it all in, Jaym felt safe. Secure. He knew immediately where he was and began heading to the most familiar place for him in the city: Dante's.

A worn, wooden sign with the name painted in white hung outside the bar. As always, it hung waiting for a breeze to give it a push and allow it to swing along its short metal rod. But this deep underground, the air was as stale as it could get—there was no breeze here. Below the sign was a metal door with two small, adjacent windows on either side. The glass hadn't been cleaned in ages, so one could barely see what was happening inside. Jaym pushed open the door and walked in.

The bar was dimly lit and sparsely populated. A few old men, regulars, sat at the table up front playing cards. One older woman read a book at a high top, while sipping some sort of dark drink. Behind the bar was Dante, with his token burly mustache and white beard. He wore his standard outfit: a discolored button-down shirt and an old, woolen vest.

Sitting at the bar was Jaym's longtime best friend, Beck. Even seated, Beck's height was still apparent. His broad shoulders tapered down to the chair, with his muscles bulging beneath his shirt. Jaym had always hated how much taller and stronger Beck was than him, despite being nearly a whole year younger.

Neither Dante nor Beck had noticed Jaym walk in; they were too engrossed in whatever conversation they were having. Jaym knew the topic before he even began listening. There was only one thing people were talking about today.

"The punishment was way too much. There must be more we don't know!" Beck's voice crescendoed as he finished the sentence, gesturing so aggressively that he would've spilled the drink in his hand if it weren't already nearly empty.

"I'm telling you they're making an *example* of him, Beck. They're not stupid. They know other secretaries and government officials bend the rules too. But if they did anything more drastic, things could get bad. Like ten years ago bad. I still can't believe Thaddeus got away with it for this long." Dante topped Beck's glass off, pouring from an unlabeled glass bottle.

Jaym approached the bar. "Hey Dante, ever think about cleaning those windows?"

"And have my bar be completely exposed to the outside street, with all its wanderers, thieves, and government watchdogs meandering about? Hell no! The more grime the better. In fact, I think they could use a fresh coat of healthy dirt."

Jaym smiled and shook hands with Dante. The old barkeep always had a way of lightening any situation, no matter how grim.

Beck looked up at Jaym and said, "Where were you? I thought we were meeting in the northeast corner of the hall?"

"I was there! I didn't see you. Place was jam-packed—I can't remember the last time I saw the hall filled to the brim like that."

"Maybe grow a few more inches!" Beck teased, flashing his pearly white teeth—an uncommon feature for someone who grew up in the Furrows. Jaym knew that Beck was very proud of them and brushed vigorously each night. He also never drank the dark rum, only the clear vodka, out of fear of staining them. Jaym glared back and gave him a friendly shove.

"Sounds like it was as crowded as the last Supreme Tribunal ten years ago," Dante interjected. "It was hell that time, way too many people. Glad I stayed here and watched from the comfort of the bar. With a nice, stiff drink to keep me company." Dante poured a glass of dark liquid and handed it to Jaym.

They called the dark drink "rum," though it tasted nothing like the rum of bygone days. At least that's what people said. No one had tasted that kind of rum in decades. Jaym took a swig and grimaced. No matter how many times he drank the cheap alcohol, he'd never get used to the bitter taste and burning sensation in the back of his throat. There wasn't much variety in alcohol available in New Boston—it was all made with leftover grains, typically the rejected stalks that weren't suitable for actual food. Dark alcohol was rum, clear was vodka, and most bars didn't have anything else to offer. You could splash a few drops of synthetic sugar to cut the harshness, but you could never quite get rid of the bitterness. Though there were rumors that, up in the high levels of the city, they had alcohol that actually had some enjoyable taste.

"Didn't want to stick around for the brawl?" Jaym asked Beck.

"I got a few good punches in and called it a day," Beck answered, throwing his fists up and shadowboxing. "I was upset. I *am* upset. The Justices went too hard on old Thaddeus. He was a good man, one who actually cared about the real people of this city, not the ones living in their high towers." Jaym nodded. "A real shame. But I don't know why anyone is surprised. After he stood up to the Council like that ... we all knew exactly what he had coming."

"True, but with everything going on right now, the Chief Justices must know this isn't going to be something people accept easily," Dante said, while pouring himself another drink.

Beck chimed in. "People are just angry. There hasn't been any explanation for the rations getting smaller. You can get arrested these days for just looking at a police officer the wrong way. This city is going to shit, I tell you."

"Did you know him, Dante?" Jaym asked.

"He actually would come in here for a drink every once in a while," Dante answered. "Told me once he liked how he could enjoy some peace and quiet down here. Last time I saw him— must've been a few months back—he wasn't exactly talking sense. Mostly mumbling to himself about the ration system, how it could only continue for so long. I think if the police hadn't caught him, he would've turned himself in or something soon. It just looked like he couldn't take it anymore." A few other men called to Dante, who moved down the bar.

Jaym looked over at Beck, who stared ahead blankly, sipping his drink. The glass looked small in his large hands. Jaym could see dried blood caked over a few fingers, though it was hard to tell how long the blood had been dried there. Jaym had never seen Beck's hands very clean. The dirt was sewn in so deep that his hands were almost leather-like. He and Jaym both worked for the construction bureau at the moment. They had frequently moved around jobs in the city over the past three years since they had finished primary school. Well, since Jaym had finished—Beck decided to drop out at fifteen to follow Jaym into the workforce, as most kids did when they turned sixteen. The rich kids continued their studies in secondary school, and then ultimately in the Academy—where they'd go on to fill their parents' roles as the real movers and shakers of New Boston.

Jaym and Beck had always stuck together. They had grown up in the same orphanage, chased each other through the Furrows from as soon as they could walk. Beck, ever the mischievous one, finding ways to get them into trouble and Jaym rescuing them out of it. Jaym sometimes wondered if he had been born in this city purely to make sure Beck got home to his own bed at night.

"Hey, guess who I ran into today. Our old friend Heath."

Jaym lowered his gaze. "That guy? He's not our friend, Beck."

"Sure he is! He's a good guy. We've basically known him our entire lives. But anyways, he said he's got a few jobs he could use help with. We both know the rumors about a pay cut coming soon. And I'm already low on cash."

"I'll pass," Jaym grunted. "That guy is bad news, Beck. I'm not getting caught up with that and neither should you."

"Come on, Jaym. Let's at least hear what he has to say," Beck chided.

Jaym took another drink, letting the dark liquor overtake his senses. The screen in the corner of the bar began to light up, and a fanfare of music interrupted the bar's quiet atmosphere. *Must be nearly 5 p.m.* The city seal faded away and the nightly news show began playing.

Beck downed the rest of the drink and stood up. "I can't stand to watch this crap. I told Heath I'd stop by tonight. You can join if you want. Unless you want me to go all by myself!" Beck grinned. He knew exactly where to push Jaym. And he always managed to stay upbeat, even when he was angry.

"Fine. I could use some cash too. We're behind on rent for the month, and you owe a third. But I'm making the ultimate call. Dante, what do we owe you?" Jaym called down to Dante at the other end of the bar.

"Don't worry about it, boys. Today was hard enough for all of us. Stay out of trouble."

Jaym and Beck smiled, grateful for the old man's kindness. Both boys had known Dante for nearly their entire lives. When they were younger, they helped clean the bar, picked up shipments and packages, and carried them down through the city streets. He was as close to a father and confidant either had ever had.

Outside the bar, Jaym couldn't tell if it was morning or evening. The street was mostly empty, and the windows of the apartments above were mostly closed. A few drifters dotted the street, most dozed off on the ground. The voices of the news anchors echoed softly from the many screens in the apartments and on street corners, but Jaym did his best to tone them out. *Well maybe whatever job this is will take my mind off things. And I can't let Beck go off on his own.* But as they ventured on, Jaym couldn't stop picturing Thaddeus's strained, worn face. Defeated.

Beck led the way. "Follow me, he told me where to find him."

Jaym shook his head and took in a breath, distancing himself from his inner thoughts. He followed Beck, who was headed down a dark alley nearby. The two were about to head even deeper into the underground.

CHAPTER 3

———

"Watch it kid!"

Jaym jumped back as a drunken man stumbled out into the street, nearly running into him.

"You watch it!" Beck yelled, putting himself between the man and Jaym.

Damn, don't be so jumpy Jaym. He was still wrapping his mind around seeing Heath. He hadn't seen the guy in over a year. Beck was right: they had grown up with Heath. He had lived with his Uncle in the Furrows but had joined the orphanage boys fairly early. His Uncle had been arrested, and ultimately executed, when Heath was only twelve. His crime: peddling Silver, the only drug left in the city. It was highly illegal to have and use, even more illegal to sell. Silver was made with iodine, the same mineral needed to manufacture KIPs. And there was only so much iodine readily accessible.

They continued along, now in one of the deepest sections of Sub3. The streets were barren. The police rarely ventured this far down, and a general rule of "finders keepers" prevailed. It was always nighttime here. The walls of Sub3 were a blend of rock and metal, giving it an industrial, mine-shaft feel. Jaym could barely hear the echoing of Velma's evening news show. Looking around, he saw a shattered news screen. Large cracks ruptured the smooth glass and distorted the pristine faces. People down here didn't want to be bothered by the aristocrats of the upper levels. Down here, a different society was brewing.

People stumbled in and out of bars, and transacted other types of business on the street. Jaym made eye contact with a woman scantily clad in lingerie, leaning against an open door frame. She smiled, beckoning to him. One could find lots of activities in these parts: there were brothels, gambling rooms, the occasional rave. If you were willing to pay, you could find almost anything you wanted.

Beck led the way through the twisting, industrial streets. Eventually they stopped in front of a metal door, and Beck knocked twice. The windows on either side had been boarded up. A few moments later, a thin slat slid open and two dark eyes looked out.

"We're here to see Heath. He's expecting us," Beck said. The eyes stared back for a few seconds.

"What's the password?"

Beck and Jaym looked at each other.

"He didn't tell us," Beck answered.

"No password, no entry." The eyes glared back, and the metal slat began to slide shut.

"We said he's expecting us!" Jaym stepped forward. "You want to explain to him why he had to come let us in himself?"

Beck tried to hide his smirk. "My friend is right. He surely wouldn't be happy about that."

The pair of eyes held their gaze a moment longer, and then the slat closed. Jaym could hear the sound of metal whining and squeaking as the door opened. A burly, muscular man stood in the entryway. His arms were covered in tattoos.

Slung over his shoulder was a black rifle—the same weapon the police had been brandishing earlier in the hall during the trial. The man moved aside, and Beck and Jaym entered. Two other men came up on either side as the first man closed the metal door, securing it with two different locks. "Arms up," one of the men said, as the two patted them down to check for weapons. "They're clean," the other replied to the first man.

They were led through a series of rooms. The place was dark and musty. In one room they passed, Jaym saw men drinking and playing cards. As they passed the open door, the men's laughter abruptly stopped. One even stood up, gripping his gun. But Jaym and Beck were ushered along by the guards before anything could devolve. Passing another room, Jaym saw men counting money, the table covered in stacks of bills and coins. And in a third, he saw men weighing a glittering, shining powder, as others packed it into small pouches—Silver.

Jaym and Beck continued down the hallway until they were led to a door at the end of the hall. The man leading them pushed the door open and they walked inside.

They were in a formal-looking office, though the musty smell remained. A large, stately wooden desk sat in front of them, with two leather chairs facing it. Behind the desk sat Heath, who was writing what seemed to be a letter. He was wearing a dark, pinstripe suit, with a bright, pink tie. His broad shoulders filled out the suit well, and Jaym felt a momentary pang of jealousy that he was the shortest guy in the room. Heath's dark hair was slicked back on his head, and his face was clean shaven.

"Gentleman!" Heath said, as he looked up from his paper. He placed the cap on his pen and stood to greet them. "Good to see you boys."

"Heath, always good to see you," Beck said. He reached

over and shook Heath's hand. Beck turned to Jaym, who was a few steps behind, and flashed a subtle, glaring look. His face emotionless, Jaym stepped forward and reached out his hand.

"Hello Heath. Long time."

Heath smiled at Jaym as they shook hands.

"Likewise, Jaym. I can't remember the last time I saw you. I was just reminiscing to the guys here about our days as kids." He motioned to the corner of the room, where two more guards sat, both with large guns on their laps. "We used to think we ran the Furrows, eh! I guess not much has changed." Heath let out a boisterous laugh. "Please, please, have a seat."

Jaym and Beck settled into the leather seats. Jaym looked about the office. The walls were lined with bookshelves and filled with an assortment of items.

"Those certainly were the days," Beck said. "How's business?"

"Business never sleeps, young Beck. Another nuclear Armageddon could start and we'd still be carrying on as usual down here." Heath leaned back in his chair. "So, what can I help you boys with?"

Heath turned and looked at Jaym. His smile was pleasant enough, but Jaym didn't return a friendly gaze. Despite having grown up together, Jaym had never quite trusted him. Even when they were kids, Heath had seemed to be looking out only for himself. He always had a suspicious tinkle in his eye, as if he were scheming about his next move. Jaym took a deep breath to try and relax.

Beck spoke up. "There's a rumor that we might take a pay cut from our jobs over at the construction bureau soon. If there's anything we can help you out with, we're interested in lending a hand for some extra cash."

Heath smiled. "Well now that is unfortunate. To be honest, Beck, I didn't know if you'd take me up on my offer.

I mostly have a few small jobs, but they won't pay much. Unless..." He looked down to the desk drawers and began tapping his fingers on the desk.

Jaym spoke up. "We're not interested in anything illegal— just need a little bit of extra padding to make rent."

"But we're also not picky," Beck chimed in. "So, if there's anything that'll pay better for two old friends, you know we'd appreciate it."

Beck looked at Jaym and gave a not-so-subtle head nod. Jaym resisted the urge to roll his eyes.

Heath looked up and leaned back in his chair. "Well, I do have one specific job I need some assistance with. It's of the utmost importance to me, for a very significant customer. To be honest, I hadn't thought about it until just now, but I probably can't send one of my guys. Need someone more inconspicuous, who will blend in. Someone like you two." Heath's eyes stared coldly at Jaym. Jaym stared back, trying not to blink. He felt as if Heath were goading him, but he couldn't tell what his eyes were hinting at.

Before Jaym could answer, Beck jumped in. "Sounds like we're the men for the job, Heath. Just tell us exactly what you need us to do."

Heath and Jaym remained locked in eye contact. After a brief pause, Heath broke from their stare and motioned to one of the men in the back corner. His expression resumed its friendly smile from before, as the man brought a box wrapped in brown paper over to his desk. Heath placed his hand gently on the package. "Like I said, precious cargo. He'll know if it's been opened or tampered with, so best to keep it in its pretty packaging."

Heath stood, followed by Beck and Jaym. Heath handed the package to Jaym. "I trust you both. After all, we go way back, don't we?" He continued smiling, though it didn't make Jaym feel any more at ease.

"Can we ask who it's going to?" Jaym asked, accepting the wrapped box.

"I'd rather keep that private as well. This customer is highly ... sensitive. You likely won't even meet him, he's a busy man who employs a staff. If he isn't there, someone else will receive the package on his behalf. Don't be armed when delivering it, and don't do anything stupid."

Jaym spoke again. "How will we know we're delivering it to the right person, if this is so ... sensitive."

Heath paused again before answering, staring at Jaym. He then pulled out a black pen and wrote the letter P on the box. "That'll do—the customer is expecting this, so I don't foresee any issues. You just focus on delivering the package."

"Okay, Heath. That all works for us. You can trust that we'll deliver it safe and sound. We'll go tomorrow, after work. What's the pay?" Beck asked.

Heath opened a drawer to his right and pulled out a wad of cash. He counted out a pile of bills and handed them to Beck, and then another to Jaym. "That's half. Once I confirm with the customer that the package made it, I'll come find you boys at Dante's and give you the second half. I won't make you come all the way back down to my ... humble abode." Heath gave a soft smile as he handed Jaym the cash.

"That works for us. We appreciate it, Heath," Beck said, stuffing the cash into his pocket.

As they turned to go, Jaym realized something. "You haven't told us the destination. I know the customer is sensitive, but we have to know where we're meeting him, right?"

Heath's smile got a bit bigger. "You boys ever been in a penthouse apartment before?"

CHAPTER 4

Jaym breathed in the air. Clean, fresh. *I'm surprised they even need to take KIPs up here.* He and Beck had just emerged from an elevator at New Boston's Justice Square, on the city's ground level. The square was filled with crisp, green synthetic grass. Massive glass skyscrapers towered around the perimeter, and at the far end of the square was the stately Grand Tribunal Hall. It looked imposing—its windowless walls bore down over the square like a fortress, with the modern, dark skyscrapers looming above. The city had grown like a fungus, especially once society emerged from below ground after the nuclear wars subsided.

Jaym stopped to orient himself and ensure they were headed in the right direction. He rarely ventured up into the city's higher levels. People eyed them as they crossed the square. He and Beck stood out in their dirty, grimy clothes. Beck had been anxious to deliver the package, so they hadn't even changed out of their work clothes from the day. Jaym tried to ignore his shoulders tensing up. Lower city folk weren't forbidden to walk around the city, but there were many stories of people being arrested for loitering, trespassing, or some other phony charge just for crossing imaginary lines. And in recent months, those stories had become more and more frequent.

Heath had given them very specific instructions for navigating to their destination. They continued crossing the square, heading into the maze of towering skyscrapers. Most of the buildings were paneled in New Boston's signature dark glass, though one on the square's perimeter was dotted with transparent panes. Through them, Jaym could see bright green plants—one of the many vertical farms dotting New Boston.

As they traversed the square, Jaym stayed fixated on the brown messenger bag over Beck's shoulder with the elusive package within. He felt a brief shudder when he thought about their last encounter with Heath before venturing above ground. He still didn't trust the guy.

"Where do you think you're going?"

Startled, Jaym stopped and looked up. A police officer had rounded the corner and was standing in front of them, just as they reached the perimeter of Justice Square. Beck had almost bumped into the man; his mouth opened but he was so caught off guard that he couldn't get a word out.

Jaym piped up before Beck could. "We're just on our way to deliver a package."

"Yep, no trouble here, sir!" Beck added, regaining his composure. He smiled at the officer, showing off his sterling, white teeth.

The officer reached his hand out. "Lemme see the address."

Jaym wasn't one to get nervous; he had been in many fights and squabbles throughout his youth living in the underbelly of the city. He and Beck had taken on larger groups just the two of them, and had usually come out on top. But this was a different world, high above the parts of the city he knew best. Jaym felt pangs of discomfort and another shudder went through his body.

"Sure. I'll read it out to you," Jaym said. He gestured to Beck, who reached into his messenger bag to retrieve the package. But as Beck started handing the package to Jaym, the officer grabbed it out of his hand. A shock went through Jaym's body, and he saw Beck's eyes go wide. Sensing both their nerves, Jaym spoke quickly. "Don't worry, Beck. This officer knows that this is a very important package, and that its recipient would be incredibly upset, if not downright furious, to know a policeman opened it without his permission just because two young, spry boys like ourselves were delivering it." A sly smile crossed his face, as Jaym's eyes met the officer's.

The policeman held his gaze for a second, and then glanced down at the package's address. Heath had written the elevator numbers on the outside of the package, so they wouldn't forget. The policeman's eyes went wide as he looked back up. Handing the package back to Beck, he said, "No loitering around. Get to your delivery and get back to wherever you came from." And with that, the policeman strode past them, not looking back.

Jaym and Beck looked at each other as they took a sigh of relief. "Man, that could've gone worse."

Beck shrugged. "Oh please, I wasn't going to let him open it."

Jaym let out a laugh. *Oh Beck. Yeah right. You could barely speak up to the guy.*

Beck continued. "You know, it's all about confidence, my dear Jaym. Confidence and acting like you belong." Beck smiled, his grin spreading from cheek to cheek. "I like it up here—so much more room and space. Life feels ... calmer ... slower and less bleak."

"Well, don't get used to it. We clearly stick out."

"*Us?* All I need to do is flash a smile at any passerby and we'll be invited over for afternoon tea and cakes." Beck's smile grew even wider.

"Yeah, okay. Let's just keep moving. I know we'll be fine, but it's just that … I don't trust Heath. He's always looking out for himself, ever since we were kids. I don't know why anything would change now. You saw the … stuff … that he was handling down there…" Jaym's voice trailed off.

"Look, I know he's not exactly dealing with the most legal activities these days. But he's never done anything to betray our trust before. He told me he's learned a ton about the operation since his uncle died. They run a tight ship now. Plus, this is gonna seriously help us this month."

Jaym nodded back, and the two continued on their way. He tried to laugh to himself, to ease his discomfort. *Oh Beck. At least you're always consistent.* For as long as he had known Beck, which was basically his entire life, Beck's confidence had been unabated. Even in the few fights he had lost, he always came out claiming he could've won had he just had a few more punches—that he let the other guy win.

Jaym led them up a staircase to a bustling street. It was a wide boulevard with short, curved trees down the middle. The sun shone down on their faces—a feeling Jaym hadn't felt in a long time. He had only been this high in the city a few times before. Jaym looked up—a few stories higher, a monorail cruised swiftly and silently between the buildings. They both paused and stared up. Beck was gleaming, his face in awe.

"Never seen one before?" Jaym teased.

"What is it?"

"A monorail. An electric train. The rich don't even have to walk between their glass towers. Come on!"

The electric monorail glided along its route, crisscrossing between the monolithic buildings. It weaved around a corner and disappeared.

Despite his jeering, Jaym was also in an awestruck daze. He thought back to the first time he had visited the ground level of the city. It was on a school field trip as a young kid. Every school—even over-crowded PS-46, which served the youth of the lowest city levels—had its students take field trips to tour the Grand Tribunal Hall. He was struck with the same awe then that he felt now—seeing the towering skyscrapers, the opaque reflective glass. He had dreamt of the shiny and gleaming windows for weeks after that trip.

Technically every school in the city was public, though it was well known that the closer to the single digits you got, the more likely it was you came from a high-class home. PS-1 was the city's most illustrious school. It catered to New Boston's top elites, including the children of the Chief Justices, government officials, and other dignitaries. Students were assigned to schools based on their housing locations; a "natural and orderly" way to organize the city's youth and education system. But in reality, it was just one of many invisible, socioeconomic barriers that kept everyone in their proper lanes. No one strayed in New Boston, and social classes didn't mix.

Walking along the boulevard, Jaym kept glancing into the various glass storefronts. A restaurant here, a café there— various stores and merchants. But the large, dark glass walls were opaque to the outside looking in. That was the most common facade one found at this level in the city: dark, unforgiving glass walls that hid everything behind them. The inner workings of the city, the behind-the-scenes artistry. *What could possibly be happening behind all these dark panels? Then again, who can say what's happening throughout all the crusted-over windows of the Furrows, and in the deep levels recesses of the city.*

"This way, Jaym," Beck called out. He was turning the corner off the main boulevard onto a smaller street, and they hopped onto Elevator Fourteen. Unlike the metal industrial elevators underground, this one was glass. It carried them a few more stories up into the city. Here the streets were suspended high above the ground floor, winding between the buildings. Jaym felt exposed and uneasy as they moved along. Soon they were back on what seemed like solid ground—platforms between the skyscrapers. They instinctively moved into the shadows that the buildings cast down.

Jaym felt a sense of comfort wash over him. Shadows were natural to him. Being exposed on the wide boulevard, standing on suspended streets, not knowing who was peering out at him from behind the thousands of dark windows towering above—these things terrified him, sending shivers down his spine. Here in the shadows, he felt in control. There, it was the opposite.

They came to a round clearing. At the far end, a set of double doors stood with "Elevator 26" etched into the stone above. Next to the door was a small screen with a standard keypad. Heath had told them the combination in advance, and, after entering it, the doors sprung open.

"There aren't any guards?" Jaym thought aloud as they entered the elevator.

Beck shrugged. "I guess they never expect to need them this high up. The thing did have a passcode."

"Strange." *They must change the code once we leave…*

The doors automatically closed behind them. A pleasant voice spoke out: "penthouse requested." And soon they were shooting into the sky, flying up to the highest levels of New Boston.

CHAPTER 5

As they flew above buildings, Jaym looked out at the expansive city. He pressed his fingers up against the glass, captivated by the view. At times, he caught glimpses of the city's edge—the buildings abruptly stopped, and a drop off led to a field of large rocks, boulders, and debris that had long since petrified from past skirmishes. It was a natural barricade that had evolved around New Boston in the city's early days. There were dark lakes and rivers, remnants of the old defenses and moats, all poisoned and radioactive now.

The elevator began to slow and soon stopped. "Penthouse, floor eighty-two." The doors opened to a round, serene garden. Elaborate plants and flowers adorned the ground and grew up along the building. While the windows bore the same dark, opaque glass, the penthouse wasn't as stark and foreboding as other buildings. Rather, long wooden beams held the windows together, artistic sculptures flanked the entrance, and a soft fountain bubbled in the center of the courtyard. It was the most beautiful thing Jaym had ever seen, a beauty he didn't know existed throughout the entirety of New Boston. Beck, too, paused to take in the scene.

"Well come on, let's get on with this!" Beck said, interrupting the moment.

They strode up to the set of double doors. Jaym looked anxiously at the confidence with which Beck crossed the courtyard. *He's walking as if he owns the place.* After knocking, a woman dressed in a simple maid's uniform opened the door.

"May I help you?"

Beck inclined his head in a slight bow. "Hello ma'am. We're here to deliver this ultra-important package to … um … Master P." He held out the wrapped package, showcasing the letter.

She eyed them suspiciously. "Come in. Wait here." She led them into the marble foyer and then moved on.

Jaym glared at Beck. "Dude, can you act normal please? What the hell was that bow thing?"

Beck grinned back. "Oh, come on, I'm just acting the part. Look at where we are!" He looked around the room, marveling at the opulence. Jaym had to admit, it was a lot to take in. The entrance had staircases circling to a second floor on both sides of the foyer, framing Jaym and Beck with majestic dignity. On the two walls were matching paintings of flowers and gardens, both in thick, golden frames. Peering up, Jaym gaped at a massive crystal chandelier hanging from the ceiling. The air was fresh and light. A bundle of freshly cut tulips sat in a vase on the table in the center of the entranceway.

Beck began walking forward toward the main hallway leading deeper into the household. "Where are you going?" Jaym whispered.

"Just a little bit of exploring! Come on, who knows the next time we'll be in a place like this. I gotta see what else is here." Beck's cunning smile spread across his face.

"Beck! This is a stupid idea!" Jaym repeated Beck's name but to no avail, as his friend continued down the hallway. Shaking his head, Jaym followed after him. The halls were lined with the same dark wood as the foyer, with more impressive art pieces hung at regular intervals. There were a few doors here and there, all closed shut. A strange quietness pervaded the entire household—as if everyone else inside was afraid to make a noise.

Beck stopped in front of a set of double doors. The right door was cracked open a few inches, allowing for a thin triangle of light to be cast out onto the floor. Beck reached out, pushed the door open, and slipped inside. Jaym could feel the muscles in his body becoming more and more tense. Reaching the door, he slid inside after Beck.

"Beck, this is stupid. Let's go back..." his voice trailed off as he took in the room. They were in a formal-looking office, filled only with a stately desk and two chairs in front. But it was what was beyond the desk that captivated them both. The entire wall was covered with large, glass windows. It was so clear and transparent, Jaym felt as if he were simply flying above the city. The windows overlooked the whole of New Boston—you could see every area of the city from this high up, with no obstructions. The sun gleamed down on its expanse. Jaym couldn't remember the last time he had seen so much sunlight. Or blue sky, for that matter—only pockets reached the lower levels of the city, even on the ground floor where they had been earlier.

"Wow," Beck said.

"We should go," Jaym responded, peeling his eyes away from the view. His heartbeat was racing as a million possible situations flashed through his mind.

In a way, the room reminded Jaym of Heath's study, miles

below on the opposite end of the city from where they stood. The desk was of a similar dark wood, as was the leather of the two chairs facing it. But there were many stark differences. This study had a dignified air to it. Leather bound books filled the bookcase along the wall to Jaym's right, and a dark leather sofa sat to the wall on the left. An imposing chair sat square behind the desk. Jaym was hit by a realization. *Whose desk is this?*

"Jaym," Beck called, his tone suddenly serious. Jaym moved to the bookshelf where Beck stood. There, in a gold frame, was a family portrait with one of the most recognizable men in all of New Boston seated in its center. Chief Justice Gregorius Marks.

Marks was wearing his traditional judicial robe, with a golden broach of the city's seal on his lapel. He didn't smile, but he also didn't frown; rather he looked as if he knew that all those staring into his eyes were below him. A man with clear knowledge there was absolutely nothing one could do to challenge his authority and power. Flanking Marks behind him were two young children, a boy and girl. Jaym knew that Marks had a son and daughter, but he had never seen what they looked like. The boy bore striking resemblances to his father and had inherited the same smug, magisterial expression. The girl had soft features and looked beautiful in a simple, gray dress, her neck adorned with pearls.

Beck broke the silence: "Of all the houses we end up in..." his voice trailed off as he wandered along the wall of books, inspecting more of the shelves. His eyes had found a small golden globe sitting on a stand, at the end of a row of books. Even from across the room, Jaym could see Beck's eyes were mesmerized as he took the globe off the stand and tossed it a few inches in the air.

"Beck, we should go back. Someone is bound to come soon," Jaym said. *This is downright stupid. The maid said someone would attend to us shortly—*

"What do you two think you're doing!" The doors had burst open, and a stately butler stood glaring at both of them. His eyes were wide in shock. "You are not to be in the Chief Justice's study!"

"Our apologies, sir," Beck said, with a calm yet confident demeanor. His hands were behind his back, but behind the corner of his head, Jaym could see the golden sphere was still missing from its stand. *He can't be serious!* Beck continued speaking: "We were just admiring his book collection. We're here to deliver a package." Beck nodded in the direction of the box, which he had placed on the desk.

The butler grabbed the package. "Consider it delivered. Now get out," he said as he ushered them out of the study. The butler had grabbed Jaym by the shoulders to turn him around and shove him out the door. They headed back to the grand entrance of the penthouse. Jaym's heartbeat was gaining speed with each step as they headed toward the door. Just as they passed the flowers, though, the doors opened.

Two young men strode into the foyer. They were both tall, roughly Beck's height, and wore similar outfits: dark blue blazers with crisp, white shirts. Their faces were cleanly shaven, which made them look slightly younger than Jaym and Beck, who both hadn't shaved in a few days. They were talking to each other, but upon entering, stopped and locked eyes with Jaym and Beck. The man in front spoke up first. "And who might you two be?"

Before either could answer, the butler interjected, "They were just delivering a package, though they seem to have the tendency to wander off. I caught them snooping in your father's study."

"Snooping you say?" the man said. "Don't you two know whose house this is?" He took on an annoyed tone, almost insulted. Focusing on the man's face, Jaym recognized him as the Chief Justice's son in the picture.

The second man now spoke up. "Well, I'm sure these boys were impressed, it's the most immaculate study in the city." The man smiled, putting Jaym even more on edge. He wasn't sure if the man meant to be condescending or was simply trying to break the awkward silence.

As if confirming his doubt, the Chief Justice's son spoke back up. "No doubt they were impressed. Judging by the looks of them, I'd guess this may be their first time in a penthouse as well kept as this one!"

Jaym's mind was quickly calculating how to best respond. But before he could, Beck spoke up.

"Our apologies, gentleman. We didn't mean to snoop. The door had been open, and the study was indeed immaculate—it caught our eyes."

Yeah right, Beck. Really convincing with that formal tone. They'll see right through us and suspect we did something.

Marks's son had fixated on the package. It didn't even seem that he had heard Beck speak. His face reddened as he turned to the butler and angrily said, "Jeffrey, this is to go *straight* to my room! Didn't I tell you that? Go now!" The man shoved the package back into the butler's arms, who nodded and scurried off up the stairs. Jaym and Beck cast each other a concerned look. *We need to get out of here*, Jaym thought, wishing he could telepathically communicate with Beck.

Marks's son turned back to Jaym and Beck. "I don't think your boss would be very happy to learn his delivery boys were snooping around a customer's penthouse apartment. Particularly someone of my—" Hearing the front door open, the man cut off his tirade and stepped back.

The doors swung open wide and in strode Chief Justice Marks himself, along with a young woman in a navy dress. He exuded power and pomp, even in the way he strode into the foyer and stood taking in the scene. Even the younger men stepped back in his presence.

He spoke calmly, though with a solid tone, "What is going on here? Piers, I could hear you yelling from the courtyard."

Jaym was too tense to move a muscle. He stood petrified— still as a statue. He had grown up seeing Chief Justice Marks on screens and posters throughout the city, but seeing the man in real life was all too captivating. When Marks turned to look in his direction, Jaym averted his eyes.

The first man, who must've been Piers, spoke up. "Apologies, father. These two boys were just delivering some food. They were lingering around, and I was just reminding them their job is to deliver and leave. Perhaps the courier service needs better ways to ensure the trustworthiness of their employees." Piers glared at Jaym and Beck.

Jaym jumped in. "Our apologies. We'll be on our way."

"You have a lovely home Mr. Chief Justice. Very impressive!" Beck chimed in. His voice was still shockingly confident.

Marks responded, "Very well. You'd best be on your way." And with that, he strode past the group in the direction of his study. Jaym's heartbeat picked up even faster. He began walking toward the door and Beck followed in lockstep close behind. The girl stood watching them head toward the door. Jaym met her eyes. He recognized her as the daughter from the portrait. She had her dark hair tied up in a bun, with a few strands falling to frame her face. The same set of pearls from the portrait hung around her neck. She didn't smile or frown, but rather stared at Jaym, studying him as one would an animal specimen. But then he was out the door. *The girls in the Furrows don't dress like that.* He turned back to get one more glimpse of her, struck by her beauty, but Piers had stepped in the doorframe. Still with a scowl on his face, he shut the door with a loud thud.

Jaym and Beck hurried across the courtyard. The serene fountain in the center and the scents of the blooming flowers did nothing to alleviate Jaym's hurried heartbeat and anxiety. Each second they waited for the elevator to arrive felt like hours on end, and all Jaym could picture was the door busting back open with Marks storming out, having discovered that Beck had stolen his golden globe. When the elevator doors finally opened and they entered, Jaym let out a big breath.

Beck slapped him on the back. "Chief Justice Gregorius Marks in the flesh, eh? Heath really could've given us at least *some* warning about whose penthouse he was sending us to!" Beck smiled, reached into his bag, and pulled out the golden sphere.

"Put that away, Beck! There could be cameras in here." Beck quickly stashed the globe back in his bag. Jaym continued eyeing him seriously. "That was stupid. What's going to happen once Marks realizes you stole that from his study? That thing looks like it's straight gold."

"Exactly. This thing is worth a ton."

Jaym anxiously turned and stared out the elevator's glass windows. His mind was racing, flipping through the scenes he just experienced: Marks's beautiful daughter, Piers's anger when he saw the package, the butler racing to stow it away. *Heath's main business is one thing and one thing only. Silver.*

CHAPTER 6

———

"Scumbags. I can't stand them." Piers scowled as he placed the package in a drawer in his desk. *If Father had seen this, I'd be screwed.*

Keats was sitting on the edge of the plush bed, looking out the window. "They weren't aggressive or anything." His voice was detached. "Hey, do you know what Gwen is up to this weekend?"

"You're thinking about my sister after that?" Piers shook his head. "The fact that those two boys were snooping around … who do they think they are! I swear, we're not keeping people in check in this city anymore. People are becoming more and more brazen, thinking they can do whatever they want." Piers's voice cracked across the room.

"Can you blame them?" Keats responded evenly. "This is one of the finest homes in the city; I can't stop myself from peeking into your father's study sometimes. Those two probably haven't even been above the ground floor before. They're Furrows boys, you could just tell." Keats was still staring listlessly out the window, seemingly distracted by the setting sun shining off the skyscrapers.

"How can you be so apathetic? It pisses me off just thinking of the two of them standing there, clueless and ignorant of how wrong they were. They have no right to walk in these halls; Jeffrey should've had them wait outside in the courtyard."

Keats turned to face Piers, studying him. "Getting this angry over something so insignificant isn't good for you, Piers. Just be happy your father didn't walk in a few minutes earlier and see what they were really here to deliver. But hey, that's your risk. You know I've told you it's a dumb idea." Keats paused and looked back out the window. "I wonder if Gwen's around tonight. She was looking radiant today in that navy dress."

"I don't know, I don't keep tabs on what my sister is doing every hour of the day. Just go ask her out already, I already told you I don't care."

"I actually already have."

Piers had already moved on. "And of course, I'm relieved with the sequence of events; but how can you just look past those two feeling so at home here? You just said it yourself—they're Furrows boys. They don't belong up here. They should know their place—wait by the door, drop the package, get back to their own city level." Piers had long felt anger toward the poor people of the city. Ever since his mother died, he had harbored resentment toward everyone who lived below ground.

"Have you ever been down to the Furrows?" Keats asked, genuine curiosity in his face.

"No, why would I go down there? Not exactly a place I'm dying to visit."

Keats stared at Piers, pondering. Then he turned back to the window, resuming his gaze. "It could do you some good, to get a better understanding of the different groups of people living in this city. I've gone on a bunch of patrols down there recently and it's a tough place to live."

Piers scowled and turned back to his desk. "I don't need to be down in that dump."

Keats continued. "I know you want to follow in your father's footsteps. If you want to be a respected person in a position of authority, you have to be able to appeal to *all* the people of New Boston. Not just those up here at the top."

"Yeah, well people also need to know their place. Ensuring justice isn't just about having people respect you. It's about understanding our system. Our rules and laws. Just like how the Chief Justices ruled yesterday on Thaddeus—he was out of line, threatening our entire system. I knew that from the start of the trial—didn't I tell you exactly how the Chief Justices were going to rule?"

"True, and I agree with the ruling—Thaddeus broke the law, plain and simple. But I can't help but wonder if the laws were right to begin with. Thaddeus knew the system well, and he never struck me as an irrational person. If he would risk his life to break the rules, he had to have good reasons. I'm sure you've heard that there has been unrest in different areas of the city … maybe certain laws need to be relaxed a bit."

Piers's eyebrows tightened. "You can't seriously believe that, can you? That would only make things worse! The law isn't to be taken lightly. Think about the grueling process the Justices go through whenever they even decide to enact new policies. They have the best interests of the entire city in mind."

"True. But didn't some ancient philosopher say 'The more laws, the less justice'?"

Piers mirrored Keats, mocking him. "Someone paid attention in philosophy class. But it was Aristotle who said, 'The law is reason, free from passion.' How about you stick to your work and I stick to mine?"

Keats shrugged. "How are things going at the Academy?" Piers rolled his eyes and turned back to his desk. "Come on, Piers. Let's talk about something else."

"The Academy is fine," Piers grumbled. "We spent the entire past two weeks talking about residential policy and eviction rules. Absolutely invigorating!"

Keats tilted his head, considering the topic. "I mean, that's a pretty important issue. You should see where half this city lives. The sublevels of New Boston, woof." Keats let out a sigh. "I'm glad I grew up where I did, to say the least."

"Yeah, I guess it's important. It's just hard to stay motivated when I sit in lecture halls all day and spend all night trying to get inspired by dense legal texts. I'm starting to think I should've followed you and joined the Police Bureau. Shooting practice, martial arts ... sounds much more exciting."

"Oh, come on, you love all that boring study stuff. Always have! Besides, you just said you don't want to be 'down in that dump.'"

Piers considered it more. Almost to himself, he said, "I guess it wouldn't be so bad, being in a uniform. With a gun to protect me."

Keats continued. "Well, the police isn't all it's cracked up to be. Plenty of paperwork and boring logistical elements. And even when I've been in the field, seeing the squalor of some parts of this city ... makes me understand a bit more about where Thaddeus was coming from."

"What does that mean?" Piers asked, confused, with a hint of indignation in his voice.

Keats responded genuinely. "Do you really think it's right for people to be starving in this city? You can't seriously think that the ration statutes are reasonable. Think about how much food we have up here..." His voice trailed off.

"We have ration statutes for a reason, Keats. The vertical farms have stringent production restraints, our distribution systems are intensely complicated. Sure, the city's leaders allow themselves to enjoy a spoil here or there, as a token of appreciation for all the work that goes into running such a fragile system. We can't be rewarding those who simply bottom feed!"

Keats nodded to himself and turned to gaze again out the window.

"Keats." Piers repeated his name, louder, after not getting a response. "Keats!" The taller boy turned and faced his friend. "Whose side are you on?"

Keats returned his focus to Piers. "I'm just playing devil's advocate, Piers. Of course, you know where I stand—my future is the same as yours, following in my father's footsteps as a leader in this city. Well, maybe not his exact position, Secretary of Radioactive Protection doesn't sound all that great, but some position. And the ration statutes and city laws, they all go over my head anyways." He stood up from the chair. "I think I'll go say hi to Gwen and then head home. I don't want to be late for dinner and have to deal with another angry father today. I'll see you tomorrow?"

Piers was still tense. "Yeah tomorrow." His mind had turned back to the two Furrows boys, especially the taller one. *He was basically smirking at me! The nerve of him.* He didn't even notice that Keats had walked out. Jeffrey's voice brought Piers back to reality. "Mr. Piers, your father would like to see you in his study."

* * *

Piers took a deep breath and pushed the large, mahogany doors of his father's study open. He tried to keep his mind off the two Furrows boys, but he was still fixated. *What does father want to talk about?* Meetings with his father only went one of two ways: bland, pointless rituals of necessity where his father pretended to care about Piers's progress at the Academy or recent social bouts. Or they were fierce arguments where Piers was scolded, castigated, and reprimanded. There was little in-between when it came to their interactions.

"Good evening, Father." Piers stood a few feet back from his father's desk and clasped his hands behind his back. He stood straight, mindful of his posture. The study never felt comfortable. From the bookcases, to the stately desk, to even the leather chairs, everything looked and felt rigid.

Marks was seated, his head down, focused on several papers. He held a black telephone up against his ear, with its coiled cord dangling to the console on the desk. Only Justices and high-ranking government officials had telephones. Marks raised his index finger to Piers without lifting up his head. Piers stood still, at attention. He looked out at the windows behind the desk, taking in the expanse of New Boston.

After a few moments, Marks said "thank you" into the phone and hung it up. He finally addressed Piers, still without looking at him. "Sit, son. I realized we hadn't even talked yesterday. I was quite busy after the trial. What did you think of it?"

"I thought you ruled fairly and swiftly." The leather cracked as Piers sat down in the chair. He leaned back, in a fleeting attempt to get comfortable.

Marks took his glasses off and looked up, meeting his son's eyes. "And how do you feel about the verdict? Thaddeus's execution?"

Piers tried to remain expressionless as he stared at his father. *What is he grasping at?* Marks's pale, gray eyes were inscrutable. He couldn't remember a time his father ever showed real emotion. Other than a few distant memories from before his mother died. "I was disappointed in him. Thaddeus broke the law and threatened our entire society. He had taken an oath to serve our city, and he broke that oath. He deserved the ruling."

Marks continued looking directly into Piers's eyes. After a moment's pause, he said, "Actually, I didn't want Thaddeus to be sentenced to death." A shocked expression spread across Piers's face. His father tilted his head slightly, studying the expression. "You're surprised to hear this?"

"Of course!" Piers couldn't hide his shock. His eyes flitted angrily. "How can that be so! You said yourself in the tribunal, he threatened the very balance of the system!"

"Yes, this is true. And what angered me the most was when he retorted back at me in public, showing a complete lack of respect for the high tribunal court and the office of the Chief Justice. And for that, I knew he needed to be punished—even more so than for breaking the ration laws. But when we were deliberating, I and a few other Chief Justices had concerns about the repercussions that such a severe verdict could have throughout the city."

Piers took a breath, calming himself down. He was now more confused than angry; it seemed his father was balancing between two schools of thought. "Keats mentioned there has been unrest across the city. Is that what you were worried about? Riots or something in the lower levels?"

"Yes. We've dealt with unrest many times throughout our city's history. Even personally so." Marks looked down solemnly. "We've always managed to quell them and ensure the status quo is maintained. But Thaddeus had a strong reputation amongst the city's lower levels, and they will not take kindly to him being executed. Even today, there were multiple clashes that erupted, just as many did yesterday after we handed down the verdict."

Piers stood and walked over toward the bookshelf along the wall, his mind racing. "So why did you allow the execution verdict to pass?"

"The Chief Justice Council must present a united front. Connally felt very strongly that, given we haven't ever had a Secretary break the law in such a grave way, we had to present an example—not just to the common folk, but to those in positions of power. He argued that if others followed Thaddeus's actions and attempted to institute their own justice through subverting the system, our society would face an even graver threat than a few riots here or there. The system is what preserves the city. I agree with Connally wholeheartedly on this, of course. After all, respecting the consequences of one's actions is the reason we publicize the Tribunals to begin with. But we, as leaders, must also be weary of the power of the crowd. Should it turn violent … we all know what could happen." He returned his attention to the papers on the desk.

Piers had begun following the various books with his fingers, stroking the spines. "I agree with Chief Justice Connally. Just like you said, even Secretaries aren't above the law. Thaddeus knew what he was doing was wrong. We can't have others attempting to follow his actions without fearing the consequences." Piers's finger had reached the end of a row of books and came upon an empty stand. His eyes suddenly widened as he realized what was missing. He distinctly remembered a moment in his childhood when he was tossing the golden globe and was rebuked by his father for playing with such an expensive object. His mother had given the globe to his father the day he was elected to the Supreme Tribunal Council. *Where could it have gone?* He then remembered; the two boys had been snooping in the study.

Piers spun around frantically. "Father!" he exclaimed, moving aside and motioning to the empty stand, "Your golden globe! It's gone! Those two Furrows boys must've stolen it—they had trespassed into your office!"

Marks looked up to the bookshelf, a puzzled yet calm look on his face. "The globe is missing?" Marks leaned back, clearly conflicted about how to react. "I need to lock this door. No one, not those two boys, not you, not Gwen, should be in my study when I'm not here!" His voice boomed as he finished the sentence. "But I have more pressing things to worry about. If those two boys come back to deliver more food in the future, I will deal with them then. Let Jeffrey know to keep an eye out around the house if they turn back up." He returned his gaze to his papers.

Piers stood facing his father, his mouth gaping open. "You don't want to go after them? Find them and punish them? They stole from you, a Chief Justice!" Piers's face was flushed, a mixture of anger but also surprise.

Marks leaned back up and looked at his son. "Piers, I am not going to take resources away from the city's police to go after one small theft. That globe is meaningless in the grand scheme of things. Think about what I was just saying—focusing on the bigger issues is what we city leaders must be doing. Like I said, if those boys come back here again, I'll deal with them. I would certainly not let the issue go unraised. But this is a trifling matter."

"I cannot believe the nerve of those two boys, first trespassing throughout our home, and then stealing. The people of this city are beginning to become too bold—too daring in challenging the system and the rule of law." Piers was muttering to himself at this point, thinking back to the tall one's smirk. *He had the globe in his bag that entire time!*

"Piers, anger results in carelessness. You need to work on your focus. Those two boys must've been barely nineteen. Right about your age. They, like you, clearly don't have a handle on the consequences for their actions. They lack restraint, self-discipline. An appreciation for the broader scheme of things."

Piers focused his eyes on his father. His heartbeat had accelerated, and he was seething. His father had a way of degrading him that always struck a chord. Speaking as evenly as he could, he said, "I do have an appreciation for the broader scheme of things."

Marks finally looked up and leaned back in his chair. "I think you need to get some exposure to the more … common areas of our city. Anyone who wishes to govern must know and understand all the people under him—from those in high positions, to those in the lowest trenches. Keats's father mentioned that Keats was recently promoted within the police bureau. Why don't you join him for an evening patrol this week? See for yourself what life is like for those in the Furrows."

It's like he and Keats already came up with this plan together. Piers hated feeling like he was out of control, not making his own decisions. But at the same time, another thought popped into his head. *Maybe I'll run into those two boys on a nightly patrol and have the opportunity to confront them.* Piers looked up. "If you think that's a good idea, sure, father."

Marks stared contemplatively at his son. "I do. I'll reach out to the Police Chief and let him know. Now I have work to do; leave me until dinner." Marks returned his focus to his papers. Piers turned to leave the study, his eyes passing over the empty globe stand on the bookshelf. His mind was racing, and he couldn't stop thinking about the two Furrows boys with their cocky smirks. *If they think they can do whatever they want in this city, they have another thing coming.*

CHAPTER 7

"You should've seen it, Dante—the marble floors were so shiny you could see your reflection in them!" Jaym rolled his eyes, listening to Beck jabber away. Dante leaned his elbows on the sticky bar surface, his hands propping up his chin while he listened to Beck's account.

"What was it like being that high up in the city? Did you see the sun? The *actual* sun?" Dante asked.

"Felt it shine right on my face!" Beck's voice was loud with excitement. "You could see the entire city from up there, it was like walking among the clouds."

"Wow, that's incredible," Dante said. His voice was listless, as if he were daydreaming.

"It really was. Right Jaym?" Beck nudged Jaym, who was sitting next to him.

Beck's voice was a distant echo to Jaym. He was exhausted from the whole experience, even after getting a night of sleep. After they left the Penthouse, he had pressed Beck to expedite their return to the Furrows. Beck had protested, wanting to relish every minute spent in the city's higher levels, but eventually gave in. They had descended back into the familiar depths of the city, where Jaym had felt a sense of relief wash over him.

After turning down Beck's invitation to head to a gambling lounge, he went home to their tiny apartment and collapsed in bed. He had popped his KIP pill, too tired to be stressed that he hadn't taken one that morning, and passed out.

"Huh?" Jaym said, as he was beckoned back to the conversation. "Sorry, I didn't hear you."

"Do you think it's fair the way they live up there? That opulent, massive penthouse?" Beck asked. The awe and excitement from his tone were gone; he spoke directly, in a matter-of-fact way.

"I mean, it was a Chief Justice's house ... one of the nine most powerful people in the entire city." Jaym's voice was distant, as he was still mentally removed from the conversation. He took a sip of vodka, appreciating the numbness the alcohol provided. His mind was still reeling from his realization of what was likely in the package. *Piers buys Silver ... but doesn't want his father to know. That much was clear.*

Dante snorted. "Yeah, as if they're the only nine people who are living in that kind of place. I bet every Secretary and Deputy Secretary has a butler and waitstaff, while the rest of us live crammed down here with barely enough rations to survive. Gonna have even less food now that we don't have ol' Thaddeus coming around." Dante shook his head and took a swig from his own vodka, not even grimacing as the harsh liquor went down.

Hearing Thaddeus's name brought Jaym's attention back. "Yeah, and look how that turned out for him. You're risking your life and other people's lives if you try and revolt. What do you even want to do, Beck? Riot outside Marks's penthouse? They'd gun everyone down in minutes!"

"You know, maybe I do. I heard there was a massive riot outside the skyscraper where Chief Justice Connally lives this morning. People went right up to the ground floor and everything! I wish I had gone."

"You have a death wish, Beck. You know how dangerous that is," Jaym cautioned.

Beck looked at Jaym, his face serious. He responded evenly and solidly. "I want to do something. Something is better than nothing. I can't stand to think that I sit down here, hungry and dirty, my skin pale from having not seen the sun in months. While those two pricks in their blue blazers and slicked back hair get to live a life of luxury for no other reason than who they were born to."

Jaym returned his eyes to his drink and took another swig. *He's not wrong.* "Have you contacted Heath yet about the other half of our payment?"

Beck downed his drink, shaking his head afterwards as the vodka burned his throat. "He should be here any minute actually. Told him we'd be here all afternoon. Well, I will be, at least."

"Listen boys," Dante spoke up. He had been quietly listening to them bicker. "I've been living in this city for a long time. Nothing has ever been equal. That's just a fact of life. But I will say, these are the smallest rations I can remember. Like I said the other day, things haven't been this tense since ten years ago, and we all know how that ended. So many innocent people killed. Even the lights seem dimmer down here these days. Back when I was a kid, I'd go up to the ground floor all the time—visit the markets, catch a few sun rays that made it through the skyscraper cracks. Now, I won't go above Sub2. With all the stories of people getting arrested for the smallest reasons, I won't risk it. Who would run this bar with me gone?" He pointed at Beck. "*You?*" Dante let out a hollow laugh.

Beck was quiet for a few minutes, and then said, "I'm just sick of living in fear, out of the sunlight, down here in this … dungeon."

Dante gave Beck a smile and a slight nod. He grabbed the bottle of vodka and emptied its last contents into Beck's and Jaym's glasses, and then moved away to clean the other end of the bar.

Jaym stared at the drink. Without looking up, he said, "You know I agree with you, right? I hate living this way. I truly hate it."

"Then let's do something about it."

"Beck, don't you realize that living in fear down here is better than not living at all? We can't take on the entire system ourselves. What good would that accomplish? It's just a wasteful death wish."

The pair sat in silence for a few minutes, until Beck pulled the golden globe out of his jacket pocket and tossed it in the air. Jaym eyed the shiny object with anger. Anger for what it represented: both the unbridled opulence of the rich, and the carelessness that Beck showed in stealing it. "That was stupid to take that from Marks's study, Beck. What are you trying to prove?"

"He has enough money to buy a dozen more of these. He won't miss it," Beck replied. "What Dante said isn't even the full truth. Not only was there a riot outside Connally's, but I heard there were raids all across the city these past few days. The police were arresting people on their watchlist for bullshit accusations of breaking into granaries and food supplies, protesting what happened to Thaddeus. The Tribunals are going to be filled for weeks."

"And you stealing that golden globe is meant to help those people?" Jaym said.

Beck slammed the globe on the bar. "No. Me taking this from Marks's study is me sending a message. On behalf of all those who live in the Furrows, it says: 'You aren't untouchable.'" Beck's voice had risen substantially, and the few other people in the bar had turned and cast their wary eyes toward the two boys.

"Hush! Keep your voices down," Dante called from down the bar.

Beck scowled, and in a quieter voice said, "Just think, Jaym. Those two boys in the blazers. They have full intentions of taking their fathers' spots at the helm of this city and continuing this way of life. Preserving the status quo."

Again, he's not wrong. Despite all the emotions of the moment, Jaym couldn't help but smile. His and Beck's relationship had truly stood the test of time. For as long as he could remember, Beck had passionately, and often naively, tried to spur the pair into action while Jaym would remind him of logic and reason, often pleading for restraint and caution. He put his arm on Beck's shoulder. "Like I said, I agree with you. But you also have to realize what we're up against. The city establishment is strong, it's fortified, armed, and has the support of the broad public. Not everyone is so ready to rock the boat like you are, Beck."

Beck looked back at him, his face grave and serious. "Yeah, well, tensions are bubbling Jaym. Maybe more people will be on my side than you realize. I hope I can count on you."

Jaym looked Beck square in the face. Without skipping a beat, he responded, "You know you can always count on me. Maybe not to put my life on the line for some stupid show of bravado, but I wouldn't let them take you away without a fight." He gave Beck a friendly push and was relieved when Beck smiled in response.

Tossing the globe again, Beck asked, "Would stealing, say, a small, expensive yet inconsequential object constitute as a 'stupid show of bravado'?" His signature smirk filled his face, as he showed off his pearly white teeth.

Jaym laughed and turned back to his drink, hearing the bar door squeak open. A moment later, Heath's familiar voice rang out from behind him. "Hello gentlemen!" Heath put his arms on both their shoulders and gave them a squeeze. "How about we go grab the booth in the back for a little more privacy, eh?"

Before waiting for an answer, Heath began heading toward the back of the bar. Jaym and Beck followed, Jaym noticing that two guards from Heath's operation were standing by the bar's entrance.

They settled into the booth, the old brown vinyl cracking as they sat. Heath continued, "So, what did you think about that penthouse? Ritzy, eh?" He smiled, raising his eyebrows.

"Oh, it was ritzy all right. Made me realize what I want to be when I get older, a Chief Justice!" Beck said, smiling back. Jaym rolled his eyes.

Heath's smile evaporated from his face. He leaned in, his voice much lower. "You keep your voice down, you're not supposed to know who that package was for!"

Jaym now spoke up. "Well, it wasn't for him, now was it? It was for his son." Jaym stared at Heath. "You should've given us a warning that we were going to the penthouse of one of the most powerful men in the entire city."

Heath leaned back. "You think so? The less you knew about where you were going, the better. Not that it would've mattered apparently. My ... customer let me know there was some ... improper behavior that you both exhibited during the handoff—care to elaborate?"

Beck jumped back in. "Our apologies, Heath. We couldn't help ourselves from peering around the penthouse; it was just so … magnificent. We promise we'll follow any and all instructions in the future." Beck was even-keeled in his response, not overly apologetic, but not sarcastic either.

Heath stared back at the two of them for a few more seconds, his face still grave. "The customer was pissed, Beck. I told you no funny business. This is a delicate operation I'm running. But the package ultimately was delivered, and that's what counts." Heath took a wad of cash out of his pocket and handed it across the table. "So here is the rest of your payment, minus thirty percent."

"Thirty percent!" Jaym snapped, alarmed.

"Yes, thirty percent. You realize what the cost to me would be if I lost that customer? Actions have consequences, Jaym. Even in … sensitive dealings. But hey, I'll give you both the chance to make the thirty percent back. I always have the need for new guys. Now I have to be going." Heath got up and they followed him back toward the bar's front door.

Heath shook Beck's hand, and then extended his toward Jaym. "Listen, Jaym. Don't take this too harshly, you're lucky I didn't take more of a cut. This is business, nothing more."

Jaym could feel his anger bubbling up inside. *Heath is as big a prick as those two blazer-wearing rich kids.* After a brief pause, he reluctantly reached out and shook Heath's hand. Heath smiled in return and turned to go. Just then, shouting erupted outside the bar door. Heath motioned to his two bodyguards who whipped out handguns and flanked their boss as they swiftly exited.

Beck was just a few steps behind, getting ready to follow Heath out.

"Beck! We should wait in here," Jaym said, grabbing his arm.

"And miss whatever party is happening? No way!" Shrugging off Jaym's grip, Beck pushed open the door and headed out.

"Beck! Get back in here!" Jaym called at his friend. He cast Dante a worried look and followed out the door in pursuit.

CHAPTER 8

———

The city emblem pin shined in the light. Piers reached up to tilt and center the pin on his left chest. *Perfect.* He smiled, excited for his first patrol.

"All spruced up and ready to go!" Keats said, slapping his hand on Piers's shoulder.

Piers didn't bother turning to face his friend. "Shut up. Where do we go now?"

"To Captain Stone to get our assignment. Follow me, let's get our stuff. I'll be showing you the ropes."

Piers gave a sarcastic, "Great!" as he peeled away from the mirror.

Keats led Piers down the halls through the massive police headquarters. Policemen milled about in small groups, streaming from various doors and hallways, all walking at a busy, quick pace. They continued to the main atrium, filled with escalators several stories high.

Seeing Piers marvel at the size of the facility, Keats said, "Weren't expecting it to be so grand, huh? This is the most organized and systematic building in all of New Boston." Piers smiled, taking a second to appreciate the chaotic orderliness of the headquarters.

They moved down to the lower levels of the facility, and Keats led Piers to a large room filled with weapons of all sizes hanging on the walls. There were many other police officers coming and going, grabbing various items from the walls and shelves below and heading out on their way. Piers found himself standing in front of a massive array of handguns, each a slightly different size than the next. His eyes grew wide as he stared at the weapons in awe. He reached up to grab one, but it wouldn't budge. He then noticed small metal pinchers holding the gun affixed to the wall.

"Now you can't just grab whatever you like," Keats said, coming up from behind. He took out a small plastic card and slid it through a reader next to the weapon. The reader let out a slight beep, and the pinchers opened. Keats pulled the gun from the wall and handed it to Piers. Raising his eyebrows, he said, "I'm Level Three now. That means I get weapon access." Piers took the gun and assumed an aiming position.

"Whoa!" Keats grabbed the gun back. "This baby is armed and ready, so be careful. Always keep the safety on until we're on the streets." Keats holstered the weapon.

"I know that," Piers snapped back. "So, what? I don't get anything to defend myself?"

Keats shook his head as he swiped his card again, grabbing two more items from the wall. "These are electrified batons. A few whacks of this will not only stun the hell out of anyone but will make them think really hard about whatever they try to do next." He handed the black rod to Piers, who holstered the heavy bat on his belt. Keats holstered a second baton himself. "We always only use a gun as a last resort. Killing an innocent civilian will bring much more harm than good."

They left the armory and headed to another large room. Policemen were moving in orderly patterns, forming lines in front of various elevated platforms. A few men stood on each platform with large, transparent computer screens framing them. Piers followed Keats until they stopped in a line of their own. "These are the Captains," Keats explained. "They'll give us our patrol orders for the shift and explain any situations that have unfolded. This whole area is called Central Command." Keats gestured around at the dozens of captains on their platforms. At the far end of the room, a massive screen showed a map of the entire city. The map was constantly changing, lit up by dozens of colors moving across the screen.

Keats kept ushering them along. Soon, they were in front of one of the platforms. A serious looking man sat with perfect posture, focused intently on the screen in front of him. Keats adjusted his posture to be similarly upright and rigid. In a loud, formal tone, he addressed the captain. "Sir, Officer Presley reporting for duty. I have with me Piers Marks, on patrol assignment by order of Chief Justice Marks."

The captain touched the screen for several seconds, and replied, "Confirmed, Presley. Marks, I'm Captain Stone. Glad to have you on board. You two are on Sub3 patrol this evening. Nothing major, just general HCS. Keep an eye out for any drugs or crime, and arrest at will. Shift time—two hours. Then report back for additional instructions." The captain was curt, with no emotion in his voice. *Efficiency at its finest.*

"Yes Sir," Keats replied. He turned and left abruptly. Piers, unsure if he should reply, nodded in affirmation and continued behind Keats. The captain continued moving things about his screen, and Piers realized that he had never even looked down at them.

"What is HCS?" Piers asked, rushing to keep up with Keats. He had quickened his pace as they moved through command central.

"Harmonious Citizen Surveillance. Basically, we're just supposed to make sure no one's starting any fights, doing Silver out on the streets, or anything else to stir up trouble." Keats stopped and turned to Piers. More quietly, he said, "You know, Silver activity constitutes severe punishment." Piers glared back at Keats. "I'm aware," he replied curtly. Piers knew Keats didn't approve of his recent escapades into recreational drugs but wasn't about to have that conversation now.

Keats caught his drift and continued on. "Even us walking through the streets keeps things calm. People need to see uniformed officers from time to time to be reminded to follow the rules. The threat is enough—we rarely take action. Remember, we always engage with citizens diplomatically first. Try to deescalate. Don't go straight for your baton unless you really need to. Now let's get going."

They exited the police headquarters and found themselves in Justice Square. The sun was setting—its last rays shining through the cracks of the skyscrapers. Piers followed Keats as they traversed the square to the large staircase heading to Sub1. The main market was emptying out, and they strolled past the shopkeepers closing up their stalls for the day. People seemed generally cheery, several nodded their heads and a few even smiled as the pair passed. Piers smiled back, feeling respected. He glanced down to make sure his badge was still centered.

Next, they descended down another staircase to Sub2. The streets were becoming narrower and more dimly lit. Piers breathed in the dry air. *And I thought the air was stale up on Sub1. Is this even safe to breathe down here? Do these people take an extra KIP to survive?* He reached down and checked to make sure his baton was still at his side, as he stepped out in the middle of the dark but busy street. Keats, a few feet ahead of him, turned back. "Everything okay Piers?"

Piers continued staring ahead, his eyes slightly wide, not in awe but rather in introspection. "Yeah, I'm good. It's just that, I've never been this far below ground before."

The streets were teeming with activity. Noises and music were coming from various buildings. Two woman stopped chatting and smiled as Piers and Keats strolled past. "Good evening, officers!" one called out. Keats tipped his hat, while Piers simply stared at the woman. Next, they came upon the large balcony of the Sub2 cavern. The massive hall was filled with people: men huddled around boxes rolling die, women chatting while clutching babies, young kids chasing each other through the crowds.

"Didn't realize there was so much happening under the surface?" Keats asked, seeing Piers stare out at the crowds.

"No. It's just…" he paused, "a different world down here." He gripped his baton with his right hand as he started walking down the staircase, Keats right behind him. As they strolled, a few people looked up here or there. They weren't frightened or even surprised. Some didn't give the pair the slightest piece of attention, while others stared directly into Piers's eyes. They looked hardened, austere.

On edge, Piers continued out of the cavern, down a quieter street. He barely noticed when Keats stopped in front of an open staircase entrance on their left and began descending to their destination. Above the entrance, the discolored stone was embossed with the words "Sublevel Three." Coming out on Sub3, Piers glanced around. The streets were eerily quiet and fairly empty. Here or there, someone came out of a door seemingly hidden within the walls but kept their heads down and hurried on their way.

They continued moving throughout the streets, a bit slower than they had been before. Keats kept trying to bring up casual conversation, but Piers was too alert. Just then, a scrawny man came stumbling out of a door from one of the walls, coming up to the pair.

"Please sir ... can I have some food!" His voice was screechy. Piers's eyes lit up, panic flushing his face.

"Go to the nearest ration distribution center. Immediately." His voice was commanding but had a slight tremble just beneath the surface.

"They're out of food!" the man wailed, inching closer to the pair.

"Get back!" Piers yelled. He went to grab the baton, but Keats stepped in between him and the man.

"Sir, we have no food. We cannot help you." Keats's voice was steady, but softer than Piers's. The man stumbled back, whimpering. Keats turned, gave Piers a wary look, and began moving away from the square. Piers was still tense but followed Keats's lead.

They had only taken a few more steps when the man lurched in front of Piers. He grabbed onto his uniform jacket.

"I ... am ... hungry!" the man screamed, his eyes bloodshot.

"Get back!" Piers shouted. He pushed the man off, who staggered back a few steps. Piers whipped out his baton and pointed it at the man. "Do as I say!"

The man was losing balance as he continued leaping toward them. Piers again started to feel panicked. He clicked the button on the end of his baton, and a blue stream of electricity glimmered down the rod. In one fell swoop, Piers struck the man. The man writhed on the ground in pain, letting out another scream. Hearing the commotion, people had opened their windows and others had come out of the shadows. From his peripherals, Piers saw two men running out of a door, both with handguns drawn.

"Put your weapons down!" Keats yelled at the men, as Piers spun to try and get his bearings of what was happening. A third man pushed through from behind the two others, and Piers immediately recognized him. They had only met on a few occasions, and typically in dark alleys on the city's ground floor, but Heath had one of those faces that was hard to forget. The two made eye contact.

"Listen to the man!" Heath yelled, putting his hands on the two weapons hoisted in the air. Turning to face Piers and Keats, Heath said, "Gentlemen, our apologies. We weren't sure what the commotion was. Let's just all be on our way, shall we?" The two men lowered their guns and looked confusingly at their boss. From behind them, two young boys emerged.

Raising his eyebrows, Keats said, "Weapons are illegal without a government issued permit."

Piers eyes nervously flitted back and forth. He was about to say something, when the writhing beggar began to stand back up.

"Stay down, you lowlife piece of shit!" Piers yelled, raising his baton again.

The taller of the two boys took a few steps forward from behind the guards. "Hey, you can't talk to him like that!" he yelled defiantly. "He deserves as much respect as you do!" As Piers got a good look at him, Piers recognized the boy, and a smile crept across his face.

Piers, flushed with adrenaline, took a few steps closer to the boy. "I can talk to him however I want. He tried to assault a police officer. Do *you* know who you're talking to?"

"This isn't a fight worth having, Beck," Heath said, putting his hand on the boy's shoulder. "Let's just all calm down."

"Listen to your friend," Piers said. "Back off." *Beck. Funny name for a stupid kid.*

"No!" Beck shoved Heath's arm off. "You can't just waltz down here to our home and harass us. You have no right!"

Annoyance surged in Piers. He took a step forward, as the gap between him and Beck closed. "Do you know who you're talking to? You don't get to address us! When I give you an order, you listen!"

With a widening, confident smirk, Beck sneered, "Get the hell out of here, you rich bastard!" Beck took a few more steps forward, closing the gap even more. Beck's frame blocked out the dim lights nearby. Piers felt his pulse picking up, and his eyebrows furrowed together. In a flash, he raised his baton and slammed it into Beck's side. Beck let out a scream and fell to the floor, shaking from the electric waves coursing through his body.

"Beck!" the other boy yelled, lurching forward a few steps. His voice was angry but tinged with fear. As he lunged forward, he raised his fists.

"Jaym, don't!" Beck managed to gasp.

"Stay back! All of you!" Piers shrieked. He stumbled backward as the shorter boy, Jaym, kept lunging forward. He was about to throw a punch when Keats jumped in between, his own baton raised. Keats brought the baton down, and Jaym fell to the ground, convulsing.

Piers's face was white with terror. He quipped at Jaym, "You just tried to attack a police officer! You'll suffer the consequences the Tribunal decides for you."

Piers's body was pulsating with energy. Keats had leaned down and was handcuffing the shorter boy, Jaym. The taller one had scuffled back toward the door. Steadying his focus, Piers watched as Heath pulled the taller boy up. Despite the commotion, he could make out Heath's loud whisper to Beck. "Stay back! Don't do anything else stupid!"

"We need to get out of here," Keats said, as he stood. He pulled Jaym up, who was beginning to stir back awake.

Piers looked around the small square, noticing that a fairly sizable crowd had congregated. He took a deep breath, having regained his composure. Adjusting his posture, he addressed the crowd. "Attacking a police officer, or any government official, is a grave crime! You people need a reminder in the importance of respect for those who keep this city safe. Now, all of you would best be about your business!"

CHAPTER 9

———

Keats led the way back through the Furrows. He had given a sedative to Jaym, who mindlessly followed as he was led up from the lower levels of the city. Keats tugged him along, not wanting Piers to be the one handling their new prisoner. He had told Piers to bring up their rear as they headed back to headquarters.

Piers appeared still flushed with adrenaline. At one point, he shouted at an onlooker. "What are you looking at! Back to your business!" Keats shook his head, not wanting to engage any further. *This has already gotten out of control. There is no need to be arresting this guy.* His mind was already focusing on the onslaught of paperwork he would have to complete. Keats recognized both boys immediately and knew Piers did too. *Talk about wrong place at the wrong time.*

After forty-five minutes, they made it back to the police headquarters. Keats led their trio through the main entrance to the prisoner processing center on the ground floor. There, Jaym's information was taken down, his fingerprints scanned, and his mugshot taken. After that, Keats stood and faced Jaym, who was flanked by two guards.

"Jaym Torrey, you have been arrested and charged for assaulting a police officer, and for disrupting the peace of the city. You have the right to a fair and expedient trial by tribunal and will answer for your actions to the Justices of New Boston. You will be held here until the date of your tribunal." Jaym's face was hard and unforgiving. He held a deadpan stare the entire time, clearly not wanting to give either of them the enjoyment of his suffering. Piers stood behind Keats, a thin, wry smile spanning across his face. Keats nodded to Jaym after speaking his sentence and began to walk off.

Piers turned to follow Keats, but just then spun back around to face Jaym. "Enjoy your cell buddy." Jaym lunged forward but was stopped as the guards on either side jumped to restrain him. "Get him out of my face," Piers said, and walked off.

Keats shook his head, waiting for Piers to rejoin him as they headed toward central command.

"Now what?" Piers said.

"Now," Keats answered, "we fill out the paperwork and processing information, and provide the Captain a summary of what happened." Keats spoke in a matter-of-fact manner, not even looking at Piers as he answered him. *I can't believe I have to deal with this on his first day. Unbelievable.*

"Okay, jeez. I don't get why you're so uptight right now."

"Uptight?" Keats spun to look at Piers, his expression sharp and alert. "Piers, this whole ordeal is all your fault! Letting the situation boil over, not having control over your emotions. All over some Furrows kid, probably our own age, who—"

"Why does any of that even matter?" Piers cut him off, raising his voice.

"It doesn't," Keats said, shaking his head. "Keep your volume down." They were back in Central Command, which was noticeably emptier than earlier that evening. A few policemen glanced their way, but had since turned back to their tasks. Most typed away on screens to report the innocuous events of their patrol, while a few spoke to Captains at various elevated podiums.

Before Piers could respond, Keats turned and said, "I'll handle explaining to Captain Stone. Why don't you just go change out of your uniform and take a breather." Piers opened his mouth, about to protest, when he was distracted by someone who had come from behind and slapped him on the shoulder.

"How was day one!"

Piers turned, revealing one of their friends. "Benji! Damn good to see you. Had a bit of a crazy first day out there, got into a brawl with some lowlifes down in the Furrows." Keats left the pair chatting. *Bragging already ... this will end well.*

As he headed to Captain Stone, Keats decided that he would leave out certain details of the evening. He had been running back through the sequence of events and kept finding himself stumped. *Why didn't Piers erupt more at those two guards with guns? He should've been freaking out. We could've easily been killed.* He also thought back to the most recent all-hands police force meeting, where the Chief of the Bureau had instructed all officers to keep the peace as much as possible. Skirmishes had become more and more common, and the Bureau didn't want policemen inciting anything even bigger. Keats wasn't even sure what the punishment was for omitting details to the Captain, but he decided no one would find out. It was a risk, especially to his newly minted Level Three status, but he wanted to get to the bottom of these questions himself.

Keats stopped in front of Captain Stone's podium and adjusted his posture. "Captain, sir. Officer Presley reporting back in from patrol. I need to file an arrest report." The Captain looked down from his screen and met Keats's eyes. "Go on. Details please." Keats went on to recount the events of the evening as simply as he could. He described Jaym as a drunk who had gotten into an argument with the police officers. He said they subdued him quickly and effectively and brought him directly back to Headquarters.

"And young Mr. Marks? How did he handle this whole escapade?" Captain Stone inquired.

"He did well, Sir. He maintained composure as best he could, though I'd recommend him for a few days off to recover if he's to join for a second patrol. It was a more tumultuous first time than most experience."

The Captain nodded and said, "I agree. Tell him to take a few days off to process and relax, and report next week if the Chief Justice wishes for him to continue. You'll both receive details of when the tribunal will be convening over the situation." Captain Stone turned back to his screen, a clear signal that the conversation was over. Keats gave a short salute, "Sir," and walked off to change out of his uniform.

He found Piers in the middle of the locker room, surrounded by a group of other newly minted policemen, excitedly recounting the events. "Keats! Come over here, I'm telling these guys about how crazy it was, almost an all-out gun fight!"

Keats eyes flashed up. *Why can't he keep his big mouth shut!* "Excuse me fellas, can I chat with Piers here for a second? Need to debrief him on what the Captain said." The group dispersed, and Keats lowered his voice. "Man, you cannot just start gossiping about what went down."

Piers recoiled from Keats, suspicion coming over his face. "So, what if I am! Why are you being so secretive? You're weirding me out."

"Because," Keats began, "I didn't tell the Captain about the men with the guns."

"Why not!" Piers raised his voice, but Keats shushed him quickly.

"Because, Piers, that would mean we'd get caught up in a whole investigation. Captain Stone would want to know who those guys were and why we didn't call for back up and arrest them. Which, to be honest, I'm not sure why we didn't. Something I want to discuss later." Keats noticed Piers lower his eyes. "Now get yourself cleaned up; Captain wants you to take the week off. Most novices don't run into such excitement on their first patrol." Keats undressed and put on a crisp blue suit as he explained his reasoning.

Piers looked up with a shrewd, devious look. "The mighty, moral Keats, lying to a Police Captain. But hey, you're the experienced one. When is the tribunal for the guy we brought in?"

"We'll know in a day or so. I'll keep you posted. Now I'm headed out—I'm supposed to meet your sister for a drink this evening."

Piers's expression changed—a calmer smile crossed his face. "Ah so that explains the suit! Gwen didn't mention anything to me. I guess I'm just kept in the dark on everything these days, eh? Go, have a good time. I'll see you later."

Keats rolled his eyes, also letting out a smile. He said goodbye to Piers and headed out of the headquarters. Dusk had settled in, and he realized he was already late. He headed to the Garden District. It was one of his favorite parts of the city. He had always admired the stately, elegant Academy buildings that populated the area. The buildings were adorned with ivy, green plants hanging down from the walls and sky walkways. Small cafés and bars dotted the streets with outdoor seating. The cafés and squares were popular meeting spots among students, like Gwen. He found her already sitting and sipping a drink at an outdoor table. She had a book laid open in front of her.

"I'm sorry I'm late," he said, as he sat down.

She didn't take her eyes up from the book, as she said, "Busy day out maintaining safety and order for the good people of New Boston?" Her tone wasn't sarcastic, but rather amused, almost seductive. Gwen was something of a celebrity. Everyone knew she was the daughter of a Chief Justice, but she was something more than that: stunningly beautiful, slender, with soft features. The book looked massive in her hands. Gwen was studying to be a historian, and even though she was a year younger than Keats, she had surpassed him intellectually a long time ago.

"Trying, I suppose. What are you reading?" *Come on Gwen, let me see those eyes.* Her eyes were her best feature—a dazzling hazel, that contrasted her dark brown hair.

"*A History of New Boston,* I'm in a seminar about the founding of the city," she said, as she turned a page. "It's actually quite fascinating. Did you know this city used to be called Des Moines before the resettlement of the eastern seaboard?"

"I think I heard that at some point during my studies." *Come on, Gwen. Stop teasing me.*

She finally closed the book and leaned forward on her elbows. "So, do tell, what kept you late from our date? If I recall correctly, you took my brother out for his first patrol this evening, no?"

There they are. Keats smiled as he looked into her eyes. She smiled back. He went on to recount the story, with all the details. She listened intently, raising her eyebrows and even rolling her eyes when he explained Piers's actions on Sub3. When he finished, she let out a sigh. "I can't believe he arrested someone. On his very first patrol, no less." Her tone wasn't angry, but disappointed. "Well, that's my brother for you. He's always had an angry bone at the..." she paused, "common people of the city."

"I think it's gotten worse recently too. His whole disposition, even in the last few months, has been more ... aggressive. Combative. I find us getting into arguments all the time."

Gwen looked away and took a long sip from her drink. "Well, this isn't anything new, he's always hated most of the people in this city. He blames them all for our mother's death. But she'd be disappointed in him for this hatred he has. She was always a supporter of those less fortunate than us."

Keats nodded. Piers rarely brought up his mother. All he knew was that she had died ten years ago, in the flare ups after the last Supreme Tribunal was called to order. He wanted to know more but wasn't sure how to ask. Instead, they sat in silence for a few more moments, Gwen still looking down at the ground.

Every time you see her, you find a way to make it awkward! Keats had been enamored with Gwen for years, but this was the first time he had asked her out. They had referred to the meetup as a date, but were both maintaining a cordial demeanor.

Keats finally broke and said, "If you ever want to talk about it, I'm always here for you." He tentatively reached out and put his hand on hers, at the base of her glass. She looked up and smiled.

"Thank you. Unlike my brother, I try not to carry a grudge against what happened. The city was rife with violence those days. People were angry. But to be honest, I'm starting to get nervous people are getting angry again. Did you hear about what happened after the Thaddeus verdict was handed down? Crowds in the lower level gathering halls were irate, with some riots breaking out. I heard there was a crowd outside Connally's house. This city has gone through so much pain, I don't want to see it happen again."

Keats nodded in agreement. "I know. I can feel it too, tensions starting to boil. And Piers arresting people in the Furrows definitely isn't going to help. Though as soon as I recognized that it was the same guys who delivered the package to your house the other day, I knew Piers was going to do something brash."

Gwen sighed again, and her shoulders dropped. She looked glum, almost morose. "He arrested one of those courier boys? What did they ever do to him!"

"Yeah, the shorter one. The taller managed to avoid getting arrested. Though Piers did give him a good whack with his electric baton." Keats tilted his head. "Though in Piers's defense, they did lunge at us. The whole thing just got out of control quickly."

Gwen let out another dismal sigh. Then, she suddenly shuddered. "Which tribunal has jurisdiction over this kind of arrest? My father's?"

Keats shook his head. "The Tribunal for Societal Conduct. Typically, Chief Justice Dent oversees that one. He's generally known for being tolerant, so I don't expect an execution sentence or anything. Plus, the punishment for attacking a police officer is generally just six months prison time and community service."

Gwen looked up at Keats, giving him a bit of a smile. "Let's hope so. I'm sure they don't deserve any harsh punishment. Plus, if the Justices have any real clue as to what's going on in this city, they'll be cautious with what they do to a young boy from the Furrows. Just think what that could incite." Gwen downed the rest of her drink. "It's getting late. Walk me back to my elevator, won't you?" She stood up and held out her arm. Keats wrapped it through his, and the two strolled off into the night.

CHAPTER 10

———

Jaym squinted as he was led through the ultra-bright halls of the police headquarters. The lights were blinding, especially after having spent so much time underground in the city's lower levels. He had a pounding headache, and his body was still sore from the baton Piers had brought down on him. To make things worse, the handcuffs were irritating his skin. *That asshole definitely put them on a notch too tight.*

"This way," the guard in front said, pausing as a set of double doors opened up. He stood to the side, letting Jaym pass through. Jaym let out a sigh of relief as he walked into the more dimly lit room, relishing the ability to relax his eyes a bit. He began to take in the scene: the room was expansive, filled with various holding cells that resembled large cages. He was prodded from behind by a baton.

"Follow the arrows," the guard said, his voice stern.

Jaym looked down, seeing a simple black arrow pointing toward the rows of cells. He kept moving forward. Some cells held people, two or three, others were empty. They went on forever, cells upon cells upon cells. Faces looked up at him from behind the bars, but the room was mostly quiet. Guards perused the aisles from time to time, all with serious looks on their faces.

After a few minutes of walking, the arrows led him to a clearing in the middle of the room. There was a guard sleeping behind a desk, leaning back in a chair with his feet kicked up in front of him.

"Steyn!" the voice yelled from behind Jaym, who perked up, startled at the sudden outburst.

The officer jumped up from his chair, nearly falling over. Still with a dazed look in his eye, Steyn mumbled, "Sorry, must've dozed off. What do we have here?" He began to reorganize the papers on the desk, getting everything in order.

"We have someone who isn't my problem anymore. He's yours," the guard said, prodding Jaym forward.

Steyn ignored the trite comment, and said, "Do you have his paperwork?"

The guard thrust forward a folded sheet of paper, and then began walking away. Steyn unfolded the document and began reading over it, writing a few things down on a pad as he did so.

Standing up, he began addressing Jaym in a monotone voice, reciting a script he clearly had memorized to a tee. "Okay … welcome to police processing. You'll be staying here for the next few days while your trial date is set by the Tribunal. You will be provided two meals a day, a set of city-issued clothes, and will be allotted one hour of recreation a day. Follow me to your cell." Steyn came around the desk, handed Jaym a folded pile of clothing, and began heading down one of the many aisles. Jaym trudged along behind him. His whole body felt numb. He moved along, unable to concentrate on the situation.

At a certain point, Steyn stopped, unlocked a cell door, and stood aside to usher Jaym in.

"Oh, let me take those off of you," Steyn said, reaching over to undo the handcuffs. Jaym was silent as he let Steyn uncuff him. For a brief moment, he considered retaliating. Steyn wasn't a large guy. He could slam Steyn's head into the metal bars and knock him out, then grab the keys and escape. But by the time he considered it, Steyn had removed the cuffs and gently nudged him into the cell.

"I'll be back shortly for your clothes." Steyn turned and left, heading back toward his desk.

Jaym turned around, taking in his cell. He suddenly realized he wasn't alone. Three men were also in the cell, all staring at him. It almost seemed like a ritual silence, a rite of passage as he was being welcomed into the jail. Two of the men were sitting facing each other on a bench. They were both older, maybe in their mid-forties, and fairly burly. The third man sat on the ground in the corner. He was much older, with a thick gray beard.

One of the men on the bench finally spoke up. "Who are you?"

"Jaym," he answered.

"You better get changed into those before that guard comes back," the other man on the bench said, pointing to the folded clothes. "Go ahead, we've all seen it before."

Jaym eyed the men suspiciously. Realizing they were right, he turned his back to the men out of instinct as he changed into the gray jumpsuit.

"Cozy, isn't it?" the first man said, as Jaym turned back around.

Jaym eyed the man cautiously, still keeping his distance.

"Don't let them bother you," an older man in the corner said, speaking up for the first time. "We're all in the same boat in here anyways. Screwed over."

"Yeah? Screwed over how?" Jaym asked.

"Me, I got caught stealing some food from a restaurant I worked at," one of the men on the bench said. "Bryson here got into a little tiff with an officer."

The other man on the bench smiled. "Grabbed his baton right off his belt and gave him a solid little whack!"

Jaym also smiled, suddenly feeling comfortable with the men. "I'm sure that felt great."

"It felt amazing," Bryson responded. "Just hope it was worth it. I've been in here for a week already and still don't have a trial scheduled. Keep getting pushed to the bottom of the pile."

"Really? I thought they usually happen fairly quickly?" Jaym asked.

"They usually do," the other man said. "The son of a bitch must be toying with the system. He doesn't want Bryson to miss any of this quality cell time."

"Yeah, well, nothing I can do about it stuck in here. Hell, nothing I could do from the outside either!" Bryson chimed in. "What about you?"

Jaym sat down on the ground a few feet from the older man. His eyes focused on the ground. "I was stupid. Attacked a police officer. This prick who was being overly aggressive with a poor, hungry man. And my friend Beck, he reacted. And this officer slammed him to the ground with his baton." Jaym looked up, looking almost confused. "I don't know what I was even trying to do. But I was just so angry. I couldn't let him attack my friend like that, merely for standing up for this poor guy! But before I knew it, the other officer hit me with his own baton, and next thing I know I'm being led away in cuffs."

The men looked at Jaym with still faces. Jaym averted his eyes again. He felt a mix of emotions: anger that he put himself in this situation, fear for what would happen next, and fury at Piers Marks.

The nameless man on the bench spoke, his tone softer. "Hey kid, it's okay. That's not worthy of a death sentence or anything."

"Well," Jaym began. "It might be. The officer I tried to attack? The asshole is Chief Justice Marks's son."

Bryson let out a whistle. "Oh man. The son of a Chief Justice!"

"Good for you!" The other man on the bench laughed. "Go finish the job when you get out of here! Kill that son of a bitch if you see him again."

The older man, who had been quietly listening, spoke up. "Don't give him such stupid advice. Going after someone like that is only going to get you killed."

Jaym looked to the older man. "I know that. But I want to stop him. Otherwise, he'll keep getting away with things like this. I just don't know how." Jaym hated how desperate he sounded, but between his exhaustion and the anxiety the cell had imbued within him, he didn't have the energy to feign confidence.

"Not much one person can do in this city," Bryson said. "That's why I say, if you get out of here and get a shot at getting even with this prick, you take it."

"Don't provoke the boy!" The older man raised his voice. "You're asking for him to get himself killed. It's bad enough he ended up here at his age. You want him to die first thing when he gets out?"

"You mean *if* he gets out of here," the other man on the bench chimed in.

"If!" Jaym cried out, louder than he expected. He shuddered as the word echoed against the dark walls of the cell and reverberated in his mind.

"Shhh," Bryson cautioned. "Let's not attract the guards."

"Don't listen to these men." The old man's voice had returned to a calm tone. "You cannot go up against the son of a Chief Justice. That boy can do whatever he wants. He could shoot you dead in the street and they'd find a way to cover it up."

"So he should do nothing?" Bryson's tone was almost mocking. "Maybe you should've taken your own advice. We're all in the same cell right now anyways."

The old man faced forward again, staring out into the darkness. "I didn't say do nothing. I said don't be violent. Don't just react out of anger, even though it's warranted. I may be in the same cell as you, but not for the same reasons. I'm an organizer. I've been holding clandestine gatherings for years, having discussions on how to change this city—create change in the hierarchy. But I was caught a few days ago—police raided a gathering I was holding and brought me here. Must've gotten a tip from someone, or we got sloppy with our communication. They're always listening. But it's okay. I knew this day would come. It's been coming for a long time."

"I'm not violent," Jaym said, more to himself than the men.

"Good. But you were stupid." The old man eyed him without turning his head. "You let your emotions get the better of you."

Jaym nodded in response. "I know. I was just so angry. Seeing him attack that poor beggar, and then attack Beck for standing up to his force ... they can't just do what they want in this city. Especially to people like you, who live their whole lives as peaceful citizens of New Boston." Hearing himself say the words brought a renewed sense of anger to Jaym, but also a sense of clarity that he didn't have before. A stronger understanding of the root cause of his anger.

"Oh I wouldn't say I'm peaceful," the old man said, grinning. "Words can hit harder than fists. And never underestimate the power that comes from old-fashioned determination and anger. A mix of those and you've got yourself a fire that will never burn out."

Jaym smiled. A strange wave of endorphins was washing over him. His arms tingled with an energetic vibration. "You've been fighting this way for years? I thought all that stuff ended after the fighting ten years ago," he asked, incredulously, almost in a sense of awe.

"Oh heavens no. After the Chief Justices dissolved the SubCity Tribunals ten years ago, people only became more inflamed. But we had to be smarter and more secretive after that—more clandestine. Without being tried by Justices from our own city levels, consequences for getting caught planning anything against the city government became much, much graver."

"What was it like, before the dissolution?" Jaym was captivated by the old man's recollections.

The old man continued staring ahead, clearly nostalgic. "Things were ... calmer—

less tense. People weren't afraid all the time. Though once Silver began proliferating in the lower city levels, and the SubCity Tribunals couldn't clamp it down, things started unraveling."

"And you've been fighting against the system all this time?"

"For years. Never stopped." The old man continued smiling into space. "Met some really great people on this journey. Sad it's coming to an end."

"An end?" Jaym asked.

"Son, when you've been around as long as I have, you have a good sense of how these tribunal trials go. I've got no shot. I'm being tried for Treason in the High Crimes Tribunal. I'll be dead by the end of next week. If it's a busy news week, I'll be executed quietly. And if nothing else is going on, maybe they'll make a spectacle of it."

"They can't! It's not right!" Jaym exploded, unable to contain his energy. His emotions were pinballing back and forth. He could feel his face becoming flush.

The old man raised his hands, motioning for Jaym to quiet down. "Shhh, son. It's okay. Yelling and screaming isn't going to make a single difference right now. Besides, I've come to terms with my fate. I've contributed to the grand plan, and I'm a small player when it comes to the game. I'm just happy to have gotten a turn."

Jaym found himself slowly shaking his head. "Just because you accept this fate doesn't mean you deserve it."

"Well, either way, deserving it doesn't change if I receive it. We can't make much of a stand from this expansive dungeon. But my hope is that young people like you keep taking up the charge. Change will come, even if it takes a generation or two. Things come and go in waves. But I haven't seen things this tense since the last time the Supreme Tribunal was called. Especially with how low rations are." The old man looked at Jaym compassionately. "I hope your fate in the tribunals is better than mine."

The conversation went quiet. *Just like what Dante said. Things are building.* Jaym shivered, feeling the coldness of the barren cell for the first time. He brought his knees closer to his chest and tightened his arms around them, relishing the slight increase in warmth.

Then, all the men's heads perked up. They heard the sound of keys jingling, and shortly after, Steyn returned from out of the dark, shadowy aisle.

"Gray looks good on you," he said, emotionless. The guard's eyes seemed almost absent, as if he were merely going through the motions without a thought in the world. "Hand me the clothes."

Jaym stood and pushed the pile of clothes over near the cell's entrance. As he got up, he felt pangs of soreness shoot through his lower back. He turned to see where he had been sitting, but it was only the hard, cold floor. Steyn reached into the cell and scooped the clothes up. He turned and began walking away, before stopping abruptly. "Oh, Jaym is it? Yeah, they've scheduled your trial. The day after tomorrow." Steyn turned and continued on his path, unaware of the gravity of the words he had just uttered.

Jaym froze, nearly stunned.

"It's okay, Jaym. Sooner is better than later. Trust me on that," one of men on the bench said.

"He's right," the old man agreed. "Sitting here wasting away does nothing of consequence. If you live to fight another day, best to get on with it. And if fate has other things in mind, best to get on with that too. Either way, one must always move forward with confidence that they can and will handle whatever the world has in store. Just be smart about it. Don't waste your youth and potential picking a fight with some measly policeman."

Jaym remained silent as he sat back down. He didn't even notice how hard the floor was anymore, nor the cold chill that had already returned to his spot. His eyes were open, but he was looking within, experiencing a moment of introspection unlike any he had experienced prior. *These men are heroes. We need more men like them in this city. I need to be more like them.*

Jaym spoke out loud, but mostly to himself. His voice soft but strong. "I won't waste my life. I'm going to get back at that bastard."

CHAPTER 11

Beck slowly stirred awake. The events of the day before were playing in his mind like a hazy dream: Heath and his armed guards had pulled him back into the bar. He remembered them placing their hands over his mouth to silence his screams. The room was spinning. He was in one of the old, leather booths. Gulping down dark rum without even feeling the burn in his throat. Heath and Dante were whispering by the bar. Dante came over to him and said something, but it didn't register. Another gulp of rum. Darkness.

Beck sat up, his head pounding. He was on an old couch, the foam visible through tears and rips. Looking around, he was in a small, crowded apartment, though it was hard to tell. The usual dim lights were blinding as he came to.

"Dante! He's up." The voice rang in his head, but Beck knew who it was immediately. "Oh Beck." His friend and third roommate, Jemma, sat looking at him with wide eyes. She put her hand gently on his shoulder.

"That he is," Dante said, standing up from a table in the corner. He put a piece of stale bread into his mouth as he walked over to Beck. He leaned in, close enough that Beck could see the crumbs in his beard. "Sit up, kid. How you feeling?"

"Ah … everyone stop shouting." Beck rubbed his temples and took a few deep breaths. "Dante … Jaym … what are we going to do?" His voice trailed off.

"Listen and listen to me good. You are to do nothing right now. You hear me? *Nothing.*" Dante's face was stone cold.

"But we have to do something!" Beck groaned, his voice cracking. His whole body hurt as he spoke. Jemma sighed and handed him a glass of murky water.

"What you're gonna do is go home, eat some food, and rest. When you're feeling up for it, you can write a letter in defense of what happened for the Tribunal. I'd expect they'll schedule it to happen in a few days from now—it should be announced sometime today. But you are not, under any circumstances, going to try and find those two cops."

"How would I even know where to start!" Beck retorted back. *He's treating me like a damn child!* Looking up at the older man though, he immediately felt bad. Dante looked even more worn than ever. Wrinkles covered his usually cheery face, which instead looked mournful.

"Don't play dumb with me, Beck. I heard what Jaym said before you two charged those guys. You knew them. And something tells me they weren't your old pals from school."

Beck looked down, remembering more of the details. *They definitely recognized us too, those rich penthouse pricks.* "So, what now then?"

"You do as I said. You lay low, get some rest, and get ready for Jaym's trial. I called Jemma over here to help get you home. Jemma," he turned, looking at her, "you make sure our friend Beck here doesn't get into any funny business, understand? Beck, come by the bar tomorrow and we'll chat when you have a clear head." Dante helped Beck up and brushed off his shoulders. "This isn't your fault, you understand?" He looked directly into Beck's eyes. "Jaym's gonna be just fine. We're gonna get through this. The punishment for fighting a cop isn't execution, and they'll likely take it easy on him since he's young and has a good record." Dante reached into his pocket and took out a KIP pill. "Take this. You're behind."

Beck nodded and tossed back the pill. "Thanks, Dante," he mumbled. He stood up from the couch, feeling the weight of the rum's hangover washing over himself. He pushed against the wall for support, the wallpaper crumbling, cracking, and flaking against his force. Jemma smiled at him in pity and led him to the door and down the stairway. They exited into the back of the bar, which was empty and quiet. Beck shuddered as the bar door came into view. An image of the rich kids—the so-called police officers—flashed in his mind, and he could almost hear the sizzle of electricity running along the police baton.

"It's okay, Beck," Jemma said, bringing him back to reality. "Jaym will be fine. He always is." She tightened her grip on his arm and smiled at him. Beck tried to smile back. He and Jemma had been friends almost as long as he and Jaym. They walked quietly through the streets and alleys of the Furrows, until they reached their small apartment. The apartment had become a bit of a commune in recent years: it had originally been Jemma's place, then Jaym moved in, and eventually Beck took up the third tiny bedroom. They had had other friends come and go for a few weeks here and there, but the three of them had stuck it out.

Once inside, Beck started heading to his room.

"Hungry?" Jemma called to him.

"Not really," Beck answered, his voice distant.

"Beck, I really do think he's going to be okay."

"I don't know, Jemma. Two days ago, we delivered a package to Chief Justice Marks's penthouse. And those two rich kid cops were there."

"Well it isn't them who get to decide what happens to Jaym," Jemma consoled.

"Jemma, the cop is Marks's son!" he blurted out. Beck could feel his mind reeling. *What am I supposed to do? What's going to happen to Jaym? Should I go to those rich kids and beg for them to help him?* The questions swirled in his mind.

Jemma walked over and hugged him tight. "Jaym has always been a smart guy. You and I both know that. He'll find a way to get out of this. I really believe so."

Beck pulled away from her, wiping a tear from his eye. "I hope you're right. I'm going to go to take a nap; I still feel exhausted." He went to his room, closed the door, and fell onto his bed, letting the weight of his emotions crash over him.

Beck spent the next day moving mindlessly about the city. He had returned to Dante's, as the barkeep had asked, the day after the incident. Dante informed him that Jaym's had been set for the following day. *Twenty-four hours ... what am I supposed to do until then?*

As he sat sipping a drink at the bar, Beck could hear whispered conversations about the upcoming trial.

"They're not content enough to go after government officials, they have to come after us too?"

"Going after the young folk. These cops are just trying to incite more riots. People are angry."

"I heard the policeman was Chief Justice Marks's son! Can you believe that?"

"Well let's just hope the kid's old man isn't overseeing the Tribunal, we all know he has it in for us. He'll execute the poor kid just like he did Thaddeus."

"I heard it's Chief Justice Dent overseeing it. He's not too bad, that one."

Beck's emotions changed by the hour. *Those damn rich kids. They aren't even old enough to be trusted in policeman uniforms.* An hour later: *I wonder what Jaym is doing right now. Probably making friends in the prison cells. Hell, he probably knows everyone at this point.* An hour after that: *Will he be stuck in a cell forever? Will the Marks boy get his father to sentence him to life?* But the worst thoughts though were of self-doubt. *I should have followed after him. I'm the stronger one. We would've been a stronger case as a pair at the Tribunal.*

After some time, he got up from the bar and wandered the Furrows aimlessly. At one point he noticed that Jemma had been trailing behind him. *I bet Dante told her to keep watch—make sure I don't do anything stupid.* But Beck didn't care. The hours flew by. The energy in the streets had begun to build. People recognized him as the friend of the Furrows boy on trial, gave him pats on the shoulder as he went about his day, and wished him good luck. Beck soon found himself reenergized with an anxious buzz. And then, when the morning of the trial came, Jemma woke him from his bed. "It's time."

They didn't talk during their hour-long journey to the ground floor of the city. Beck could feel his heartbeat accelerate with each step. It started racing as they crossed Justice Square to the Grand Tribunal Hall. Tribunal trials were a daily occurrence. They were organized by various crimes: interpersonal relations, rations and sustenance, high crimes. Jaym would be tried in the Tribunal on Societal Conduct. Typically, only High Crime Tribunals, or the few instances the Supreme Tribunal was called to order, like that of Thaddeus, were screened to the full public across the city. However, one could always go witness a trial in person. New Boston encouraged interest in its governing system. As the city's leaders always said, "Justice is about all of us."

Standing in front of the massive steps leading up to the building, Beck froze. Probably sensing he wasn't next to her, Jemma turned and walked back down to him.

"It's going to be alright, Beck." She reached down and gripped his hand. "I'm right here with you." She gave him another tight hug, as people flowed past them into the building. Jaym's trial had already garnered more news than what was typical; there were dozens of people streaming into the building. Beck, still silent, smiled in appreciation of Jemma's support. He was glad he wasn't alone. Together they walked up the steps and into the massive, stately building. Inside was an even more impressive atrium. They crossed the room to a large board showing the day's trials. Next to Jaym's name was "Tribunal Hall G." They continued on into the building.

"Beck! Over here," Dante called as they approached a set of large, oak doors. "I saved us seats in the front." Beck nodded and followed him into the room. There were no windows—only dark, wooden walls. Massive oil paintings of past Justices hung, reminding Beck of those from Marks's penthouse. The ceilings were high, at least two stories, making Beck feel small for the first time in a while as they made their way to the front of the room. He wasn't even sure if he was walking in a straight line; the commotion was giving him vertigo. "It should start any minute. Sit here," Dante said as he pushed Beck down into the seat.

They were in the first row behind a low barrier, and the table beyond sat empty. Everyone in New Boston knew how the Tribunals worked. They were taught the protocol at a young age in school, and most people bore witness to at least a handful of trials each year. Beck looked to his right and saw the prosecution table was already filled. The two policemen, the guys from the penthouse, sat in their uniforms. The one who Beck now knew was Piers Marks turned, and they made eye contact. Piers's lips curled into a soft, confident smile. Beck's eyes grew closer together, and anger boiled up in him. "This place is packed. A decent number of high-ranking-looking people too," Jemma said, looking around the room. Hearing her voice calmed Beck a bit. His shoulders lowered slightly. He looked about at the people, mainly the ones near Piers. A few rows behind him, he recognized the girl who had entered the penthouse with the Chief Justice that same day.

"She's beautiful, isn't she," Jemma said.

"Huh? Who?" Beck jumped.

Jemma nodded toward the girl, clearly having seen where Beck's eyes had been focused. "Gwen Marks. Chief Justice Marks's daughter." Gwen looked a few years older than he remembered her in the painting in Marks's office. But she was just as dolled up as she was in the portrait.

Just then, a loud noise grabbed their attention as the doors in the front left corner opened. The volume of the room went up a notch, as people saw Jaym walk into the courtroom flanked by two heavily armed guards. He was in a solid gray jumpsuit, as was common for anyone taken into police custody. Beck overheard the woman behind him say "My God, he's so young!"

Jaym was led to the table just a few feet in front of Beck. He flashed Jaym his signature smile in a show of support, just before the guards spun him around and seated him at the table. "You got this!" Beck whispered, hoping it was loud enough for Jaym to hear. Up on either side of the high bench, two vertical screens showed Jaym's face. The Tribunal's theatrical design ensured all those watching had full view of each party's emotions and responses. Everything was on display.

The Court Sergeant, wearing his stately black robe with golden cords, bellowed out, "All rise for the Justices of New Boston's Tribunal Court for Societal Conduct." The robe-clad Justices began striding into the room on their dais, several feet higher than everyone else. As the fifth Justice—the Chief Justice—walked out into the courtroom, the crowd murmured. Beck's face went white as Chief Justice Marks concluded the parade of dignitaries.

"Where is Chief Justice Dent?" Beck whispered to Dante. Dante's eyes had gone wide. He slightly shook his head, a clear motion to remain silent. Marks banged his gavel a few times, as the volume in the room had continued to rise.

"Order, order! We have much to do today, with several trials on the docket. Everyone, please respect the decorum of this sacred Tribunal," Marks declared, his voice booming throughout the hall.

Beck's eyes darted about the room. He looked over to Piers. The boy's relaxed look had dissipated, and he had straightened up in his chair. He stared ahead with intent. The second boy, the other policeman, was whispering into his ear. A few rows behind, Gwen Marks also looked slightly unsettled.

Marks banged his gavel again, and the room finally fell silent. "Commencing the Trial of Jaym Torrey, accused of disruption of harmonious citizenry and assaulting a police officer. Trial five-six-six-four." One of the other Justices, a much older man with a frail voice, had read out the decree. Marks, sitting in the center of the five men, calmly said, "How do you plead?"

Jaym stood. "Guilty." His voice was firm and unwavering as he looked ahead, emotionless. His words evoked more murmuring from the room.

Beck frantically whispered to Dante "What is he doing!"

"The right thing. He shouldn't lie. Who knows what other witnesses they have? Better to own up to it."

"Witnesses would back Jaym up! Who wouldn't want to support a young Furrows boy?"

Dante peered back over at Beck. "Don't be so naïve, Beck."

Another one of the Justices now spoke, "To the accusers, do you have anything in addition about the aforementioned events that you'd like the Tribunal to be aware of?"

Piers stood. "My esteemed Justices. This man is a threat to the public safety of New Boston. He charged at me and my fellow officer, unprovoked, while we were on patrol. He likely would've killed us in his attack had we not defended ourselves. I, of course, did not use lethal violence, but believe I would've been justified in doing so. I believe this man," Piers motioned to Jaym, "aimed to take my life. Perhaps it is only fitting that this Tribunal take his for retribution."

A few shouts erupted in the room again as Marks immediately banged his gavel. Piers sat down, trying to remain solemn, but his smile was too pervasive.

Beck looked up at the screen, as Jaym's face shown for all to see. His eyes remained locked and focused, though he looked paler than before.

"Order!" Marks said, his voice now booming. "And to the defendant, would you like to say anything to this forum?"

Jaym stood, bringing his handcuffed hands together in front. "Yes, your honor. With all due respect to the Police Officer, I did not do anything unprovoked. There was another man, a poor beggar, who had approached the pair of officers.

I was too far away to see or hear what their exchange was, but I recognized this man. He is harmless. His arms are weak due to malnutrition from the city's rations. He would barely be able to lift himself up to a bed each night, if he were fortunate enough to sleep on one. And I watched this officer," Jaym gestured toward Piers, "beat this poor beggar to a pulp. I could not stand idly by. I recognize what I did was illegal, and hence plead guilty to accept the consequences."

The air in the room was tense and heavy. "I see. Thank you for your testimony," Marks said. Turning to look directly at his son, he continued. "Officer, do you acknowledge what this man has said to be true?"

Now it was Piers who looked pale. "Well, yes—but the beggar had attacked us as well! He too—" Piers voice wavered, but he was cut off by his father. Piers looked to the other officer for support. The second officer stared ahead, his face serious and devoid of emotion.

"Very well. That is all the testimony I believe we need. We shall quickly confer amongst ourselves." Marks leaned and spoke softly to the two Justices on either side. The courtroom's volume rose, as the spectators murmured and gossiped to each other. Jaym sat like a statue, staring straight ahead, emotionless.

Beck heard Jemma speaking to him, but he wasn't listening. He was trying to remain calm. But then the gavel came down, bringing the room back to order. *So soon?*

Marks leaned into the microphone. "Honest admission of guilt and direct candor are prized values within our society. Without them, we cannot ever hope to achieve justice and peace. While we cannot forgive your actions, we shall not give undue punishment in light of your commitment to these pillars of integrity. Your sentence is three months of community service at the Ration Distribution Centers of New Boston, to help feed the very people you sought to protect."

Beck and Dante both let out happy gasps, as the whole room reacted in surprise. Beck wanted to jump up and run to Jaym, as he felt ecstasy wash over him. He looked around and saw mostly smiles and joy. The majority of the people in the room were from the lower levels of the city. It wasn't often that a boy from the Furrows came out on top in a Tribunal. But even more shocking was Marks's stance against his son.

The gavel came down again.

"Order! We are not finished. To the policeman," Marks cast his stern gaze down toward his son, "we are concerned about the events that unfolded on the night in question. We also recognize that this was your first patrol, and that you are not a career policeman. We request your Captain open an investigation into the situation and recommend that you take a leave of absence from this foray into law enforcement until said investigation concludes. Undue force must never be used on the citizens of New Boston. Mr. Torrey, you are free to go. We shall move on to the next Tribunal after a brief recess." Marks banged the gavel again, stood, and led the slew of Justices back through the door they had entered from.

Beck looked at Piers, whose face was now drained of all color. The second officer was pulling him up from his seat as the crowd began to get up and mill about. Several of the people had begun shouting and pointing at the pair, as they began to rush out of the hall. Jaym, once uncuffed, leaned over the railing and gave both Beck and Jemma big hugs. Jaym and Jemma were exchanging some conversation, but Beck was so elated, he didn't even register what they were saying.

At one point, he heard Jaym say, "Beck, are you *crying?*" He wiped a few tears back. "Shut up. I'm just happy you're coming home."

"What? Please, you think this little thing would've stopped me from coming home?" Jaym grinned. He then looked back to the now-empty prosecutor's table. "We haven't won yet, Beck. This is just the beginning."

CHAPTER 12

————

The procession out of the courtroom was nothing short of jubilant. Jaym's smiled spanned from ear to ear. He let out a few laughs for the first time in days. Beck and Jemma flanked his sides as they moved through the crowds. *Wow, everyone is here.* Hands shot out to shake his hand as he moved down the Grand Tribunal Hallway. There were dozens of familiar faces from his sector of the Furrows, and countless others whose faces blended into the crowd. He hadn't realized the sheer number of people who had turned out for the trial.

"This is insane!" Beck yelled over to him.

Jaym yelled back even louder, "Absolutely crazy!"

Jaym felt elated as they exited the building and entered the square, where the crowds had dispersed into the open space. Most were headed toward the gaping tunnel entrance to Sub1. As they headed that way, Jaym saw a small group of policemen. Anger bubbled back up inside him. He craned his neck to see if Piers was there.

Just then, Dante's big, smiling face blocked his view. "You're a hero today, boy!" Dante bellowed. Jaym returned a smile and shook Dante's hand, before pushing past him to try and get one last look to spot Piers. Jaym's mind flashed back to the trial's final moments. He had gotten a quick glance at Piers's face when the verdict was handed. His face had shown not the embarrassment that Jaym had expected, but rather hatred—loathing. And though he thought he'd enjoy seeing that, Jaym instead felt a renewed surge of fear.

"Alright, let's get you home," Jemma said, nudging Jaym along. They had to move past the group of policemen in order to get to the square's exit. As they approached, it became apparent to Jaym how young they were. All about his own age.

"Pricks," Beck said, under his breath.

"Guys," Jemma's voice was cautious. "Let's not start something else."

As they moved past the policemen, someone called Jaym's name out. He stopped and turned to face the group. He could feel Jemma tugging at his arm, but shrugged it off.

Piers's co-patrolman stepped forward from the uniformed boys, rolling his shoulders back as he faced Jaym. He thought he heard Beck whisper something else, but it didn't register. He eyed the other policemen, who had formed a loose circle around the pair.

The young policeman reached out his hand. "I know you and I have not formally met. I'm Keats Presley. Congratulations on the verdict."

Jaym eyed the hand. "Don't think I forgot who hit me with the baton."

Keats expression softened. "I know. I wanted to apologize. And say I'm glad about the verdict. You didn't deserve anything harsher."

Jaym was suspicious of Keats's friendly attitude. "Where'd your friend run off to? I'd rather hear the congrats from him."

Jemma stepped forward from behind him. "Come on, Jaym. Just say thanks."

"I can understand the anger," Keats said. His voice was even, almost sympathetic. "I didn't want any of what happened to have unfurled the way it did. I'd say I've even felt quite a bit of regret the past few days."

"Oh, well isn't that nice to hear!" Jaym cracked back.

Keats sighed and looked down. But as he opened his mouth to respond, a voice called out to him.

"Keats, you here?"

Gwen Marks pushed between two guards into the circle.

"Keats—" she began to say, as her eyes met Jaym's. "Oh, ah, hello," she managed to get out, stumbling over her words. "Mr. Torrey, I'm Gwen Marks. Congratulations on the verdict. I was glad that you received such a light sentence and that my father was lenient and merciful. He isn't always so forgiving..." Her voice trailed off.

"I agree," Keats said, "today, justice was served."

"Was it?" Jaym responded, his voice hard and tense. He turned to Gwen. "It looks like your brother walked out of this courtroom with not as much as a slap on the wrist."

"Jaym!" Jemma whispered, her voice anxious. From his peripherals, Jaym could see Beck standing tall next to him, looking like his own personal bodyguard.

"No, Jemma," Jaym said, "they know I'm right. Piers was overly violent that night in the Furrows. And then today he blatantly lied to the entire Tribunal—in front of his father!"

Keats cast Gwen a nervous glance, waiting for her to respond. After a moment, she said, "I agree with you." Her voice was even and calm. "I'm going to do what I can to stop my brother from reacting so violently in the future. I'm sorry for how he treated you."

Jaym didn't know exactly how to respond. Gwen sounded serious. Articulate and poised.

Keats chimed in. "Plus, the embarrassment Piers got today ... that's punishment in and of itself. He was humiliated by his own father, in front of the entire city."

"Why do you two even care?" Beck jumped in.

Gwen turned to him. "It's Beck, right? Listen, I hated having to watch all of this today too. This isn't good for anyone."

Jaym felt his shoulders drop a bit as he bought into the sincerity in her voice. In a softer voice, he responded, "We appreciate the kind words. Not everyone is so ... sympathetic to us guys from the Furrows."

Gwen smiled, clearly appreciating the change in tone. "This city needs some more sympathy."

Jaym nodded. "You know what, I agree. It could also use people like him staying out of the Furrows." He shot Keats a glance. "Anyways, we better be going."

Gwen nodded, her serious expression back. "Us too. Nice to meet you, Jaym from the Furrows." And with that, she and Keats turned and disappeared into the crowd.

***

Beck and Jaym made their way through the thinning crowds in Justice Square as they headed back down into the Furrows. They were in a group of people following Dante, who had invited everyone to the bar to celebrate.

"They were just trying to be nice," Jemma said, giving Jaym a squeeze on the shoulder. "Lighten up and let's just enjoy today!"

Jaym rolled his eyes. "Yeah, yeah, I guess." *I've had enough of the Marks family today.* He smiled as they entered the lower city levels. The energy was happy and bubbly in the streets. Jaym paused as they passed a news screen. Velma, in a light blue suit today, was delivering the news. Her brown hair was tied up in a bun as always.

"And in Tribunal news today, a young man from the Furrows was let off with community service charge for disruption of harmonious citizenry and assaulting a police officer. Chief Justice Marks delivered the sentence, commending the man for his admittance of guilt and candor. The Chief Justice highlighted the importance of these values to our society..."

Velma's voice droned on, as a video clip of the Tribunal room showed the moment the verdict was handed down.

"Would you look at that. You're famous!"

Jaym turned, not recognizing the voice. A woman he had never seen before was watching the screen next to him. A proud smile crossed his face before he continued on his way. He quickened his pace to catch up to the party of people behind Dante.

When they arrived at the bar, Dante started passing around bottles of liquor. Jaym found himself shaking hand after hand as the bar filled up with people. Eventually, he, Beck, and Jemma made their way to the back of the bar. Jaym dropped into a booth. "Damn, I'm exhausted!"

"Oh yeah, being a celebrity is a ton of work!" Jemma teased.

Jaym laughed. "Oh yeah, super famous." They laughed and sipped more drinks. After a few moments, Jaym spoke up again. "Thank you, guys."

"For what?" Beck asked. The group was flush with energy from the day and heat from the alcohol.

"For always being there for me."

The three clinked their glasses and took big, hearty swigs. As Jaym slammed his glass down on the table, a familiar voice boomed into their quiet corner.

"Ah, look who it is!"

Heath was looking down jubilantly at the group. Jaym's smile evaporated as he looked up. Before he could say anything, Beck said, "Heath! Sit down, have a drink with us. You remember Jemma?"

"I would love to join you all. And of course! Jemma, good to see you." Heath plopped down next to Jaym.

Jemma forced a smile and said hello but couldn't hide her apprehension. Jaym reluctantly edged along the booth, allowing Heath some room. He cast Beck a frustrated look. Sensing the group's unease, Heath spoke up.

"What a day!" Heath slapped his hand on Jaym's shoulder, who grimaced. "I'm glad you got off easy, Jaym. Now we can finally put that night behind us. Maybe another day we can talk about getting back at those two cops. But for today, celebration is all the doctor ordered." He reached into his coat pocket and pulled out a small canister. He slid it across the table to Jaym. Winking, he said, "A congratulations present."

Jaym eyed the canister suspiciously. "What is it?" he asked.

"Oh, just a little something to keep the energy up." Heath narrowed his eyebrows, in an almost evil smile.

Jaym opened the canister and dumped out a bit of shiny powder. He shot his eyes up, meeting Beck's and then Heath's.

"What the hell, Heath. Are you trying to put me right back in one of those cells!" Jaym's voice amplified, tinged with shock and anger.

"Whoa, Jaym, of course not. Calm down, it's just for a special occasion. What better way to stick it back to the man, right?"

"You know, I've never done it before," Beck said, his voice softer.

"Well, no time like the present! No one will know. Just put a little dab on your tongue." Heath licked his finger and reached over to the small bit of powder on the table.

He placed his finger in his mouth and closed his eyes as he sucked the powder off.

Beck shrugged. "Why not?" he asked, looking at Jaym. Jaym could see Beck's drunken eyes losing their focus. He licked his finger and began dipping it into the canister.

"Beck," Jemma said quietly, her eyes disapproving.

"Seriously, Beck?" Jaym asked. His voice too was low but filled with clear frustration.

Heath instead answered. "Come on, Jaym. Live a little! This is your party after all."

"I'm good, thanks," Jaym said. He tried to sound casual, but his voice was still a bit harsh.

Heath leaned back in his chair. "Listen, Jaym. We're all on the same team. It's us in here against them out there," Heath motioned to the door. "Don't judge Beck and me here for indulging ourselves a little. Keep your eye on the real enemies."

Jaym crossed his arms and leaned back. "I just don't want to be back in that Tribunal hall anytime soon. Do you Beck? Do you want to be in my spot next time?"

Beck dipped his finger into the canister a second time. As he deposited the powder on his tongue, he perked up. "Maybe I do. Is that better than living at the whim of Piers Marks? I just can't accept that he gets to go home tonight to that penthouse apartment, have a big fancy dinner with his father, and sleep in his comfy bed. He's the one who should be tried in the Tribunal!"

Jaym could see the drug begin to flush through Beck's body. His eyes had focused as he finished his rant, and his voice had gotten louder—harsher.

Standing up, Jaym mustered all his strength to remain calm. "Listen, I know that this whole thing has been hard on all of us. But if you want to sit here, get high, and then go get yourself arrested, be my guest. I've been in those cells, and I don't want to be back anytime soon. At least not for something as stupid as this. They are better ways to take down Piers that don't result in us all getting thrown in a cell and killed. Smarter ways. And if you think we've seen the last of him, you're definitely wrong. That I'm sure of."

"I'm sorry, Jaym. I didn't mean to work you up." Heath sounded earnest. "I came by to offer my help. You and me, we can take this on together. Get back at that Marks bastard. Make him wish he never called for you dead."

Jaym didn't skip a beat. "I'm good, thanks. I'm going to get back at Piers, but I'm going to do it my way. No more stupid moves."

As Jaym started to walk away, Heath called out, "Just remember that he's the real enemy, Jaym. You and I, we're on the same team here."

CHAPTER 13

———

Piers could feel people looking at him as he walked through the corridors of the Grand Tribunal Hall. His head was down, and his eyes averted. He kept replaying the events of the trial in his mind: the tempered verdict, his father's stern gaze, Jaym's satisfied sneer. Beads of sweat had begun accumulating on his forehead. Turning a corner, he saw a bathroom and dashed inside.

Seeing another man at the sink, Piers growled at him. "Get out."

"Excuse me?" the man asked, confusingly. He gave a sideway glance at Piers in the mirror as he washed his hands.

"Get out!" Piers exploded. The man scoffed and pushed past Piers. He closed and locked the door as the man left. At the sink, he splashed some cold water on his face. He took a few deep breaths, letting his temperature cool. Looking up at his reflection in the mirror, Piers stared into his own eyes. The weight of the humiliation was just beginning to truly set in. He could feel tears welling up, but he forced them down. *Channel it, Piers.*

"This is not over," he said aloud. The deafening silence of the pristine bathroom faded, and the room slowly stopped spinning.

Piers splashed his face a few more times, and then dried it off. He pulled out a comb from his uniform's pocket and fixed his hair, which had lost its coiffed structure. Smiling satisfyingly at his rejuvenated self, he adjusted his shirt and policeman badge and left the bathroom.

He stopped at a window looking out to the square, which was still filled with people. *No way I'm going out there. Best to take the back door—quieter.* He made his way through the Grand Tribunal Hall. His footsteps echoed softly down the dark, wooden floors. He had spent a lot of time in the massive building, especially in recent years during his studies. So, he navigated the halls with ease until he came upon the back entrance. He nodded to the sleepy guard who sat at the security desk and headed out onto the streets of the city, taking the most direct path back to his family's penthouse. He passed a news screen and paused. His eyes went wide as he saw himself on camera, floating next to Velma.

"...the Chief Justice suspended the policeman temporarily, and requested a formal investigation be opened into the events. He reminded the young patrol that undue force was never to be used on New Boston citizens. The young policeman, Piers Marks, is Chief Justice Marks's son, and it was the Chief Justice who delivered this verdict. We expect..."

Beads of sweat returned to Piers's newly washed face. A brief tremble shot through his body as his heartbeat began accelerating again. He whipped his head away from the screen and continued on his way. *What was father doing there today anyways? Where was Justice Dent?* He reflected on his last conversation with his father, the day before. Marks had called him into his study. "How did your first patrol go?" he had asked, his face looking down, focused on whatever papers he had been reading. Piers listlessly recounted the events. He highlighted that he was attacked by a beggar, and then by a delinquent Furrows boy who had stood up for the downtrodden man. He noted how proud he was for having arrested a troublemaker on his first day on the job. Afterwards, Marks had nodded and merely said "Sounds like it was an eventful first experience." And that had been all their conversation about the event.

It was wrong for him to embarrass me like that. Accuse his own son of using "excessive force" on two worthless Furrows boys—after being attacked! Where was his concern for my safety? The more he thought about it, the angrier he became.

"Deep breaths. Anger will get you nowhere right now," he said to himself out loud. He made a point to take a relaxed pace for the final stretch of the walk to the elevator on his way back to the penthouse. By the time he crossed the garden and entered the apartment, his heartbeat had calmed again.

"I'll take my dinner in my room," he called down to the house staff as he bounded up the steps. He closed his door and began pacing about the room. He sat down in a plush armchair. Then he went and looked out the window at the glistening city as dusk fell. *A well-reasoned argument is what father will respect most. Exactly how and why I reacted the way I did, why Jaym and those like him are dangerous to the stability of the city. How we must be treated with respect as the future leaders of the city. Reprimanded in private, so as not to diminish how the common people view us.* "I should write this down," he said out loud, as he went to his desk and began scribbling the thoughts on paper. He barely noticed when Jeffrey knocked on his door, leaving his dinner plate outside. After he was satisfied, he moved on to some of his Academy homework, attempting to take his mind off things.

He then heard the front door thud closed, followed by an even louder thud as the large wooden study doors closed afterwards. *Good, he's finally home. I must've lost track of time.* He grabbed the notes he had written down and left his bedroom. As he headed down the hallway to the study, he passed a bar cart. On it sat a few gleaming crystal glasses and a decanter filled with his father's favorite whiskey. He poured the caramel liquid into two glasses. With his notes under his arm and the two glasses balanced in his left hand, he knocked on the study door.

"Come in," Marks said, muffled by the thickness of the wood.

Piers walked in. "Good evening, father."

As per usual, Chief Justice Marks did not look up from the desk to respond. "Piers. I'm quite busy. What is it?"

Piers placed the glasses on the wooden desk. "I figured we should toast to our first Tribunal together. The first of many more, I hope." Piers didn't smile, nor did he scowl. He spoke evenly and looked straight at his father, waiting to meet his cool, gray eyes.

Marks looked up and leaned back in his chair. He stared for a few moments at his son, studying him.

"And to what are we toasting exactly? I can't imagine you're happy with the verdict." He reached out, taking the glass from his son.

Piers blinked a few times and nodded his head. "Admittedly, yes, I was a bit disappointed. I ... wrote down some thoughts." He placed the whiskey down on the desk and took out his notes, but before he could resume speaking, Marks interjected.

"What, did you write a whole speech?" He snorted and returned his attention to the papers. "I'm not discussing this now. Get out."

Piers's mouth gaped open as he stared at his father. Rage began bubbling up inside him.

"You … humiliated me today," he said. His voice was noticeably quieter than before.

Marks lifted his head up. "Excuse me?" Unlike Piers's tone, his was stronger. His eyebrows narrowed together in a mix of anger and frustration.

"You—"

"*I* did absolutely nothing wrong today. You are the one who managed to find yourself inciting violence on your very first—and only—day in that uniform."

"I was attacked!" Piers countered in agitation.

"Oh please," Marks scoffed. "You were flaunting yourself on a little power trip, and that boy today pointed it out to you—quite eloquently, might I add."

"You believe that idiot over me? He's the one who stole the globe out of this very study! He's a liar and a thief. Is it wrong for a police officer to defend himself when a crazed Furrows drunk lunges at him?" Piers was nearly yelling, and his eyes had gone wide. He grabbed his whiskey from the desk and took a big swig.

Marks shook his head. "Where did I go wrong in raising you?" He looked back down. To himself, he said, "If you mother hadn't died, perhaps you wouldn't be so angry at the world."

Piers had walked over to the bookshelf. He ignored his father's comment about his mother, and instead said, "You weren't even supposed to be there today."

"Piers." Marks's tone was incredulous. Frustrated, verging on angry. "Do you think I oversaw the trial today because *you* were involved? This city does not revolve around you!" His voice boomed, shaking the study. The tone shocked Piers, who turned around to face him. "Chief Justice Dent had an emergency, and I was the only one available. It wasn't until just before the trial that I knew the details of the case. If anything, you should be thanking me for how the events unfolded today. Had anyone else been in your shoes, or perhaps mine, you may have received a harsher reprimand."

Piers stared at his father's cold, gray eyes. After a brief moment, he responded. "I stand by my actions. I'd do it again if I were given the chance."

"Well, luckily for us, you won't be given that chance. You won't be returning to the police force."

"They haven't even begun the investigation! I deserve—"

"There won't be an investigation!" Marks bellowed, cutting Piers off. "That was a formality. You will go to Captain Stone and tell him that your foray into the patrol squadrons is at an end. That you wish to focus your attention on your legal studies. Have you forgotten where your future is?"

"I don't see any reason why I can't continue with the police force on the side of my studies."

"Because you, son, think you are above the law. You do not respect authority. You are too young, too immature to wield any real power. Perhaps are even incapable of ever doing so."

Piers held his stare with his father, taking in what he had just said. He was paralyzed, unable to move or speak. Finally, he managed to bring the whiskey up to his mouth. His grip was so tight that, for a moment, he thought he might shatter the glass in his hand.

"I'll leave you to your work, father." Piers slammed the glass down on the small table. He looked one last time into his father's piercing, gray eyes, before spinning on his heels and leaving the study.

Piers moped down the hall, feeling heavy. He glared as he passed the family portrait that hung on the wall on his way to the living room. Like the other rooms in the penthouse, the living room had floor-to-ceiling windows showcasing the grandeur of the city beyond. He poured himself another whiskey and collapsed into the couch. He shuffled his shoulders, feigning to find comfort in the rigid piece of furniture.

His ears perked up as he heard the front door open and close again. Hushed voices and his sister's signature giggle reverberated down the hall.

"Oh, just one drink. You have time!" Piers sat upright, hearing Gwen's voice. A moment later, she and Keats entered the room. "Oh Piers, hi. We didn't know you were in here." She smiled at her brother.

"Yeah, I was just telling Gwen I had to go grab you from your room. Poker is starting soon," Keats said, as he and Gwen came around the couch. "How's it going?"

Piers let out a sigh. "Just had one of those meaningful father-son chats."

Gwen sat down next to her brother and put a hand on his back. "You'll get through this. You always do."

"I don't know," he responded, looking up at his sister. His anger had subdued, and he felt tired and hurt. "Father humiliated me in front of the entire city. He didn't have his own son's back—after I was attacked!" Narrowing his eyes, he looked away from his sister. "These Furrows boys will only be fueled by this. They already thought they could steal from us with no consequence before—I can only imagine how untouchable they think they are now!" His voice became louder as his rant went on.

Gwen recoiled slightly. "Piers," she began, her voice slow.

"No one is out to get you—not father, and not those Furrows boys."

"You really believe that?" his mouth hung open in disbelief.

"This has just all gotten out of hand," Keats said. "They didn't want to start a fight."

"How could you say that?" Piers quipped at Keats. His eyes went even wider. "You were there! You saw the rage in that Jaym boy's eyes. That wasn't just anger at me, how did he describe it, 'disrespecting' someone. That was hatred. Pure, seething, hatred."

Gwen chimed in, her voice still soft and compassionate. "Piers we talked to them after the Tribunal. They don't hate us. They—"

"You spoke to them?" Piers's tone escalated. His initial annoyance was quickly turning to resentment—indignation.

"It wasn't like we ran up to hug them," Keats said, slightly shaking his head. "We just sort of bumped into them in the square. When the crowds were dispersing."

Piers jumped up from the couch. He pointed at Keats, and then Gwen. "They tried to kill *us*. They stole from *us*. And you two are acting like they've done nothing wrong. Like once this all calms down, we should invite them over for a dinner party!" His voice had taken on a hysterical tone.

"Piers, calm down," Gwen said. "We were merely being cordial. We're not inviting them over for dinner, we're just trying not to start a war."

Piers let out a sigh and sat back down. "These people don't respect us. That's all I want. Respect." He narrowed his eyes and stared out into the abyss.

"In time they will," Gwen said comfortingly. "Give them some credit. They're just trying to live in this crazy city that none of us can ever escape from. They barely get to see the sun, let alone drink fine whiskey!" She gestured to the crystal glass that Piers had picked back up.

Piers snorted and finished the rest of the glass. Standing up, he looked to Keats. "Come on, we should get going. Thanks, Gwen." He smiled at his sister, who smiled back.

Keats nodded. "Talk to you later. Good night," he said to Gwen. She sighed in return and reclined on the couch as the two boys began to leave.

"Do me a favor and stay away from those boys Gwen. They're not like us." Piers's face was solemn and serious, as he looked back at his sister. "But they do need us. Hell, the whole city does. None of this works without us pulling the strings. You know I'm right."

CHAPTER 14

———

Piers leaned his back up against the glass wall of the elevator and took in a deep breath. Keats stood across from him, gazing out at the city as they descended. With its tempered, darkened glass, the lit-up windows had a subdued aura to them. The city never truly sparkled and lit up, but rather glowed like an expanse of neon lights.

"Gwen only wants what's best for you," Keats said, still looking out the window. "You know I do too."

"Then why do I get the feeling that you two are teaming up against me? Just like my father?" Piers said. His eyes narrowed, and his tone was still charged.

"Piers. Come on."

"Let's just drop it. I want to have some fun. Come on, we're going to be late."

The elevator doors opened, and Piers walked out with Keats trailing behind. They began traversing various alleyways of the ground level, Piers navigating the labyrinth of the streets with ease. The streets were empty, and the glass window-like walls of the buildings gave the city a cold feel. They were like one-way mirrors, where one could see one's own reflection, looking questioningly at what may lay beyond the glass—what was hidden in plain sight.

They soon came to a station and hopped on the monorail. The thin, sleek train began weaving through the buildings. After a few minutes, they exited, already at the far edge of the city. After moving down a few more dark, very dimly lit streets, they came to a thick metal door. Keats looked around as Piers knocked. *Sometimes it's hard to tell if you're above or below the ground floor.* The door was opened by a large guard who stepped aside. Piers followed Keats down a hallway to another door, this one wooden, at the other end. On the other side of that door was a bustling scene: women scantily clad in lingerie, dancing on poles and tables. Young men watching, drinks in hand, playing card games at side tables. A few even smoked cigarettes. Tobacco was only grown in very small quantities, making smoking a true luxury.

A tall woman wearing a short, black dress came up to them. She had matching black hair, cut short above her shoulders. "Mr. Marks, welcome back. Your usual table?"

"Krista." Piers gave the woman a good look up and down, and nodded in greeting. "Actually, I believe we have some friends waiting for us in the back room."

"Of course. Right this way," Krista said, leading Piers and Keats through the club. Aside from a few glances here or there, no one paid any attention to them as they traversed the floor past the dancers. Krista led them down another hallway to a door flanked by two guards. She nodded to the men and opened the door. "Enjoy yourselves. You know where to find me when you're done playing—if you need anything else." She winked at Piers, who turned and entered the room.

"Look who finally made it!" A tall, olive-skinned man noticed Piers and Keats enter. There were six other men in the room, all the same age as Piers and Keats. The men wore dark, trim suits, some with ties and some without. A few were standing near a self-serve bar in the corner pouring themselves drinks, while the others were standing around the large card table in the center of the room. The room was better lit than the club outside, and had dark leather couches and chairs lining the perimeter.

"Apologies, gentlemen," Piers said. He gave a little laugh. "Been quite the day. You boys ready to play?"

"I'd say," another one of the men chimed in. He wore a navy suit with a bright red tie. A tie pin glinted in the room's light. "Quite the scene at the Tribunal. I think we all would've put our money on your father handing down a bit of a different sentence."

"Yeah, definitely didn't play out as I would've expected," another man said. "But hey, now you're famous!" He slapped his hand on Piers back, who scowled.

"Yeah, your face was plastered all over the city news screens. Better hope the girls at the academy don't think *you* were the one on trial today!" The red-tie man laughed.

"Shut up, Zakk," Piers said, pointedly. He pushed past Zakk and walked over to the table. He sat down next to the olive-skinned man. "Less talk about my shitty father and more fun. I'm here to win some money. Why don't we get ourselves a little more awake, eh Alyx?" Piers pulled a dark vial out from his jacket pocket.

"Oh hell yes," Alyx said. Piers dumped silvery powder out from the vial and began arranging it into small lines.

"Keats?" Piers asked, looking up at his friend. He raised his eyebrows.

"I think I'll just get a drink," Keats said, and walked over to the bar in the corner. Piers scoffed, shaking his head as he, Alyx, and a few other men all did lines of the drug. Piers snorted the longest line, let out an exhale, and leaned back in his chair.

"Now then, let's get this game going!" he yelled, his eyes bright and eyebrows high. Alyx laughed next to him, as the drug began to take its effect. Keats and the rest of the group began congregating around the table and taking their seats. A few threw chips down as antes, and Zakk dealt out the cards.

"You know, Piers," Zakk began as he finished dealing the cards. "What your father did to you today was completely unjustified. My father said it was a disgrace, he had no right to call you out like that in front of the entire city. He actually told me to tell you he's sorry he couldn't preside over the Tribunal as he was supposed to."

"I agree," another said. The rest around the table all nodded as they examined their cards, except for Keats. His face was detached and emotionless as he focused on the game.

"And that sentence, I mean come on. The guy attacked you!" Alyx spoke up this time. "I call."

"Thanks boys, I appreciate the support," Piers said, looking around the table. His heartbeat had picked up substantially, but he managed to keep his voice steady. He paused when he got to Keats, who was sitting across from him. "I'm starting to think this city is unraveling. Criminals and thieves don't fear the system. Especially when they see that there aren't consequences for their actions. I call as well."

More nods in agreement around the table as the game continued.

"I think we need more police patrols. More eyes on the ground," one man said.

Zakk flipped the last card. "Alright, turn 'em over." Looking at the cards, he pointed to Alyx. "Two pair takes it."

Alyx gathered his chips, and Zakk passed the deck to Keats. Another round began.

"What good are more patrols if people down in the Furrows know they won't even go to jail if they break a law?" another man responded.

"Of course, they are afraid of going to jail," Keats said, speaking up for the first time. "Just look what happened to Thaddeus. One light sentence and you're all acting like the whole system is about to come crashing down."

The entire table turned and looked at Keats. Piers stared at his friend. His leg had started shaking slightly. "Thaddeus was one of us. Not one of them." Alyx and the other men shifted their focus to their cards, averting their eyes. The group fell into an awkward silence for a few moments. Bets were called sans words.

"I fold." Piers tossed his cards to the middle. He pulled the vial out from his blazer's pocket and began tapping more silver back onto the table, preparing another line for himself. "Of course, I was happy to see Thaddeus punished appropriately for his crimes. But think of how long he had been subverting the system. If anything, he served as a signal to others that the system is slowing down, lessening its reins." Piers bent over and snorted up another line of silver.

"I agree." Alyx nodded toward Piers. "Thaddeus served as a good reminder of the power of the Tribunals, but it wasn't an example that resonated with the entire city. That Furrows boy should have been punished to the full extent of the law to show everyone that we don't allow for people to subvert our laws and get away with it."

"Exactly!" Piers responded emphatically and loudly, shaking his fist. "I understand my father's concern about riots and rebellions from the underbelly of the city. But it is beyond me how he isn't concerned about how his lax sentencing could incite things just as bad."

"What are you so afraid of, Piers?" Keats asked. "People in the Furrows don't want to see the city burn to the ground. They live here too. And they all remember what happened ten years ago."

"No, they don't!" Piers retorted. "Those people don't think like we do. They don't care at all about the survival of this city. They only care about where they're getting their next drink." He snorted and took a swig from his own glass. The game had paused as everyone's attention became consumed by the discussion at hand. "Maybe we need to repeat what happened ten years ago."

"Thousands of people died in the fighting then," Keats spoke slowly, clearly shocked.

"I agree with Piers," Alyx said. "New Boston entered its most prosperous era after the SubCity Tribunals were dissolved. People learned to comply with the laws. They learned to respect city officials. Clearly, that respect has been lost on the younger generations. They don't appreciate the care and planning it takes to bring this city to the next era. Meanwhile, we're the ones pledging our lives to the future of New Boston. Following in our fathers' footsteps." Alyx took out a cigarette and lit it.

An echo of yeses came from around the table. Piers spoke up again. "And if someone like Jaym Torrey thinks he can get away with stealing from my house, and then get away with attacking me, an armed police officer, in the streets, what do you think he's going to try to get away with next?"

"He stole from your house?" Zakk asked, his eyes going wide.

"Sure did," Piers responded. "Sniped this stupid, meaningless golden globe that was sitting on a bookshelf in my father's study. He and his annoying friend were delivering a package, when our butler found them snooping around the house and sneaking into the study. A bit ironic to think what they were delivering, now that I think about it." He smiled and laughed softly to himself, glancing at Alyx to his right. "But you know what the worst part of it all was?" Piers paused for dramatic effect. "My father didn't even care they stole the globe."

"How could he not care?" Alyx asked, dumbfounded. Everyone around the table had gaping mouths, with looks of disbelief on their faces.

His lips curled into a frown and he looked down at the center of the table. "I don't know. My mother gave him that globe. And he just shrugged it off as no big deal." Piers could feel his face flushing, and his muscles tightened. *He doesn't even care about what happened ten years ago.*

"That's pathetic."

"Disgraceful."

The responses were all similar around the table. Keats sat quietly.

Piers nodded, still focused on a point in the middle of the table. "Pathetic is exactly right. My father has been weak in the face of all this. I used to respect him immensely, with his staunch backbone, his unwavering love of the law and Tribunal system. But now all I feel is disgust at how he's acted these past few days. He's been a coward. A weak, spineless coward."

The table was silent for a few moments. Keats finally spoke up.

"What about his execution sentence to Thaddeus? Was that weak and spineless?"

The whole table turned to look at Keats and then back to Piers. The smoke from Alyx's cigarette hung in the air, as if time were suspended.

"No. It wasn't," Piers conceded, his voice firm. "But that doesn't make up for how he passed judgment today. Or his lack of care about the theft."

The rest of the table nodded slowly.

"Well maybe there's something we can do about it," Alyx said. He stroked his chin and narrowed his eyes as he looked to Piers.

"Like what?" Piers asked.

"Well, Keats, Zakk, and I are all Level Three policemen now. We can run our own patrol units. And if we just so happened to find ourselves in another scuffle down in the Furrows..." his voice trailed off.

"No way the Justices could let that slide again. But we'd have to be very smart. You're not supposed to be on patrol," Zakk said, mischievously.

Piers smiled. "My father would have to recognize that these repetitive Furrow criminals are a threat to the safety and security of all New Boston citizens."

"Exactly," Alyx agreed, smiling in return. "Plus, if we do happen to run into Jaym, we can remind him what the full extent of the law really does look like."

"What exactly are you all proposing?" Keats asked. Piers looked over to him, studying his face. He was trying to look calm, but Piers could sense the dread in his question.

Alyx cast a frustrated glance toward Keats. "Oh come on, Keats. You and I both know how we could report a patrol gone awry. Silver bust. As easy as that."

"I think this is a great idea. Tomorrow night? The night after?" Piers asked.

"You're suspended!" Keats yelled, shocked.

Piers looked across the table, astonished. "Whose side are you on, Keats?" The table fell silent again. "I doubt Captain

Stone will notice if I slip into the unit. I'll join you when you leave headquarters. It'll be easy. Clandestine."

Keats shook his head. "This is how a war starts. This is how we repeat what happened ten years ago."

"There won't be any war, Keats," Alyx said. "We're simply illuminating to the great Justices of the city what they are clearly overlooking—that the Furrows need to be kept in check."

"Exactly," Piers agreed. "Not that I'd complain if it did start a war. But either way, this time, we'll make sure the Tribunal sentencing goes according to expectations. Then all will be restored." He and Alyx smiled at each other. "Alright let's get back to this game. I'm ready to take all your money, you sons of bitches! Ante up!"

CHAPTER 15

————

"Hey Jaym, Beck is looking for you," Jemma said. Jaym lifted open his eyelids, which felt heavy. He was laying on his bed in his room, the dim lights from the street poking through the blinds. You could never really tell what time it was underground, but he guessed it was around 8 p.m. He groaned and sat up from the bed. "Thanks, Jemma. Where is he?"

"He said he'd be in the cavern square. Let me know when you're ready, I'll join."

Jaym went to the bathroom and jumped in the shower. A weak, cold stream came down on him. His eyes shot open as he shivered and quickly washed himself. Much more awake, he got dressed and headed downstairs. It had been a few days since his Tribunal. *Where has Beck even been?* The day after the trial, Jaym had recounted to Beck his experience in the cell with the other men. Beck had listened in awe, calling them "revolutionaries." But for the two days after that, he had all but disappeared. Jaym wasn't even sure where he had been sleeping. Jaym had gone to work at the construction site the next day, but Beck didn't show. And the day after the project was abruptly put on pause. "Backup on supplies" was the excuse the foreman had given, but Jaym suspected they were just waiting for things to calm down.

Jaym had been too consumed with his own affairs to worry. He had become a bit of a local celebrity and was feeling inspired by the old man from the cell. He spent the days wandering the city and squares, talking and meeting with people about their run-ins with the system of New Boston. The more he listened, the more he realized how angry people were. There had been two more armed encounters in other parts of the city. It was rumored that a few people had been shot and killed in one of the brawls, but it hadn't been confirmed by the news yet. And rations had continued to be lowered, citing reasons that another vertical farm in the city had recently been contaminated.

Coming down the steps, Jaym frowned as he looked about the apartment. *God, this place is disgusting.* The stairway was littered with dirty clothes and random objects, and clearly hadn't been cleaned in months if not years. Jemma was stirring a few pieces of processed food cubes around in her bowl of off-white, synthetic milk—New Boston's version of cereal.

"Ready. Let's go," Jaym said. Jemma pushed herself away from the table and the two of them set off into the Furrow streets. They didn't talk much as they made their way to the cavern. At one point, they paused in front of a news screen showcasing Velma's familiar face.

"Vertical farming production is up fifteen percent this quarter, and it looks like it'll be a promising harvest. Chief Justice Connally's wife has completed her surgery and is feeling great, the Chief Justice has reported. All of New Boston is wishing her a speedy recovery. In Tribunal news, there are only forty-five trials for low crimes set to appear before Justices this week, marking the fourth straight week of declining

Tribunals. We can all admit this is an exciting metric, highlighting the peaceful times here in New Boston…"

"I think I hate her," Jemma said, turning to Jaym.

Jaym grinned wide. "She's the worst."

"And how is her bun always so perfect!" Jemma nearly spat the words out as she laughed. "Come on, we don't need to listen to more of this nonsense."

As they continued on, Jaym noticed several policemen walking down the streets.

"I've never seen this many guards down here before," he muttered.

Jemma cast him an anxious look but didn't respond. Shortly after, they arrived at the cavern which was in its usual buzz of activity. They wandered through the busy rows of vendors and booths. Men crowded around crates, and woman gossiped, holding babies. "There he is!" Jemma said, taking the lead. They weaved through the crowds, and Jaym spotted Beck leaned up against a light pole on the perimeter of the action. He was staring off into the distance, looking aloof—distracted.

"Hey Beck!" Jemma said, running up to him and giving him a hug.

"Hey Jemma. Jaym." Beck nodded.

Why is he so serious? "Where the hell have you been the past few days? Didn't see you at the construction site the other day." Jaym's voice was sharp.

"Yeah, I'm done with that place," Beck said. "I've been helping Heath with some stuff."

"Oh yeah? Delivering flowers?" Jaym asked, raising his eyebrows.

"Dude, what's your deal with him?" Beck stood up from leaning on the pole. His shoulders were hunched and tense.

"What?" Confusion rang through Jaym's tone.

"You've been so hostile to him ever since we delivered the package to that Marks bastard. Actually, even before that. When we first went down to his office."

"Excuse me?" Jaym's voice was harsh, as he took a step closer to Beck. "Were you the one who was just put on a Tribunal where that Marks bastard requested you to be executed?"

"Guys! Calm down." Jemma stepped between the two boys, pushing them back by their chests. "Beck, what's the matter? Why so angry?"

Jaym let out a breath. "Jemma's right. I'm sorry. Are you okay man?"

"I'm fine," Beck answered. "Sorry. Just been a busy few days." He smiled, and tried to return to his typical, light tone. But Jaym could still sense the tension underneath. "I actually called you here because of Heath. He wants to talk to you. I know the construction site was shut down, so don't bother trying to tell me your days are busy. Come on, I'll take you down to him."

Jaym's tone shifted back to serious. "Why?"

"Listen, Jaym. Things are happening in this city. Things bigger than you and me. Heath is on our side, and I'm going to help him. I know you see it and want to be a part of it. The least you could do is hear the guy out."

Jaym was quiet for a few seconds. *Heath could be a good ally in this. He has men, weapons. He's cunning.* "Okay, Beck," Jaym conceded. "I'll chat with Heath. Maybe I've been a bit harsh on him. But I'm not going to throw myself in front of the police again just to save your ass if you follow him into a war. That's not going to help us with whatever is happening in the city."

Beck nodded and smiled. "Fair enough. Jemma, want to join?"

"I think I'll let you two handle this one on your own. See you both later." Jemma turned and disappeared into the busyness of the cavern, as Jaym followed Beck. They navigated through to the city's lowest levels to where they had visited Heath a week prior. As they left the square, the streets quieted.

"Jaym," Beck said, the first time he spoke since leaving the square.

"Yeah?"

"I'm really happy you got off with the light sentence that you did."

Jaym relaxed a bit and put his hand on his friend's shoulder. "Me too. Don't run off again without telling me. I almost started to assume the worst."

"I'm old enough to care for myself you know." Beck gave Jaym a playful push and continued on.

They didn't speak the rest of the way. Jaym found himself breathing easier though, having cleared the air. They soon came upon the same thick, metal door, and followed the procedure as before. The guard let them in, but this time Beck led the way down the hall. He nodded to the two guards outside the double wooden doors and let himself into Heath's office.

Heath was hunched over his desk, his brows furrowed in deep thought. His head jerked up when the door opened, and a smile crossed his face.

"Beck, my friend!"

Beck nodded and stepped aside. "Heath, I brought Jaym with me to see you. I know you had some things you wanted to discuss with him." Beck took a few steps away and leaned up against the bookshelf. Jaym eyed him from the side, feeling isolated without Beck next to him—threatened, almost.

"Please, have a seat," Heath said, his tone friendly.

Jaym sat down in one of the seats in front of the desk. He leaned back, trying to strike a relaxed pose, but only felt more uncomfortable and awkward. Fidgeting, he shifted forward and gripped the arms of the chair. "Hello, Heath. What can I help you with?"

Heath smiled. "You know, Jaym, I was hoping you were going to come see me a few days ago. You and I both know that we'd be a stronger team together. We could jump start a movement, with your celebrity status and my assets. And I know you're out of work. What's stopped you from coming to see me?"

Jaym tried to stay still and control his breathing. "Let's just say I think there are smarter ways. Ways that won't get me right back in a Tribunal." He shot a glance over at Beck, who stared straight back.

"Of course, I don't want you back in a Tribunal! I wouldn't want any of us being arrested. What good would that do?" Heath leaned back in his chair. "But getting back at Marks requires more than just brains. It requires resources, men, and strategy. I've been running a successful enterprise at the center of all of those things. A smart guy like you would be a major asset to our operation here."

"You're telling me there isn't any risk to your business, Heath?"

"There is risk in everything in life, Jaym. And with risk comes reward. Do you think you can get back at Piers without any risk? Or are you content to spend your days trying to organize the chaos down here in the Furrows—waiting for another cop to pick you up and end it all before you even tried to change anything?"

Jaym resisted the urge to look down. *Stay confident.* "Of course, I'm not content with that. But even if I play a small part in helping to organize this, that's better than risking my life unnecessarily. The Furrows is better than whatever a second tribunal may sentence me to."

"You talk as if it's so black and white. Tribunal or not. Life isn't so simple, Jaym."

Beck chimed in. "Besides, the Tribunals aren't all that bad. Some might say they're a risk worth taking." His tone had a subtle coldness to it. "You of all people should know that."

"I don't need to take any chances working with a drug dealer, Beck." Jaym looked his friend dead in the eyes. *What has happened to him? Where is this coming from?*

"That's not all Heath does, Jaym," Beck shot back, straightening up from the bookshelf.

"Boys, boys," Heath said, fanning the air with his hands. "No one is asking you to do anything you don't want to do, Jaym."

"Then what *are* you asking me to do?"

Heath leaned back in his chair. "Simple, easy things. You see, the events of the past week, starting with the exchange outside Dante's, have opened all of our eyes to the injustices in this city—reminded us that what those in the past have sacrificed has been for nothing."

"I think we can all agree it's time for a change. Things are only going to be worse once people like Piers Marks are in charge," Beck quipped.

"I agree," Jaym responded. "But what exactly are you trying to do? What do you want *me* to do?"

"Well, for starters, just keeping an eye on what's going on out there for us. I am..." Heath paused, "a bit too well known to really keep my ears to the ground." Heath walked out from behind the desk and leaned on the front side. "I also heard you spoke with Piers's co-officer—Keats—and Piers's sister.

I'd like you to get close to them. Keep the relationship up. It could prove useful as this whole thing progresses. How does that sound?"

"I barely know them," Jaym said. "They just came up to me after the trial."

Heath continued. "Well, we've done a bit of recon. We happen to know that Gwen, I believe that's her name, yes? She frequents a particular café in the Garden District—The Dandelion. Go and bump into her. Pretend you're delivering a package. Lay some groundwork. That's all we're asking of you."

"See, easy. No drugs." Beck's face was devoid of its usual cheery grin.

"Okay," Jaym said, pointedly. He was ready to end the conversation and leave. "I'll go try to find Gwen tomorrow and get to know her better. Now if that's all, I best be going." *It could be useful for me too.*

"Great!" Heath clapped his hands and stood. "Beck, why don't you lead Jaym out." Heath went back around his desk as Jaym stood up. Beck nodded and led Jaym out of the office, back down the dark corridor.

Jaym slowed his pace, trying to see what activities were going on in the various rooms. *What is this all about? Is he really doing this for the good of the city?*

"Jaym."

He barely heard Beck call his name. Beck repeated it, and he came back to attention.

"Just give Heath a chance, okay? We're all on the same team here."

Jaym puffed his nostrils and headed out, exhausted from the short encounter.

CHAPTER 16

Gwen yawned as she brushed her hair. She was sitting in front of her mirror, looking at herself listlessly. She scanned the many colored vials of makeup in front of her and selected one indifferently. *What a crazy few days.* After finishing, she stood and looked over at her desk. Sighing, she packed a few of the books into her tote bag. *I'm so behind on readings.* She left the room and headed downstairs.

She heard the tinkling of silverware as she reached the foyer. Turning, she saw her father seated at the dining room table, having his breakfast. A spread of pastries was laid out on the table, and a pitcher of orange juice sat to his left. His eyes were focused on a paper he held up in the light.

"Good morning," she said warmly.

Marks looked up and put the paper down. "Gwen. Good morning. Join me?" He smiled at her and gestured to the empty chair on his left.

Gwen walked into the dining room and sat on the edge of the chairs. Jeffrey quickly walked over and placed a teacup next to her.

"Sorry father. I actually don't have much time. Have a lot of work to catch up on."

"Ah yes. It has been a ... busy past few days."

Gwen's smile faded. She looked down at the teacup and tenderly touched the porcelain. She traced the intricate blue vine of the flowers. Memories of setting out the delicate cups for tea parties with her mother flooded her mind.

"What is it dear?" Marks's voice was tender.

"I just miss her." Gwen looked up at her father, her eyes heavy.

"I do too." They sat quietly for a few moments.

"I'm worried about Piers, father," Gwen said, breaking the silence.

Marks scoffed. "He's acting spoiled. Self-righteous and arrogant."

"He's angry, father. He feels you humiliated him."

Marks lifted the china teacup in front of him, admiring it. "Our city is a fragile one, Gwen. Humans weren't meant to live in such close quarters. Breathing in poisoned air, slowly dying. Acting on emotional impulse, creating frenzied upheavals ... it's a surefire way to bring the entire system down." He looked at her fondly. "You've always appreciated fragility. Your brother certainly does not."

As Gwen listened, she felt a pit in her stomach. "I want to help him. I just don't know how."

"Talk to him and try to reason with him. We must make him understand how delicate the system is. And that he does indeed have a part to play. But I will not have him threaten the stability of this city." Marks's face had soured. He looked down at the pastry in front of him. "Things are already unstable. Things out of our control."

Gwen nodded. "Okay. I'll try." She stood up from the chair. "I'd best be going."

Marks feigned an attempt at smiling goodbye to Gwen, and quickly returned his focus to the papers. Gwen picked up her bag and departed the dining room. She softly closed the front door and exited into the courtyard.

* * *

Outside, Gwen saw Piers standing next to the fountain, his friend Alyx by his side. They were both in exercise clothing, with sweat dripping from their faces. Their voices were hushed, but in the quiet courtyard Gwen managed to overhear a bit of their conversation.

"...submitted a request for authorization, so we should be set," Alyx said.

"You're sure he'll be there?" Piers asked.

Alyx jerked his head as he noticed Gwen heading down from the front door. "Hey Gwen," he said, waving.

"Gwen," Piers turned to face his sister. "Beautiful day out."

"Good run?" she asked. "Smells like it." She took a few steps back and laughed.

"Yeah, I better shower. Alyx, talk to you later." Piers dashed past Gwen and headed to the penthouse.

"I'll head down with you," Alyx said, turning to head to the elevator. "Sorry about the smell." He grinned mischievously. Gwen eyed him, barely smiling. She had always been suspicious of Alyx.

Following him into the elevator, she asked, "What were you two talking about? An authorization? Sounded serious." She feigned an impressed tone.

Alyx shrugged. "Oh, just police stuff." The elevator began zooming down.

"Police stuff? With my brother?" Gwen looked at him confused. "Isn't he suspended?"

Alyx stiffened a bit and cracked his knuckles. Gwen couldn't tell if he was swaying slightly or if it was just an effect of the elevator's vertigo. "Yeah, I was just updating him on some stuff we had talked about before the Tribunal."

Gwen eyed him suspiciously. "Is he breaking his suspension, Alyx?" Her voice was direct, stern.

"Hey, your brothers' business with Captain Stone is his business. I don't interfere. We had just been talking about getting him on one of our drug patrols before this Tribunal stuff went down. So I just wanted to keep him in the loop. This was all a learning experience for him, you know." The elevator slowed to its stop, and the electric doors slid open. "Anyways, gotta run. See you later, Gwen." Alyx ran off before she could push him any further on the topic.

She headed out to the Garden District. She opted for one of her favorite routes along a sky walk instead of the monorail. The path was suspended several stories in the air, weaving between the buildings. *I knew he wouldn't just sit back and accept this. Piers is definitely breaking his suspension. Probably still going after that poor Jaym.*

Gwen walked at a leisurely pace, breathing in the crisp air. At one point, the sun's rays came down through the skyscrapers, and she stopped to soak in the light. Continuing on her way, she arrived in the Garden District ten minutes later. She reached out and ran her hand along the plants growing from the wall, feeling the leaves and vines. Rounding a corner, she came to her favorite café, The Dandelion, and grabbed an open table outside. Soon, she was lost in her textbook, with a warm cup of tea in front of her.

It must've been thirty minutes later or so that she finally

looked up, tearing her eyes away from the text. *Man that's dense.* She closed the book and looked about the square. She started squinting at someone who was partially hidden by the building at the edge of the small square. *Is that … that Furrows boy?* Jaym was peeking out from the corner of the building. She made eye contact with him and smiled. He looked back nervously as he emerged from his partial hiding and quickly crossed toward her. He was holding a small brown parcel.

"Hello there," she said, her tone friendly.

"Hi Gwen," he managed to spurt out, stumbling over the words.

She let out a small laugh. "What are you doing here?"

"Oh I was just wasting some time before delivering this package. I come up here for air sometimes. I like the plants." His eyes darted up and down, but he grinned sheepishly. *He's cute, in his own innocent, gentle way.*

"Take a seat." Gwen motioned to the empty chair across from her. He fiddled with his hands debating her offer, before sliding down. *His clothes look like they haven't been washed in days.* He wore an old, corduroy utility shirt with a gray t-shirt underneath. His dark pants looked worn, but not as worn as the brown boots he had on his feet. *He looks so out of place. This must've taken some confidence to come up here.* "How's everything been since your Tribunal? Do you want something to drink?"

"No, thanks. And I'm okay. Things went back to normal fairly quickly." Jaym glanced down at the book. "What are you reading?"

"Oh this? *A History of the Early Tribunals.* Riveting stuff, let me tell you. But I'm sure you don't want to hear about that."

Jaym laughed, his smile widening. "No, I'm curious. Tell me about it."

Gwen cocked her head, looking at him curiously. She delved into a brief overview. She started with an explanation of how the initial Tribunal system was unorganized and lacked clarity on jurisdiction. Then, she moved on to the evolution of the Chief Justice system and the Supreme Tribunal, and the dividing of the city into various judicial sectors. Jaym's eyes were locked on her the whole time. He nodded intently, asked a question here or there.

"Wow, you really know your stuff!" Jaym said, impressed. Gwen blushed. "Well, I've been studying it in the Academy for a few years now." *He's so genuine.*

"I always liked learning about history in school. It's been a while." He looked about the square nostalgically. "I got kicked out of the orphanage though at fifteen, so had to start working." Gwen's eyes felt heavy and her eyebrows turned down. Jaym turned back to her, clearly surprised at her downcast look. "What's the matter?"

Gwen started to answer but had trouble finding the words. "I just ... didn't realize you didn't have a family. It must be so hard growing up in the Furrows."

Jaym smiled and shrugged. "It's not too bad. And I may not have parents, but I have Beck and my friend Jemma. We're our own little family of sorts down there. It's not as bad as you might think. You should come visit sometime."

Gwen felt her lips curl into a smile. "I'd like that."

The two were silent for a few moments. Gwen could tell Jaym had begun to feel awkward, and he abruptly stood up and picked the package up from the ground. "Well, I should be going. But it was nice talking to you, Gwen."

"Wait. Jaym," Gwen began as he turned to go. "Be careful down there. I don't know what my brother is up to, but I don't think he's moved on from your tribunal."

Jaym's smile evaporated. "He's suspended from the police though. So, he can't be too dangerous, right?"

Gwen looked down, unable to hide her concern. "I have a feeling Piers isn't going to simply accept his suspension. Plus, his friends are in the police force. And recently they've all been promoted. I overheard him and one of them talking, and it sounded like they were planning something. "

"What do you think he's going to do?" His eyes had gone wide in a sense of panic.

"I don't know. If I find out anything, I'll be sure to tell you. Piers just always finds a way to even the score."

"Why does he hate us so much? Us Furrows folk?"

Gwen looked down, her eyelids heavy. "He blames people in the Furrows for our mother's death. She died leaving the Grand Tribunal Hall ... ten years ago. Caught up in the violence in the square. When the Furrows people were rioting after the dissolution of the SubCity Tribunals."

"I'm ... so sorry, Gwen." Jaym's voice was soft and solemn. "Thanks for the tip about your brother. I better go."

Gwen didn't have anything else to say. She simply nodded as he turned and hurried off.

CHAPTER 17

———

Jaym felt dizzy as he left the Garden District. His mind was spinning, oscillating between the urgency to alert Heath and Beck about Gwen's warning, but also how he felt about Gwen. *Damn she was beautiful. Funny, kind. Genuine.* "Hey, watch it!" a man yelled as Jaym shouldered his way past. The man's shouting brought Jaym back to reality. *Focus, Jaym. You have to get to Heath and Beck.* The fear and panic came rushing back, coursing through his body. But also, an appreciation for Gwen. *She warned me.* He rushed down a set of stairs and began heading back to the center city square at a fervent pace. He could feel people looking at him but he didn't care.

The streets were busy with people shopping and going out their days, but he pushed through the crowds. *Nothing is going to happen right away. Deep breaths. Just get down there and tell them.* Despite his attempts to relax, his heartbeat continued thumping. *I knew this wasn't over.*

It took him an hour to get all the way to Sub3. He was nearly out of breath by the time he came to the now-familiar metal door, nestled inconspicuously in the dark street. He gave a few heavy bangs and dropped his hands to his knees to try and catch his breath.

The metal lookout slid open, and the guard's dark eyes stared out.

"I need to talk to Heath," Jaym said, frantically.

"He's not here."

"Where is he? When is he coming back?" Jaym yelled as the metal opening slid shut. He put his back up against the door, leaned his head back and closed his eyes. *He'll be back. I'll just come back later.* He wandered through the streets listlessly and had a few drinks at Dante's, where the old barkeep tried to cheer up his gloomy demeanor, but to no avail.

"Jaym, why so down? You should be happy! You're a free man, a local celebrity. A hero!" Dante smiled wide, his thick mustache popping up on the corners of his mouth.

Jaym continued staring down at his drink. "I'm just nervous, Dante. This isn't over. That Piers guy has it out for me."

"Just because his dad is the Chief Justice doesn't mean he can waltz around and do what he pleases. You saw the way Marks spoke down to him at the Tribunal. Put him right back in his place, he did."

"I don't know, Dante." Jaym looked up. He could feel his fear showing in his eyes. "You didn't see the hate in his eyes. His mother died in the aftermath of the last Supreme Tribunal. Ten years ago. And he blames the people down here."

Dante slowly nodded, his expression turning morose. "New Boston hasn't been the same since that day."

"I barely remember what it was like before."

Dante smiled again and took a swig of his drink. "Things were better before. Happier. But the violence that happened after that verdict... it was mayhem. Riots. Revolt. So many people died in the chaos and fighting."

Jaym looked back down at his drink. He was too anxious to keep chatting.

Later in the evening, he returned to the metal door and knocked again. The eyepiece slid open again, but before Jaym could say anything, the guard spoke.

"He's still not here. Go away."

"I need to talk to him! This is serious!" Jaym yelled and banged on the door, but the guard had slid the opening shut immediately after speaking. He stalked angrily away from the door, unsure of what to do. Just then, he saw two men heading toward him. He paused and moved out of their way. *They look like they could be Heath's guys.* He quietly followed behind them. Sure enough, they stopped outside the metal door and one went to knock. The slot opened and closed quickly, and the door began to open.

Jaym didn't give himself the moment to think or consider his options. He leapt a few steps ahead and walked through the door before the guard could close it.

"You! I told you to go away!" the guard slammed the door shut and pinned Jaym up against the wall. The two other men immediately pulled out handguns and aimed them at Jaym.

"I know Heath! Tell him I'm here!"

"Shut the hell up!" one of the men yelled.

"Just let me talk to him!" Jaym's voice was filled with panic.

"Hey, hey," a familiar voice rang out, as someone emerged from an open doorway, hearing the commotion. "It's okay, I know him." Beck pushed between the two men with the guns. "He's a friend."

The guard eyed Beck for a moment, and then slowly released Jaym. Jaym glared back at the man and adjusted his jacket. His shoulders were already sore from the impact of the guard throwing him against the wall.

"You do?" one of the men asked.

"Yes, let him go! He isn't lying; he's been helping Heath." The guard slowly released his grip, and Jaym threw his arms off of him as soon as he could. "Come on, Jaym," Beck motioned. The men nodded and left, and the guard turned to resume his position. As they started heading down the hallway, Beck put his arm around Jaym. "Sorry, they're a lot nicer once they get to know you. Things are just a bit tense right now."

"I need to talk to Heath—right now." They reached the end of the hallway and were outside Heath's office.

Nodding, Beck said, "Well let's go chat." He knocked twice, and then opened the door to the office.

Heath was sitting at his desk, laughing with a man seated in front of him. As Jaym and Beck entered, two guards on either side of the door stood up. When they recognized Beck, they relaxed and sat back down.

"Jaym! Wasn't expecting to see you." Heath smiled wide.

Jaym got straight to the point. "Listen, Heath. I met with Gwen, like you asked."

"Great!" Heath threw up his hands and leaned back in his chair.

Beck gave Jaym a slap on the back. "Good job, Jaym."

"No, listen," Jaym continued, his tone serious. "She told me that she thinks Piers is planning something with his other police friends. She doesn't think he's going to abide by his suspension. And she said he's angry. Like really, really angry."

Heath's eyes narrowed as he took in the information. The room was quiet for a few moments, the air clearly having changed.

"He wouldn't try to break in here," Beck said defiantly.

"He might," Heath responded, still staring ahead.

"He absolutely would. He thinks he's untouchable." Jaym's expression was stern—sober.

"Rich scum," Beck said, with unmistakable resentment.

"Beck," Heath cautioned, raising his hand. "Let's focus on the situation at hand. Jaym, did Gwen have any additional information? Like when Piers may launch an attack?"

"She didn't. But she's going to try and find out more."

"Good. Thank you, Jaym, for telling me. You've done well." Heath said evenly, maintaining his calm. "Go home and relax. You too Beck. I'll handle everything here."

"What are you going to do?" Beck asked, fear in his voice.

"I'll put more people on guard, move some of our assets to other locations." Heath smiled. "Not to worry, Beck. We can handle this."

Beck and Jaym both nodded. Just then, shouting was heard from the hall.

"Police! Police are here!"

Heath's smile vanished and his face went white. The two guards on either side of the door sprang up, as more shouting started from the hallway.

"Emergency procedures! Let's get the hell out of here now!" Heath yelled at both guards. Gunfire began erupting from down the hall. Jaym turned to Beck as his eyes went wide. He could feel his heart rate begin pounding.

"We gotta get out of here now," Jaym said.

"This way!" Heath shouted. He grabbed something on the bookshelf, and a second later the shelf swung open to reveal a hidden door.

"There is more than one exit to this place," Heath said, following the guards through the door. Yelling and gunfire continued, and Jaym's heart rate went up another few ticks. They emerged into another dark room with computer screens. Heath went to one and began typing away, with the two guards standing above him. Shots rang out, louder this time. Too loud. *Are they in here?* Another man had run up past Beck and pushed aside a metal sheet hanging on the wall, revealing a dark passageway. "This way!" he yelled to Beck, and ran in.

More loud noises erupted, and soon shooting was coming from nearby. One of the guards near Heath fell to the ground. Heath reached down and grabbed the semiautomatic weapon from the guard's hands, whipping it around to the direction of the gunfire.

"You think you can take me in!" Heath screamed as he unleashed the bullets. Then the shooting abruptly stopped, as Heath was hit in the arm and dropped the gun. He let out a scream in pain.

Jaym and Beck had crossed the room and were at the entrance to the dark passageway.

"Go Jaym!" Beck yelled, pushing him ahead. Once Jaym was beyond the dark entrance, he turned. Beck was falling, tripping over something, as more bullets rained out.

"Beck!" Jaym's voice was shrill, filled with panic.

"Go!" Beck yelled back, and as he did, a policeman stepped over Beck. A bullet hit and ricocheted off his helmet. The officer's face, covered by tinted glass, looked straight at Jaym as he pulled the helmet off. And the face that had become all too familiar to Jaym stared back at him, smiling. *Piers Marks.* He felt all his emotions go up a notch. A mix of terror, fear, panic, anger. But most of all, loathing. It was consuming him.

"Listen to your friend," Piers said. Fury swept over Jaym, but before he could say anything, one of the men slammed the door shut, and darkness enveloped him.

CHAPTER 18

───

"I would say that went as well as it could have," Piers said, smiling to Alyx.

"Agreed." Alyx smiled back, satisfied. The two stood outside Police Headquarters, watching the other policemen take Beck inside. "Kind of wish we had gotten the first guy for a second time. Or if we had gotten the drug kingpin. Captain Stone won't be happy that we didn't bring him in."

"Well, the man has a lot of firepower. And as I told you, I think he could be an asset." Piers continued looking ahead. *Yes, Heath will see things my way. I'll be sure of that.*

"You might be right. Who's that?" Alyx pointed to a man walking toward them from the headquarters.

"Well, I do believe that looks like Keats," Piers answered in a mocking tone. He straightened his posture, looking smug and confident.

Keats walked up to the pair. He looked dead-pan at them, serious. *I'm not in the mood for another lecture. Not going to let him ruin this day for me.*

"I thought you two might be out here. I passed guards escorting that tall Furrows boy inside."

"The mission was a success," Piers said. "No thanks to you."

Keats stared back, his look cold. "I told you I wasn't going to be a part of you breaking your probation."

"And I told you I simply couldn't miss seeing the look in that poor asshole's eyes when we slapped handcuffs on him. Best part was Jaym basically watched me do it. Plus, getting to gun down a few of his pals was an added bonus." Piers's blood was boiling. *Who does Keats think he is? So holier-than-thou these days.*

"How did you even know he was going to be there?" Keats was still unconvinced.

"Come on Keats," Alyx answered. "You know we've been tracking all recent criminals after their release from the Tribunals. We knew there was a high chance Jaym would be there. And those two seem to run together."

Keats looked from Alyx to Piers. He was clearly still angry, almost distrustful.

"Anyways, I better be going. Captain Stone will want a full report," Alyx said. "See you both later." Alyx and Piers shook hands, and then he headed off toward the headquarters.

Turning to Keats, Piers said, "I don't appreciate you chastising me."

Keats looked back, his look becoming graver. "I'm just nervous for you. If Captain Stone finds out you went on this raid, or worse, your father…"

"They won't." Piers spoke pointedly. He reached into his pocket and pulled out the golden globe that the two boys had stolen from his father's office. "Look what I found."

Keats eyed the sphere apprehensively. "Piers. Don't go and do something stupid. Gloating to your father isn't going to help anything."

"I know what I'm doing. I've thought through everything. So, don't you worry." Piers slipped the globe back into his pocket. "I'd better get going."

Keats nodded. In a grave, grim tone he said, "You're walking a fine line, Piers. Tensions are running high in this city. Making enemies isn't going to help calm things down. Think about how bad things were last time things got out of control."

Piers turned serious and austere. "And think about how much better the city was after that! I'm doing what's best for this city. Our city. I only want justice to be administered swiftly, consistently, and effectively. And if people hate me for that, well then they can hate me. Now I have to get going, I'll see you later." He turned and headed off into the dimly lit streets of the ground level.

Piers strode through the city with a confident, strong energy. It felt like a second pulse inside his body. He was finally taking charge instead of letting others dictate actions to him. He looked at his reflection in the opaque, dark glass running along the street. He puffed out his chest and stood tall, admiring himself. *This is my city. No one can take it away from me.*

Soon, he was rising above the streets in the elevator heading to his penthouse. The streetlights faded to dim specks of light, as if he were staring at the stars in the universe rather than down into the depths of the city. He exited the elevator and crossed the courtyard, with its peaceful fountain and adorning flowers.

He went to bed feeling satisfied. The next day, he went to the Academy for the first time in a week. Things felt normal, as if he had returned to the status quo from the chaos of the past few days. He kept thinking ahead to how his father would react when he returned the golden globe. Piers smiled to himself. *He has to be proud.*

In the evening, Piers returned home. Inside the penthouse, he saw Jeffrey crossing the foyer.

"Is my father in?"

"Yes, Master Marks. I believe he's in his study."

Piers nodded. He walked down the hall and knocked on the two, large wooden doors. Without waiting for an answer, he pushed them open and walked in. "Hello father."

As usual, Gregorius Marks had his head bent down over his desk. His eyes were intently focused on the papers in front of him, with his hands placed framing either side.

"What do you need, son? I'm quite busy." Marks addressed Piers without looking up.

"I have something to return to you," Piers answered, and pulled out the golden globe. He held it in his hand, letting the light reflect off its shiny surface.

Marks looked up, focusing on the globe.

"Where did you find that?" Marks's voice was severe.

"Alyx has just completed a raid of a drug den in the lower levels of the Furrows. The Torrey boy you so carelessly let back onto the streets was there, but he evaded arrest. They arrested his friend though and found this in his possession."

Piers smiled, his smug expression still on his face.

Marks held his gaze. "How did Alyx know this belonged to me?"

Piers's eyes suddenly went wide. He grasped for words but struggled. "He ... I told him about—"

"You went on this raid, didn't you?" Marks cut him off.

"I—" Piers fumbled over his words.

"Answer me!" Marks's voice rose quickly as he stood from his chair.

"Yes. I did." Piers's tone was fueled with resentment.

Marks grumbled, letting out a slow breath. "You deliberately disobeyed your probation. A decision, you might recall, that I made."

"The patrol squad needed men for the raid. They were presented with an opportunity and had to act on it. Surely you can understand—"

"You deliberately disobeyed me!" Marks erupted, slamming his hands down on the desk. He stood up and walked out from behind the desk. "You are not above the law, Piers! You cannot just do whatever you like!"

Rage filled his eyes. "That boy stole from you! He humiliated me! The raid was successful, and we got back what was rightfully ours. How can you not be proud of that!"

"Because, you weren't to be on those streets!" Marks yelled, his volume increasing. "Actions have consequences, Piers!"

Piers was incensed. He looked away from his father, staring ahead at the glass window. Impulsively, he lifted his arm and threw the golden globe as hard as he could at the window. The glass cracked and lines began spreading out along the pane.

"Where is this coming from? At what point did you become so sour that you are blinded by what is actually right and wrong in this world, thinking you are the white knight this city needs?" Marks sneered at his son.

Piers stepped closer to his father. "When I realized that you and the other Justices are failing to do your job. You're leading this city down a dark path and it will not recover. We're all going to end up just like mother, killed by the very people you claim to be protecting."

Marks stood still while staring at his son. "So that's it, this is about revenge for what happened to your mother?" The air hung between the two men, tense and heavy. "Revenge clouds one's mind and soul, Piers. It blocks one from reason and logic. It—"

"No, it's not about her!" Piers yelled. He spun around, his back to his father. "She's just one example. It's about all of them: it's about Thaddeus thinking he can subvert the rules. It's about Jaym and the other Furrows boy, thinking they can steal from us. It's about Gwen and Keats, congratulating a criminal that *you* set free. It's about the system being off balance, and everyone in this godforsaken city thinking they can do whatever they want whenever they want."

Silence hung in the air for a moment, while Marks continued staring at Piers from behind. Then, in a steady tone, with a subtle tinge of fear, he said, "You have no respect for justice. You don't think justice is about all of us. You think justice is only about you. But you, in fact, are worse than any of those people who you claim are cancers in our society. You, Piers, are causing destruction and instability. You're going to be the downfall of this city. But I won't let that happen."

"And what are you going to do about it, father?" Piers asked, his back still to Marks.

"I don't know yet. I'll confer with the other Chief Justices. But you are not to leave this house until I decide what to do with you."

"I may be your son, but you can't control me!" Piers shrieked, spinning around and running up to his father.

"You're a disgrace of a son!" Marks roared back.

"And you're a disgrace of a father!" Fury and rage spread to fill every inch of Piers's body. His eyes glared with scorn, and his heart was pounding. He put his hands on his father's chest and shoved him toward the cracked window.

Marks gained momentum as he stumbled backward and crashed into the glass pane, which gave way under his body. He hung in the air for a moment, his eyes wide and white in pure horror, as he looked back at Piers. And then he fell to the city depths below.

CHAPTER 19

Piers stumbled back, catching himself on the desk. He stared down at the shattered window, unable to bring himself to peer out of it. He felt frozen. A cool breeze blew through the room, as he stood in silence.

What have I done? He slowly backed away from the window and moved to the corner of the office, where a crystal decanter sat with whiskey. He poured himself a glass and downed it, gulping the liquor. He sat down in his father's chair and put his hands on the arm rests. He slowly came out of his shock. *I need a plan.* Just then, he heard footsteps approaching.

"Father, I need to talk to—" Gwen said, as she burst open through the doors. She stopped abruptly. Piers stared at her as she took in the scene. Her face shifted to a look of pure terror.

"What did you do, Piers?" Gwen said, almost at a whisper. The words seemed to slow and die as she finished her sentence.

"Gwen," Piers started to say, but he was cut off.

"Where is our father?" Gwen yelled, her voice raising. She rushed to the window and leaned out. Piers felt frozen again, not knowing what to say. He knew she couldn't see anything from as high up. She slowly turned around and asked the question he knew was coming.

"Did you do this? Did you ... push him?"

"No!" Piers stood up from the desk defiantly. "I would never!" His eyes were wide.

"You're a monster," she said, looking up at him with teary, fearful eyes. Her voice was shaky.

"It had to be Jeffrey." Piers's voice was cold and emotionless. "I'll call for the police immediately." He went to the government phone on the corner of his father's desk. *Yes, this can work. Think, Piers. Stay calm, but not too calm.*

"You're going to frame him? Jeffrey has been with us since we were children!" Tears streamed down Gwen's face. "What happened to the brother I used to know?"

"Gwen," Piers said, his voice grave and serious. "I didn't do this."

Gwen had started backing up toward the door. "I'm getting out of this house and the hell away from you." With that, Gwen turned and ran out of the study.

Piers exhaled again, realizing his heartbeat had picked back up. He poured another whiskey and gulped it down. *I can do this. This can work.* He picked up the black phone on the desk, and heard an operator answer on the other end.

"Yes, Chief Justice Marks?"

"This is Piers Marks. There has been an attack. Our butler has pushed my father out a window of his study. Send guards to arrest him immediately." He hung up the phone before the operator could ask any additional questions. Piers sat for a moment in silence, gathering himself.

He finally walked over the shattered window and peered out. He could barely make out the small dots of people that seemed to be gathering below. *Yes, this can work.*

* * *

Gwen's heart hadn't stopped racing. The scene of her brother in front of the shattered window was seared into her mind. *How could he do this? I have to get out of here.* She sped through the penthouse and out the front door, heading straight to the elevator. She jabbed the button multiple times, panting. The doors finally opened, and she threw herself up against the elevator wall. As the doors closed, she let out a sob.

Pull yourself together, Gwen. She looked at her reflection in the glass elevator. Her eyes were puffy and red. *Do I turn him in? My only brother?* Tears started streaming down her cheeks, falling in heavy droplets to the elevator floor. Wiping the tears away, she spoke out loud, "If I don't, he could come for me next." *I have no choice. I'll go to the police headquarters, find Keats, and tell him it was Piers.* She nodded to herself, feeling slightly safer as she came up with her plan.

The doors slid open, and she took a few steps out of the elevator. She found herself frozen. A small crowd had gathered nearby. She felt her heart drop as she realized what they were likely gathered around. *Oh, father.* She couldn't bring herself to go see him. *There's no time.* She started running through the city streets, away from the penthouse. Tears streamed down her cheeks and flew off, but she tried to empty her mind. *Keep moving.*

It took her twenty minutes of straight racing through the streets and skywalks to reach the police headquarters. When she finally did, she had to drop to her knees to gather her breath. She walked into the entrance, which was abuzz with activity. She looked around, feeling lost and overwhelmed.

"Can I help you miss?"

She turned her head toward the direction of the voice. A policeman sat behind an elevated desk. He was leaning down, looking at her curiously.

"Yes. I ... I need to find Keats Presley. I need to see him immediately." She stammered out the words, trying to even her voice.

The policeman typed away at the screen in front of him. "Looks like he should be here, he checked in not too long ago. I can radio for him to come out."

"No! I need to go see him! Can't someone take me?" Her voice returned to verging on hysterical.

"Only authorized personnel are allowed in the headquarters," the policeman began. *He clearly doesn't recognize me.* Gwen began to muster the energy to explain who she was, when she heard her name called.

"Gwen?"

She turned to see Alyx, who had just walked in. Gwen felt her heartbeat pick up again.

"What are you doing here?" he asked in a friendly tone.

He must not know yet. "Can you take me to see Keats?"

"We're not supposed to take people back—"

"Please, Alyx. It's an emergency."

Alyx shrugged and walked in front of Gwen to the guard's desk. He raised his ID badge. "I'm a Level Three officer, I'll escort her back. Come on, this way."

"Thanks, Alyx," she said, as they began heading down the hallway.

"No problem. Anything for Piers's little sister." He smiled cordially at her.

She tried to smile back, but hearing Piers's name made her stomach churn. *Focus, Gwen.* She started moving, following him as they moved past the desk. They came around into a room full of desks and screens. Alyx led her to a corner where several officers were seated. "He's right there. Just have him take you back out when you're done."

Gwen nodded, thanked Alyx, and went over to Keats. "Gwen! What are you doing here?" Gwen felt her tears start welling back up. Keats asked quieter, "What's the matter?"

She whispered back, "Can we go somewhere to talk?"

He stood up and grabbed her hand. They walked back out into the hallway until no one was nearby.

"What's going on Gwen?"

She tripped over the words, barely getting them out. "Piers has gone insane. I think he just killed my father. He—"

"Whoa, what? He did *what?*"

"I didn't see it happen; a window was shattered. Keats, I think he pushed him. I don't know what to do. I'm freaking out."

Keats was silent for a moment. "Wait here." He dashed away before she could say anything. She looked down at the ground and rubbed her arms, trying to avoid the eyes of the few policemen who passed by.

Keats returned quickly. "I just checked the system. Piers called in to send a unit to the penthouse. It said the butler had thrown Chief Justice Marks out the window."

"It wasn't Jeffrey. It was Piers." Gwen's voice was still shaky, but her volume had increased.

"Shh," Keats quieted her. "How do you know for certain?"

"I came into the study and saw him sitting behind the desk. The window was shattered. Father was eighty stories below, strewn across the ground. Piers looked scared. Panicked. Keats, he's become delusional lately. You have to believe me."

Keats listened to her with a flat stare. Gwen looked back

at him, annoyed at his ability to hide his emotions. *Maybe this was a mistake.*

In a grave voice, Keats said, "Okay, Gwen. I do believe you. But I don't know who else is going to."

"I don't know what to do." Tears had begun welling up in her eyes again.

"Is there anywhere you can go that's safe? Wait out the day until we see how this unfolds?"

Gwen's eyebrows furrowed as she tried to strategize. "I don't want to stay at any government official's house. They wouldn't understand why I'm not with my brother. Comforting him. The whole city will know about this soon."

Keats nodded in agreement. "Yeah I think somewhere people wouldn't expect would be better." They stood in silence for a few moments, contemplating what to do. Offhandedly, Keats said, "Honestly, somewhere in the Furrows would be best."

Gwen tilted her head as she considered the idea. *Where could I go in the Furrows?* Suddenly an idea came to her. "I could go find Jaym."

"Jaym? The same guy who attacked your brother?" Keats raised his eyebrows as he looked back at her, confused.

"I ran into him at The Dandelion the other day. He's a nice guy. He seemed sincere, trustworthy. And he lives in the Furrows." *Yes, being with Jaym will be safe. No one will even know where to find me down there. Especially not Piers.*

Keats let out a breath. "If that's our only option, I guess it's all you can do. If Piers finds out that's where you went though..."

"You can't tell him. He can't know."

"I understand." Keats nodded. "We arrested Jaym in a small square outside this bar in Sub3. I'd start there and ask around. His face has been on news screens all over the city since his Tribunal, so I'm sure someone will know where to find him."

Sub3—I've never even been to Sub1. Gwen took a deep breath and steadied herself. "Okay. I can do this."

"Come on, I'll walk you out. Here's exactly how to get there." Keats proceeded to give Gwen instructions on how to find her way to the square in Sub3 as he led her to the headquarters exit. "Be careful, okay?" Keats leaned in and gave Gwen a kiss.

She felt a momentarily relief from the stress of the day, until he pulled back. "You too." And with that, she exited the police headquarters and headed toward Justice Square.

Soon, she was descending into the lower city levels. People eyed her as she moved past, and she slowed her pace to appear less conspicuous. She squinted her eyes. *Everything is so dark down here.* She passed a news screen and stopped. An image quickly caught her eye. *Oh no. More arrests? Beck arrested?* She paused in front of the anchor and listened as Velma recounted a drug raid in the lower levels of the city, how multiple criminals had been apprehended. One of the mugshots stood out: Jaym's friend.

"...but the head of the drug operations, according to the police, evaded capture. We have yet to be given a name, but the police have said this man is dangerous, and for all New Boston citizens to exercise caution when moving about the city, especially in less-trafficked areas. Other drug raids took place this evening in various sectors..."

"He's trying to start a civil war," Gwen said out loud, her eyes wide. She continued running, picking up her pace. Reciting the directions in her head over and over again, she prayed she wouldn't forget a step. *It's a maze down here. Everything looks the same.* But soon, she came across the staircase Keats had told her of, the words "Sublevel Three" barely legible over the stone doorway. She descended, feeling immediately how the air was cooler. A hint of sulfur wafted into her nose.

Out of breath, she finally came upon the small square—her final destination. The same spot where her brother had started the fight a week earlier when he let loose his rage and arrested Jaym. It was empty. In fact, all of Sub3 seemed empty—desolate. She slowly walked the perimeter of the square and stopped in front of a wooden door. A small sign hung above with the words "Dante's."

Gwen took a deep breath. *You can do this.* She pulled her hair back into a ponytail, as it had fallen during her sprint, and gave the door a confident push.

The bar was quiet, with very few people inside. No one paid her any attention as she walked in, but she stopped a few feet inside nevertheless. Scanning the room, she felt her heart sink for the second time today. *Jaym.* She recognized him immediately. He was hunched over the bar with a drink in front of him, at the far end.

"Jaym!" Gwen called out, as she ran up to him. She threw her arms around him and hugged him, but then pulled back. "Sorry," she mumbled.

The unexpected hug didn't seem to affect him at all. He looked sullen, as if all the energy had been drained out of him. "Gwen, what are you doing here?"

"I didn't know where else to go," Gwen said. She felt calm coming over her for the first time all day. "Jaym, Piers killed my father. I walked into his study and saw the glass wall shattered—Piers sitting behind his desk..." her voice trailed off.

"What?" Jaym perked up with nervous energy. He shook his head and turned back to his drink, taking a gulp. "I'm sorry, Gwen. I guess no one is safe." As he spoke, Dante walked over to the pair.

"You're not lost miss, are you?" Dante asked, aimlessly cleaning a glass.

"She's with me, Dante," Jaym said, before Gwen could respond. "And I'm sure she could use a drink right about now." He smiled at Gwen.

"A drink would be incredible, thanks," she said, smiling back. He poured her a glass of dark liquid. She took a sip and almost spit it out.

Dante grinned, showing his stained teeth. "That's the nicest stuff we have down here. But it tastes better the more you drink it!" He laughed to himself as he walked away.

The two sat quietly for some time, both sipping their drinks. Gwen allowed her heartbeat to slow, and relished the dark, quiet refuge of the bar.

After a while, she finally spoke. "Jaym, I'm sorry for everything my family has done to you—especially my brother."

"You don't have to apologize," he said softly. "None of this is your fault. I'd never blame you for the actions of your brother. I'm sorry about your father. No matter what he did in this world, he didn't deserve to be murdered."

"Thank you." Gwen smiled. "This is the best I've felt all day. Listen, I came down here actually to find you. I can't go home after what just happened. I need someplace to stay, at least until things have calmed down a bit. Can I stay with you?"

Jaym began smiling. He opened his mouth to say something, but then something caught his eye. Gwen turned around to look where his focus had gone. The door to the bar had opened, and a man in a black leather jacket with slicked back hair entered, with a burly man behind him. The second man held a gun. *Who are they?* Gwen turned back to

Jaym. She saw his shoulders tense up as he sat up in his chair. A sense of panic began setting in.

"You've got to be kidding me," Jaym said as he stood up, and began walking toward the man.

"Jaym," the man said, "I'm so glad you're okay. I—"

"You've got a lot of nerve coming in here, Heath!" Jaym yelled. He reached out and shoved the man, his face becoming flush with fury. The guard came from behind quickly and shoved Jaym back.

"Jaym!" Dante and Gwen both yelled. Dante dropped the glass he had been cleaning, and it shattered on the bar.

"It's okay," Heath said to the guard, stepping out from behind him. "I know you're upset Jaym, but listen to me—"

"How did you escape? Where's Beck? What did they do to him!" Jaym yelled. Dante now flanked him.

"I was able to break free and escape in the commotion. The Marks boy was more interested in Beck than me. Look I would've come sooner, but I wasn't sure it was safe yet for me to come out. As soon as I knew they didn't have my face plastered across the news screens, I set out to find you." Heath spoke earnestly, passionately. "Jaym, I didn't want this to happen either. You have to believe me about that."

"Yeah well you knew this could happen at any minute. That's the risk you take when you run an illegal underground drug ring. You should've been clearer to Beck about the risks," Jaym said, anger imbued in his words.

Gwen looked from one man to the other, trying to determine what was going on. Her own heartbeat had picked up again.

Heath let out a sigh. "Of course, I was clear to him about that. You know Beck, he didn't care about the risks. You can't punish me for his decisions."

"You can't blame me for not trusting you, Heath," Jaym said.

"I don't. And I'm not here to argue about what happened to Beck, or the role either of us played. I'm here to make a plan to save him. I've had plenty of guys arrested before, and we've been putting together a map of the Tribunal Hall and prison complex for years. If there's ever a time to use it, I'd say it's now."

"You mean you want to break him out?" Gwen asked, stepping up next to Jaym. The men both turned to her, clearly having forgotten she was even there.

"You brought *her* down here?" Heath's tone was surprised, but also a bit accusatory.

"She's on our side," Jaym said defensively.

Heath stared back, clearly still suspicious. Gwen ignored him and looked to Jaym. "Jaym, trying to break Beck out is a death sentence. The Grand Tribunal Hall is always heavily guarded," Gwen cautioned.

Heath answered. "Well we either risk saving him or leave him to face the Tribunal. I don't expect your father to be as kind he was to Jaym."

Gwen stepped between the two men and looked Jaym in the eyes. "If you do this, you'll end up back in the Tribunal yourself, Jaym."

Jaym's face was hardened, and his eyes darted back and forth. Gwen looked at him pleadingly, waiting for his answer. "We owe it to Beck to at least try," he finally said.

Heath's sinister smile had returned. "I agree. Let's stick it to the bastards and break him out. I'll get the plans ready and come find you again tomorrow. Timing is going to be key with all of this, so we need to think strategically. Now, if you'll excuse me, I think I need a drink." Heath headed to the back of the bar and settled into a booth.

"I know you don't think this is a good idea," Jaym said, turning back to Gwen.

Gwen's eyes were still downcast. "I don't know what's a good or bad idea at this point." She looked up at him, tears welling back up. She felt overwhelmed at everything. "Jaym I can't go back to my house. I'm scared what my brother will do to me. I…" her voice trailed off.

"Hey, it's okay," Jaym responded, putting his hands on her shoulders. "You can stay down here as long as you want. You'll be safe here, I promise."

Gwen wiped a tear away. "Thanks. I really appreciate it."

"No problem. Things are crazy right now. And we're both clearly exhausted. I'll take you to my place. Tomorrow we can talk about what to do next."

Gwen nodded and followed him out of the bar and into the cool alleys of the Furrows. *He's right, I'm spent.* She tried to think about more mundane things, like the industrial surroundings that were so foreign to her. But she kept finding herself focusing back on Jaym. She was surprised how comfortable she felt with this young boy who was almost a complete stranger. While part of her thought that this may be a mistake, with each step she felt more and more confident that she was moving in the right direction. And for a moment, she almost forgot about the events that brought her down to the Furrows in the first place.

CHAPTER 20

Piers sat in the second pew of the New Boston Cathedral, one of the few religious buildings of the past. *Have I even been inside here before? Maybe as a kid. Either way, must've been ages ago.* Piers sat alone. He had asked for some time to himself to reflect before the funeral ceremonies were to begin. He shuffled uncomfortably; he almost never wore this black suit. The fabric was stiff.

His father's brown, oak casket lay near the altar. A bouquet of red roses sat on top, and a picture of him propped up beside. Piers cocked his head back, reminiscing on his father's face: those hard lines, angled chin, sharp cheek bones. *I wonder how he thought he would die. Definitely not at the hands of his son. Am I a horrible person? He was a terrible father, after all.*

It had been two days since his father fell from the penthouse study. They had been a blur. The police had arrived, shortly after Gwen left, to arrest Jeffrey. Piers had stood in the foyer and watched them take him away, avoiding making eye contact. His emotions ricocheted back and forth. One minute he felt ashamed and moody, and the next resolute and proud. He continually found himself looking in the mirror and saying aloud, "Stop punishing yourself. What's done is done."

Piers heard the doors open and shut quickly. Footsteps followed as someone walked up the aisle. He stiffened his posture and scowled. *I told them no visitors unless absolutely necessary.*

"Piers. I'm so sorry for your loss," a voice said from behind him. The voice was sincere and formal. Piers turned his head slightly to get a glimpse of who had come in.

"Chief Justice Connally. Thank you." He turned back to face his father's coffin. *Why is he here?*

"And at the hands of someone you've known and trusted your entire life. I can only imagine."

Piers's eyes narrowed. *Does he suspect something else? Is this him trying to tell me?* He stared ahead, avoiding having to face Connally. "Yes. I'm still processing it all. It is shocking to say the least." He felt empty all of a sudden. "I just can't believe he's gone," he said, softly.

"Gregorius was a great man. Know that I am here for you in any way I can be of assistance. The other Chief Justices and I will be meeting soon to discuss moving forward and electing a new Chief Justice to fill your father's chair. I'm happy to keep you informed on the matter."

"Yes, I'd appreciate that. Who do you think is the forerunner?"

"Oh, there are a few who have been vying for a spot for some time now. It will certainly be interesting to see how it all shakes out. But whoever does wind up in the seat, they will certainly never live up to your father. That I am sure of."

Piers spun around. "You know, Chief Justice Connally, my father always had aspirations for me to one day take his seat on the Chief Justice Council. So, while it may sit empty of a Marks for a brief period of time, know that one day I shall occupy it." He spoke with conviction.

"Only time shall tell, dear boy. While your father was indeed a great and fair Chief Justice, his position does not automatically guarantee you the seat in the future. But you have many years to go until you could sit on the Council, so best to not stress now."

Piers turned back away from the Chief Justice. "My family is the stability this city needs," he said defiantly. *Even if my father wasn't strong enough in this city's most dire time.*

"A young man of your age shouldn't be so concerned with such lofty problems as the stability of New Boston." Connally paused and spoke simply and earnestly. "You just lost your father. Let the rest of us worry about New Boston, and you take some time to mourn. It's a lot to process."

Piers scowled as he looked on at the coffin. *Did he come here to patronize me? What has he done recently for this city? The gall of these old, dying men. They don't even know what's happening right under their noses.* "You're right, Chief Justice. Thank you for your wisdom. I've always just tried to live up to my father in serving this great city, but it has definitely been a tough few days." Piers tried to mimic Connally's earnestness in his voice.

Connally placed his hand on Piers's shoulder and stood up. "Good. It's almost time for the ceremonies to begin. Where is your sister?"

Anger bubbled up inside him. "Gwen isn't coming. She said this is all too much for her." Piers hadn't seen Gwen since she stormed out two nights ago. But he had too much on his mind to worry about her at the moment.

Connally looked frustrated. "That is disappointing. She should be here. This isn't just her own father's funeral, but something the entire city should rally for. It's not every day a Chief Justice dies."

"I know," Piers grumbled. Gwen and he had always been close. But after the recent events, he felt betrayed. First when Gwen seemed to sympathize with the Furrows boys, and then in the study. And the wound of betrayal was quickly souring into resentment.

"No matter, we'll go on as planned," Connally said. He looked about the large hall. "I haven't been in this place in ages. Beautiful, truly. One of the first buildings built in New Boston, an architectural relic of the past."

As he was thinking of Gwen and Jaym, a concern came to Piers. He whirled around to face Connally. "Chief Justice, can I ask something of you?"

"Of course, son. What?"

"I'm sure you're aware, but the night my father was killed, there was a police raid. I wasn't on the patrol squad but saw on the news that a culprit was arrested. A young man from the Furrows—Beck McGullan. It seems this man keeps popping up where bad things happen. A week or so back, this man and his friend attacked me while I was on a patrol in Sub3. That time, he avoided arrest, and his friend was giving a lenient sentence by my father during his tribunal."

"Yes, I remember reading about that briefly. So, this man is now in custody of the city?" Connally raised his eyebrows, intrigued at where this was going.

"Yes. He should've been arrested during my first run-in with him, but we were only two patrolmen and didn't have the manpower. But there's more. That wasn't the first time I had a run-in with this man. Prior to him attacking me, Mr. McGullan and the other man, Jaym Torrey, showed up to our home claiming to be delivering a sensitive package.

Our butler let them in, told them to wait in the foyer, and stupidly didn't keep an eye on them. It wasn't until after the fact that we found out the package was empty, and they had snuck into my father's study and stolen a golden globe. A gift from my mother."

Connally looked inquisitively at Piers, clearly trying to determine whether or not this was all truthful. "Why would your father hand down such a light sentence at this man's trial if he knew he was a criminal? Your father was a rational man who believed in the core of our justice system."

"I disagreed as well. I confronted my father about it, and he said he was concerned about repercussions in the stability of the city. He said unrest was rampant. I guess he thought a heavy sentence on such a young man would be received poorly by the masses. Perhaps he was concerned things could escalate as they did ten years ago. I swear, Chief Justice Connally, I'm telling you the truth."

Connally took off his glasses and wiped them with a handkerchief. "I believe you Piers. Your passion shines through your words. I can't say I agree or disagree with how your father ruled, naturally every situation is unique. Instability is indeed rampant in New Boston right now, especially given the precarious situation with the vertical farms. But what are you asking of me now?"

What's happening with the farms? Piers shrugged off the thought and continued. "Beck's trial is slated for a few days from now. All I want is for justice to be served. Please, oversee the tribunal, and ensure Beck does not end up back on the streets. He is a stain on this great city."

The large doors thudded open again, grabbing Connally's attention. "Okay, Piers. I'll oversee the trial. Ah, they're arriving."

"He deserves to die, Chief Justice." Piers's voice was strong, full of conviction.

Connally gave Piers one last look, his face suddenly grave. Piers couldn't tell if it was concern, fear, or indignation. But then Connally turned to welcome the incoming people into the hall.

Piers took a moment to adjust his somber expression, a perfect balance of anguish and reservation. He wouldn't cry until the exact right moment. After all, that was something his father had taught him. "Men only cry when they have truly been broken. But even then, they must channel this into strength," his father had said. *Don't worry, father. I'll honor you today with the perfect timing for your tears.*

Piers took his place next to the coffin, as a steady stream of people began filing into the grand cathedral. First the Chief Justices, then various ministers and secretaries from different areas within the government, then the families of the high society. Outside, crowds of others were gathering, and would watch the ceremonies on large screens. This was the case throughout the city—in the many squares and caverns dotting the different levels, Piers's face would soon be shown throughout New Boston.

Each person came up and shook Piers's hand, offered their condolences, and then went on their way. As the only surviving family member at the funeral, given Gwen's lack of appearance, Connally and the other Chief Justices remained next to Piers. The hall slowly filled with people, and soon everyone took their seats. Various government officials spoke briefly about Marks and the legacy he left behind. Connally spoke on behalf of the Chief Justice Council, about how Marks was a leader and guardian of justice. Tolerant, yet sturdy. Then it came time for Piers to speak.

Piers approached the podium and took out the speech he had written the night before. He looked out at the room, filled with people. A simple camera system stood facing him, along with all the faces of New Boston's elite. But he knew they weren't here for him. They were here for his father. *Almost none of them even knew him. They just know what they saw: a pious, stern guardian of justice. Protector of our society. Not the ignorant, stubborn, terrible man he was. A man who was a coward in the face of criminals.* Piers took a visible deep breath.

"Fellow citizens. Thank you for coming today and supporting me in this trying time. Whether you are here in this great cathedral or watching across our great city, I thank you. My father would thank you if he could. I am still processing the fact that my father, the great Chief Justice Marks, is no longer with us. He will no longer be in his study, pouring over papers, when I come home each night. Will no longer be there to give me advice and help me through my endless problems. Will not attend my graduation from the Academy, or any other milestone in my own life." Piers paused, surveying the crowd. A few women had begun wiping their eyes, and he thought he even heard a few muffled cries. He wanted to smile with satisfaction but caught himself before he did.

He continued. "My father was a great man. He loved New Boston and all our great city stood for. He always reminded me how lucky we were to be living in this era. Free from the fears of nuclear war in the past, and free from the rising ocean levels that threatened previous cities. We live in the greatest city in the world. We live in a time of peace and prosperity. We live in a time of justice. And until a few days ago, I had always believed my father. I, too, love this city. But then, my father was murdered. My father, a man who devoted his life to guarding peace, prosperity, and justice for all the citizens of this city. All he ever did was try to make this city a better place for everyone. He may have appeared stern to all of you, but he was a kind man." Piers's voice became more and more emotional, and his eyes began to water.

"I will miss him greatly," Piers said, turning to look at the casket to his right, and allowing a few tears to stream down his cheeks. "Father, your death will not have been in vain." Piers turned back to face the camera and crowd. Many women were now full-on sobbing. Even a few of the men and Justices were wiping their eyes with handkerchiefs. Piers gave them his own teary attention for a few moments, soaking in the experience. Everyone was in their best, formal attire. Bouquets of flowers dotted the room. He looked down as a teardrop fell on his handwritten speech. *Enough tears for you all? You're not getting anymore.*

Piers's face hardened, and his eyes narrowed. "It is a disgrace to us as a people that this happened. My father didn't deserve this. He deserved to live out his full life, as a servant of the people. I will not let his death be in vain. I pledge, today, to dedicate myself to following in his footsteps and one day sitting in his chair on the Chief Justice Council. But until then, I will do whatever I can to help restore peace to this city. To all of you out there fueling unrest, we will stop you. To all of you breaking the law, we will stop you. To anyone thinking of committing another heinous murder, we will stop you. I will stop you. That, I promise you."

CHAPTER 21

Gwen could hear her hairbrush pull on the knots in her hair as she yanked it down. She looked at her reflection in the small mirror in Jaym's bedroom. Despite feeling emotionally drained the past two days, it had almost been refreshing to walk around and have fewer people know who she was. She wore tattered jeans and an old flannel shirt she had found in Jaym's apartment. She had let her hair down, without straightening it, for the first time since she was a young teenager.

She felt so grateful Jaym had been a source of refuge. He had given up his bed to her and slept on the couch. Though Jemma, Jaym's roommate, hadn't been as quick to warm up to her. Gwen could feel the girl glaring at her from behind, but she tried to shrug it off. She had too much on her mind anyway.

Jaym had been on the offensive since she had come down to the Furrows. Each night he met with Heath at Dante's, discussing plans for how to save Beck. During the day, he went from square to square, bar to bar, all across the Furrows meeting with other community leaders. It seemed that everyone speaking out against the city government found themselves with a target on their backs. Gwen followed Jaym through the dark twisting alleys, learning more and more about life in the Furrows. She felt sympathetic but knew this wasn't her place to speak out. *People are angry. The odds are stacked against them. Who wouldn't lash out in that position?*

Following Jaym around had distracted her from everything else going on above the surface of the city, but today she couldn't escape it anymore. Today was her father's funeral. And Piers had won—Jeffrey would be convicted of the murder and likely executed. Gwen felt defeated as she reflected on the day prior, when she had gone back to visit Keats a second time at the police headquarters.

She thought back to what Keats had said. "There's nothing I can do, Gwen. Unless you want to go before a Tribunal and accuse your brother, it's your word against his. Jeffrey has already been taken in, and the Chief Justices all seem to believe the story. After all, they have no reason not to."

She peeled her eyes away from her reflection, feeling herself tearing up. *You can do this Gwen. You are strong. Don't let them see you cry.* Any tears today would be a disgrace to her father. He always told her never to show tears unless absolutely necessary, and even then to use them to her strategic advantage. She smiled at her face sans makeup—she hadn't even made an effort to find any down here. *Be strong, Gwen. This isn't over yet.*

Gwen left the bedroom and went downstairs to the kitchen. The apartment was crowded, even without Beck. Jaym and Jemma both sat at the table; Jemma was moving her spoon around her cereal mindlessly while Jaym was reading something.

"Good morning," Gwen said, trying to sound cheery.

"Morning," Jaym said, looking up and smiling as she descended the stairs.

"Big day," Jemma said, raising her eyebrows. Jaym kicked her under the table, eliciting a loud "Ow!"

"Come on, Jemma. Be nice." Jaym eyed the other girl.

"It's okay. We all know what today is," Gwen said, sitting down. Jaym stood up and poured her a fresh bowl of the cereal from the pot on the stove. He put the bland hot cereal in front of her, along with a small white KIP pill.

"Thanks," Gwen said, smiling at Jaym. She picked up the little pill and popped it into her mouth, swallowing it quickly. "Funny, some things are so different between up there and down here, but some things are exactly the same."

"Yeah, at the end of the day, radiation kills everyone at the same pace," Jemma said sarcastically.

"Ignore her," Jaym said, "and sorry, we ran out of sugar yesterday."

"Who doesn't love bland oatmeal! Made with some lovely synthetic milk. So much better than the eggs Benedict you usually enjoy on your penthouse terrace," Jemma spat out. Jaym's eyes lit up as he glared at her. "Sorry. I'm leaving anyways. Want to get a good spot for the big show today." Jemma turned and went into the other bedroom and closed the door.

Jaym flashed Gwen an apologetic look. "I'm sorry about her. She'll come around."

"It's okay. I don't expect anyone here to like me. Hell, I'm impressed she's even tolerating me." *Not just Jemma. You too. I don't deserve this treatment from either of you.* She knew she couldn't stay down in the Furrows with him forever; she would have to confront her brother sooner or later.

"You ready for this? We don't have to go, you know," Jaym said. His voice was soft, consoling.

"I'm ready." Gwen relieved herself of her ignorant, blissful smile. She put on a stern, composed look. "I just wonder how Piers is answering all those people when they ask where I am. Chief Justice Marks's only daughter, missing in action at his funeral." She looked down at her oatmeal, trying to suppress her guilt.

"We can go, if you want. It's not that far. I can take you there."

"What, looking like *this*?" Gwen raised her eyebrows and put her arms out, showcasing her outfit. "Plus, after seeing what's been happening down here in the Furrows, I want nothing to do with all those people up there. They're all criminals. Maybe not all murderers outright like my brother, but they've contributed to a system of brutality, evil, and death."

"You're starting to sound a lot like us."

"There shouldn't be an 'us.' There shouldn't be a 'they.' There should only be a 'we.'"

"There will be—soon. Just know I'm here for you, whatever happens today." Jaym put his hand on Gwen's, sitting on the table. Gwen looked up at him with a look of surprise. After a brief moment, she pulled her hand back.

"We should get going, the ceremonies will start soon. Where are we watching the funeral?"

"They'll be broadcasting it nearly everywhere, but I figured we'd go to the cavern. It's the center of the action for this area of the Furrows. I'll lead the way."

They left their unfinished oatmeal on the table and headed out into the streets. The darkness of the Furrows was still jarring to Gwen. Sure, she was used to darker areas of the city, like the ground floor. But even there, on a sunny morning, rays made it through the skyscrapers that towered and joined together into the massive canopy of buildings. Here it was always nighttime.

She followed close to Jaym through the twisting alleys. There were throngs of people moving about. The funeral had been hyped up for the past two days since the news broke. And given the recent unrest, people were anxious to see what the leaders of the city would say. The Chief Justice Council had been quiet through the recent violence, and today was the city leaders' first public appearance in weeks.

They soon came out into the cavern. Gwen was struck by the size of it. They were standing on the large balcony overlooking the room. The crowd milled about, vibrating from the energy of the people. Huge screens hung in all four corners of the room, broadcasting the inside of the cathedral. Along the perimeter were policemen. They carried massive machine guns, clearly armed to ensure nothing got out of hand. People eyed them cautiously—bitterly.

Gwen watched the screens as the cameras focused in on her brother, standing among the Chief Justices at the front of the sanctuary. *There he is. Damn him for looking so glum.* A long line of dignitaries snaked through the aisle, all waiting to shake Piers's hands and offer their condolences.

"You okay?" Jaym asked. She felt him watching her, but her stare was stuck to her brother.

"Yeah, I'm fine. It's just…" she started to say, but her voice trailed off.

"Hey, like I said. We can always go." Jaym gave her hand another comforting squeeze, and this time she didn't pull back.

She turned to face Jaym. "I'm just worried about what lies he's spreading about me there. I'm sure people are asking about me. What if he's telling everyone I've gone to join some group of anarchists? Or worse, that I'm complicit in my father's murder!" Her face had turned to sheer panic.

"Gwen. Gwen!" Jaym grabbed her shoulders, squaring himself with her. "You don't need them." He reached down and took her hand. "We're going to get through this. And we're going to get real justice for your father."

"Okay. Thanks. You're right." Gwen tried to muster up a smile. "We will." Shouting from below pulled their attention away. The masses were teeming below in the cavern. Every few seconds, someone yelled out something, and small bouts of applause or clapping echoed behind. From all corners of the room, they could hear cries:

"Down with the Tribunals! Down with the Justices!"

"Furrows forever!"

"Free Beck!"

Gwen looked at Jaym. "Did you hear that? Free Beck?"

"Yeah. If only he knew ... he was already upset about how 'famous' I had become after my Tribunal. I can only imagine what he'll say when he comes back. He'll be insufferable." Jaym managed a smile, but Gwen could tell it was fake. She tightened her grip on his hand, smiling back.

They watched in quiet for a few more minutes before Velma flashed back on the screen to describe the events and what was to come. Next were the speeches: various government dignitaries, several Justices and Chief Justices. And then he was up at the podium—Piers. Gwen's face went pale. She was gripping the railing so hard her knuckles were turning white. Her heart was pounding.

She listened to Piers's attempt to pour his heart out— watched as the cameras panned to the audience in the cathedral, focusing on faces of women in tears. And then the ultimate knife to her stomach: Piers began to cry. She hadn't seen her brother cry since their mother's funeral. "Pathetic," she said, under her breath.

Jaym must've heard it, because he responded, "Theatrics," and shook his head in disapproval. But then Piers's tears stopped, as he stared right into the camera.

"To all of you out there fueling unrest, we will stop you. To all of you breaking the law, we will stop you. To anyone thinking of committing another heinous murder, we will stop you. I will stop you. That, I promise you."

Gwen stared on in horror. *It's as if he's talking directly to me—to us.*

As Piers's speech came to a close, the crowd grew more and more restless. Like a pot about to boil over. The yelling intensified. Suddenly, someone launched a large rock up at one of the screens. It struck the screen, sending large cracks across the picture. The crowd erupted with applause and more rock throwing, now at all four screens in each corner. Sparks were flying and chunks of glass were raining down on the people.

Several of the police started attempting to enter the crowd, electric batons out at the ready. They were met with punches, as people used their fists and other odds and ends as weapons. Police on the balconies aimed their guns down but didn't have a clear shot. The chaos masked the individual perpetrators, and the crowd had many women and children milling about. Other guards had already begun running for the exits, trying to ascend to the safety of the higher city levels. Gunshots rang out from a few places as the skirmishes escalated.

"We should go," Jaym said, as he reached down and grabbed Gwen's hand again. His grip was firm. Gwen looked back, unafraid. The anger of the crowd had struck a chord in her.

"I want to stay and fight," she demanded.

"Staying will only result in trouble. We can't do anything if we get arrested—or worse, killed." Jaym turned and began pulling her away from the balcony's edge. The crowd that had assembled behind them was also thick, and the unruliness was spreading. They pushed their way toward the tunnel exit, and just as they almost made it, they heard screams and the wrenching of metal from the main floor. Turning back, Gwen watched in horror as the first screen that had been struck began to fall from the ceiling.

"Oh no," she uttered. The screen seemed to slow in its descent, crashing into the crowd below.

"Gwen!" Jaym yelled pulling her away. She watched the massive screen detach and fall, the cries of the crowd piercing her ears.

CHAPTER 22

———

The streets were chaotic. Jaym and Gwen found themselves swept up in swarms of people moving through the alleys of the Furrows. Yelling, chanting. Crashes were heard as rocks were thrown at news screens, the sound of shattering glass thereafter. Jaym was leading Gwen against the grain of the people. The crowds were amassing, moving toward the opening tunnels that led to the ground floor of the city.

Gwen swiveled her head back and forth, clearly confused in the chaos. Jaym pulled her forward, wanting to get away from the commotion. All of a sudden, she freed herself from his grip and stood. He turned to face her.

"Gwen! Come on, we have to go."

"No. I won't run away—not this time." Gwen turned around and joined the flow.

"Gwen!" Jaym yelled, leaping after her. She had melted into the river of people. Jaym kept moving forward, pushing his way through the throngs, but every time he got a glimpse of her she evaded him. He kept at it, moving through the crowds. The crowd's energy was quickening, like an anxious heartbeat growing faster and faster. Jaym felt a sense of vertigo. He paused to catch his breath and took in the surroundings. People looked out windows at the crowd, waving and showing signs of support. The people were pouring out of the gaping tunnel that led to Justice Square. Despite the anxiety, the scene was extraordinary.

Pangs of panic set in. The massive square was filled with hundreds of thousands of people. *I'll never find her in this.* He began pushing past people, his eyes darting rapidly, trying to get a glimpse of anything that resembled Gwen. He continued moving, quickening his pace. And then he bumped into someone standing in front of him.

"Gwen!" he yelled, exasperated. As she turned around, he hugged her, embracing her tight. "I..." his voice trailed off; he wasn't sure what to say.

"Have you ever seen anything like this?" Gwen asked in awe, turning back to look out at the crowd. "Are they rebelling or mourning? I can't tell."

"People aren't stupid. They know something is wrong about all of this." Jaym felt small as he looked up at the skyscrapers towering around the square. Despite being out from underground, he still felt trapped. Ahead, the Grand Tribunal Hall loomed. Its hardline architecture looked unyielding in the face of the crowd.

They stood looking a moment longer, when suddenly a loud voice began booming throughout the square. "Return to your homes immediately. Curfew is in effect. Return to your homes immediately. Curfew is in effect." The robotic voice droned on, repeating the same commands.

"Come on, Gwen. Getting arrested isn't going to help anything," Jaym said, reaching down for her hand.

"No," she said, pushing his hand away. "I'm done obeying, Jaym. I'm done running."

Jaym's eyes went wide as he looked into hers. "We won't

let them win. Your brother won't get away with this, Gwen. I promise you. But this isn't the right way to do it. We have to be smart."

"You really promise?"

"Yes." His voice was confident despite the commotion. Jaym felt a wave of awareness wash over him. But then, explosions began rocking the square, inching his heart rate higher. "I have a plan. Come on."

She looked up at him with a sense of admiration he hadn't seen before. Whistling noises distracted both their attentions. "What is that?" Gwen's asked nervously, as whistling noises started to be heard. A few screams rang out, and someone slammed into Jaym's shoulder.

"Tear gas. Gwen, we have to go." He took a few steps toward the tunnel and beckoned to her. "Like I said, this isn't over. I promise."

Gwen took one more look at the crowd, and then turned and followed Jaym. They began moving quickly back into the tunnel's entrance, back into the Furrows.

"Okay, where are we going to go?" she said.

"Dante's—Dante's is always safe."

The streets and alleys were even crazier than before, with people running frantically in all directions back into the Furrows. They picked up their pace as they moved along. Some people huddled together, crying in pain from the gas. Others disappeared quickly into thin alleys and doorways. As they went deeper and deeper, the crowds thinned and the yelling quieted down.

Soon they were outside of Dante's, so far below that it was nearly silent. The familiar alley was deserted, save for one woman leaning up against the light pole in the small square. Jaym paused as Gwen carried on toward the door.

Gwen turned. "What's wrong?"

"Looking for some fun?" the woman asked, smiling seductively at Jaym. He ignored the woman. He trembled a bit. Gwen walked back up to him. "Jaym," she said softly.

"I'm just..." his voice trailed off for a second. Then his eyes met hers. "Nothing, I'm fine. Just thinking how much has happened in the past few days, all from that one stupid encounter in this square."

"I know. It's been a lot for me too."

Jaym looked down at his feet. *She just lost her father, and you have the nerve to act like you're the one suffering?* He looked up and gathered himself. "Gwen, I'm going to keep my promise. We're going to stop Piers. But you have to know that things aren't going to go back to the way they were. Are you okay with that?"

Gwen's looked back at him. Her face was a mix of fear and anger. She started nodding. "Yes, I know that. I knew that the moment I realized what Piers had done. He needs to pay."

Jaym looked into Gwen's eyes, thinking back to the first time he met her. Despite only having known each other for a few days, he felt so comfortable around her. And though she didn't have on her usual makeup and fancy dress, he thought she looked as beautiful as ever—even in the dim, industrial lighting of Sub3. Without thinking of how she would react, he leaned in and kissed her. After a moment, he pulled away.

"I'm sorry," he fumbled out. "It felt right."

Gwen gave a soft smile as she reached down and grabbed his hand. "Come on, let's get out of the street. I don't know about you, but I could use a drink."

"I'll be out here if you change your mind!" the woman called behind them as they entered the bar.

Dante's was mostly empty, save for a few regulars sitting in the back. Dante was sipping a drink, leaning back against the shelves behind the bar. His somber eyes glistened as if he had been crying.

"Hey Dante," Jaym said, taking a seat at the bar. "Can we get two rums?"

Dante continued staring off in the distance. "Don't have any, son."

"What do you mean?" Gwen asked, sitting down next to Jaym. She leaned forward on the sticky bar.

Dante came back to reality and walked over to them, pouring them two glasses of clear liquid. "My suppliers said that there was a bad riot outside the alcohol plant over on the other side of the city. People broke into the building and smashed bottles in the storage rooms. The police locked down the building. They said it'll be another week until production is back up and running. This stuff doesn't taste great, but it'll get the job done." He pushed the two glasses toward them. "Did you two go up to the square?"

"Yeah. It was crazy," Jaym said, bringing the glass up to his mouth. The smell alone made him wince. *People breaking bottles ... why would anyone do that?* He looked at Gwen, who grimaced as well. "Desperate times," he said, and took a sip. The liquid burned his throat as it went down. Gwen coughed, gagging on the liquor. Jaym leaned back in the stool and took a breath, relishing the familiar, musty smell. He felt exhausted, but also newly invigorated. *I'm going to keep this promise. Piers won't get away with this. I owe it to Beck—and Gwen.*

"So what now?" Gwen asked, bringing him back to attention.

Before he could answer, the door to the bar opened. Jaym gripped the counter, ready for anything. Panic washed over him as a man holding a massive machine gun strode in. The man moved to the side, revealing Heath and a second armed guard behind him. Jaym let out a sigh of relief.

"Good, I was hoping I'd find you here," Heath said, strolling up to Jaym. "Hello to you again, Miss Marks," he said, nodding to Gwen.

Gwen looked back at him blankly.

Heath turned his attention to Dante. "Oh, nothing for me tonight, thanks Dante." Dante nodded and placed a glass back on the shelf. Still sullen, he moved away from the group. "Well, I have good news and bad news. Which do you want first?" Jaym didn't answer. He stared at Heath, his eyes cold, unwavering.

Heath nodded a few times, saying "I know, I know. Not the ideal way you'd like me to start this conversation. But I'm being straight with you two … The good news is I found out where they're holding Beck. I know exactly where it is; we have strong intel on that area of the building."

"Good. That's good," Gwen said, speaking up for the pair. "What about the bad news?"

Heath looked from one to the other. "I was hoping you already knew. They've moved up Beck's trial." Heath paused, and looked away for a moment, gathering himself.

"To when?" Jaym asked.

"To tomorrow."

Jaym's shock paralyzed him. Ringing screamed in his ears. But he pushed past it, trying to focus. His mind began reeling.

When are we going to break him out? We don't have time to organize something tonight. Why would they expedite this, right after the funeral of a Chief Justice? Is this Piers trying to get back at me? Or get back at Gwen?

"Tomorrow?" Gwen asked. "Why would they do that? The city is in chaos right now!"

Jaym was nodding to himself, still running through options. His head spiked up, as he came to a realization. "This could actually work. We could go in tonight, while the chaos is still fresh. It'll be easier to slip in." He looked directly at Heath and began standing up. "What time is the next guard change? Let's get mobilized ASAP."

Heath fanned the air with his hands. "Whoa, Jaym. Deep breaths. We can't go tonight. The city is on lockdown after the riot today. We need to wait until after the Tribunal."

"We might not have time!" Jaym slammed his fist down on the bar. "You promised me you'd help break him out, Heath."

"And we will. But not tonight. Look at you, you're exhausted. Justice Square is crawling with police. Attempting to do this tonight is a death sentence for all of us."

Jaym glared at Heath. *He's not wrong. But we are tight on time. We need to strategize and be ready to go as soon as the Tribunal ends.*

"I agree with him." Gwen's voice was so soft it was almost a whisper. She lifted her head and spoke a bit louder, "No matter what happens tomorrow, even if we get the worst news, we'll have some more time before anything happens to Beck."

Jaym scoffed. He knew they were right, and he had no choice, but he wasn't about to admit that to Heath. "Fine. We'll move tomorrow night, after the trial."

"That'll work," Heath responded. "I'll tell my guys to be ready."

"Good. Tomorrow night we break him out," Jaym said, with renewed strength in his voice. "And I'm going to the Tribunal. I'm not going to let Beck be all up there alone. He needs to know we're here for him."

"I'll come too," Gwen echoed. "I want my brother to see me in the crowd."

"I don't think that's a great idea," Heath began. Jaym flashed him another look of indignation. "Hey, look, I'm not going to stop you from going. Just don't provoke anyone, especially not your brother." Heath looked at Gwen. "Last thing we need is you two getting arrested on some bogus charge before we go through with this. We'll meet back here tomorrow after the trial and gear up." Heath stood up and adjusted his black leather jacket. Looking Jaym straight in the eyes, he said, "We're going to get him out, Jaym." And then he turned and left the bar, his guard following him out.

Jaym and Gwen sat still watching Heath leave. Once he was gone, Gwen turned to Jaym. Her voice quiet, she asked, "Do you think we'll be able to do it? Get him out?"

"Yes," he said, his voice strong and confident. Jaym reached down and grabbed her hand. "And we'll find Piers. After tomorrow, things will be different. We're not going back to the way things were."

CHAPTER 23

———

Gwen tossed and turned all night, failing to get comfortable. She turned to look at the dim lights of the alarm clock. 5:30 a.m. She groaned and forced herself to get up and stretch. As she reached out her arms, she could hear her stomach groaning. She left the bedroom and went downstairs. In the living room, she paused and looked over at Jaym, asleep on the couch. *He looks so peaceful.* Moving to the small kitchen, she quietly rummaged through the cabinets to find something. *Come on, there's got to be something here.* The cabinets were bare. Jemma had said the merchants' stalls had been empty when she went shopping.

I guess it wasn't just the distillery that was attacked. Food is already so scarce, why would people attack the farms? All it would take is a few small cracks to let the outside air seep in and an entire farm could be ruined. She spotted a tiny box of tea bags in a cabinet. *Finally!* Pulling a bag out, she frowned as she held the transparent bag up to the light. *There are barely five tea leaves in here.*

She started heating a kettle on the stove.

"Can't sleep either?"

In the quiet kitchen, even the soft voice startled her. Gwen turned to see Jemma leaning against the door frame. She attempted a friendly smile. "Not a wink. Want some tea?"

"If you can even call it that," Jemma said, rolling her eyes. "But thanks, that sounds nice." They both took a seat at the table and waited in silence as the water heated. When the kettle started humming, Gwen jumped up to take it off before it could reach a whistle. "Don't want to wake him up," she whispered as she poured the water into two mugs with the small bags inside and sat down next to Jemma.

"You really think you're going to be able to get him out?" Jemma asked, gripping her hands around the mug.

"Jaym thinks so. And we can't afford to think otherwise." She bent over her mug and let the faint chamomile scent waft up. She took a sip and shivered with bliss. The hot water warmed her entire body. She hadn't even realized how cold she had been until then. She had been numb to most of her senses for the past several days.

Jemma didn't respond. They both sat silently again for several moments, sipping their teas. In a quiet, almost meek voice, Gwen said, "Thanks for letting me stay here. I'm guessing Jaym sprung it on you, since I sprung it on him too, but I really do—"

"It's okay." Jemma cut her off. But her voice was noticeably gentler.

After a few more quiet moments, Jemma spoke up. "I'm sorry I've been so hard on you. I know you're going through a lot."

Gwen smiled in thanks. "It's okay. We're all going through a lot."

Jemma looked up from her tea, a sad harshness having returned to her eyes. "It's just, you grew up with tea bags

packed full of chamomile leaves. And I grew up with this."
She nodded down to her mug. "I'm trying not to let that spite get the better of me."

"I can't blame you," Gwen acknowledged.

Jemma continued. "You just have no idea how hard life is down here."

"You're right, I don't," Gwen confirmed. She looked up from her cup and met Jemma's eyes. "But I'm learning. And I want to see change in this city too."

Jemma nodded, smiling back at Gwen for the first time. She finished her tea and stood up, walking to the kitchen's entrance. "Come on, we still have some time to sleep. You're going to need it. Here, try the armchair." She reached around the corner and pulled out a pillow. She fluffed it, looking down nostalgically. "It's Beck's favorite place to nap."

"Thanks," Gwen said, and moved to the chair. She looked over at Jaym, still sound asleep, as the silence returned. She laid her head on the pillow and drifted off to sleep.

* * *

Gwen lifted her heavy eyelids. *Is that smell ... eggs?* The scent of warm, cooked eggs wafted into the living room. She sat up slowly, relishing the smell. Looking over, Jaym was gone from his couch.

She moseyed into the kitchen and saw Jaym standing over the stove.

"Good morning. Went out and bought something special today. Was able to get us each an egg. It isn't much, but—"

"It smells wonderful," she said, beaming.

"What is that smell?" Jemma's voice came through before she even entered the kitchen. "Eggs! Jaym, how much did you spend on these! We should be conserving our money. We could've—"

"It's a big day, Jemma. Take a bite. Just be happy for a minute!" Jemma glared at Jaym, who merely laughed back and put the eggs on the table. They all sat down and began wolfing down the breakfast.

Gwen finally glanced at the clock on the stove. "It's already ten? I didn't realize we slept so late."

"It's okay, the trial doesn't start for another two hours. We have plenty of time."

Jemma looked ahead with a tense expression. "I can't believe we all have to go through this again. It can't go half as well as the last time." She looked over at Jaym. "We should probably leave in an hour to get a good spot. The cavern is going to be teeming with people."

"We're not watching in the cavern. We're going to the Grand Tribunal Hall," Jaym said, standing.

"*What?*" Jemma blurted out. "Why would we go *there*? After all that's happened, it's not safe, it's—"

"It's not a discussion," Jaym interrupted her. "Beck needs to see us. He needs to know we're there for him. We're not going to watch scared from underground, like they expect us to. We're citizens of this city too. We have every right to be up there, supporting our friend."

"I agree," Gwen said. "We'll be together, Jemma. Nothing bad will happen."

Jemma nodded back, realizing it wasn't worth a fight. "We best get ready then. We might as well look damn good if we're going all the way up there." She turned to Gwen. "Why don't you borrow one of my dresses? I only have two, but hopefully one fits."

"I'd really appreciate that." Gwen, delighted, followed

Jemma into her bedroom.

Twenty minutes later, Gwen emerged. She had pulled back her hair and put on a simple, blue dress. Jemma even had a few vials of makeup, and Gwen had put on a light coat. She felt clean and fresh for the first time in days. And she could tell it clearly showed—as she came into the kitchen, Jaym was staring at her with his mouth ajar.

"What?" she asked.

"Nothing. You just look ... very pretty." He stumbled over his words but managed to smile.

"Thank you." She returned the smile.

Jemma came up behind her. She wore a similar dress of dark navy. "She looks downright gorgeous. The dress fits perfectly." She admired Gwen's outfit.

"You look great too, Jemma," Jaym said, still fumbling.

Jemma rolled her eyes. "Thanks. Now come on, we should get going." Gwen flashed an amused look Jaym's way as she followed Jemma out the apartment.

The streets were coming alive, though slowly so. It seemed people were just now beginning to wake up and start their day. But the air felt ominous, tense. There were shattered news screens everywhere, bloody bricks and rocks littering the streets. They even noticed a few people on the ground in corners. *Are they dead? Or just passed out?* Gwen wasn't sure. They continued on, heading up toward the ground level. By the time they had arrived at Justice Square, crowds had already begun forming.

Tribunals always garnered the attention of the people, but this time felt different. After the protests and riots the night before, the city seemed on edge. They waded slowly through the crowds, past people who stared up at the large screens still hung from the funeral the day before. People looked ahead, dazed. Gwen had started leading the way at this point, beelining straight toward the Tribunal Hall.

On the steps outside the hall were more police than Gwen had ever seen. They were heavily armed, with massive machine guns armed and ready. Large concrete barricades had been set up, blocking people from getting to the steps and entrance. The guard at the space between two of the blocks perked up as Gwen approached. His hands moved quickly to grip the gun, as a few other guards nearby also prepared themselves.

"We're here for the Tribunal," Gwen said. Her voice was strong, with no sign of wavering.

"I'm sorry, miss. The Tribunal is closed to the general public, due to safety concerns," the guard responded. He was straightforward, no emotion in his voice. He continued, "You can view the proceedings from the screens—"

"Do you know who I am?" Gwen cut the guard off. "I'm sure you saw my father's funeral yesterday streamed for the entire city to see."

The guard stammered over his words. "I'm sorry, Miss Marks, but our orders are that no one is allowed in without prior authorization."

A second guard had walked over. Gwen eyed him skeptically. He had his helmet and visor on, shielding his face.

"Do you know who this is?" the guard said, motioning to Gwen. He then lifted his helmet off and smiled back at Gwen.

"Keats!"

"Yes … I recognize Miss Marks. But our orders are—"

"I don't give a damn what our orders are. Come on, Gwen. You and your friends can come through." Keats pushed his way in front of the other policeman and beckoned to the trio.

"Thanks, Keats," Gwen said, her expression still one of surprise. She glanced at Jaym, whose face didn't give anything away. They began walking up the stairs. Gwen swiveled her head slightly, noticing how immense the crowds truly were.

"Gwen, I..." Keats started saying, but seemed to be at a loss for words. She turned back to face him as they continued moving toward the Hall's entrance. "I'm so sorry—for everything."

Her expression softened. "It's okay, Keats. I don't have time to talk right now, the trial is about to start. Let's chat later. Come on, guys." Gwen motioned to Jaym and Jemma. They had reached the large entrance doors, and Gwen began leading the group inside.

"Who's that?" Jemma asked in a loud whisper to Gwen. She looked back at Keats seductively.

"Just a friend," she responded.

"Come on, let's get inside," Jaym said, bounding ahead of the two women.

Inside, the usually bustling building was fairly quiet. People in dark suits and dresses darted across the open atrium. A few were having hushed conversations in corners. Gwen moved confidently through the grand entrance, ignoring the looks that were thrown her way. She stopped in front of the large screen hanging across from the doors, listing the day's events and trials.

"There," Gwen said, pointing to the words: Beck McGullan: Hall C, 12 p.m. "Let's go." She led the way, moving forward into the main hallway.

"How do you know where to go?" Jaym asked, his eyes also wandering about the halls.

"I spent a lot of time here when I was younger. My father wanted me to see the Tribunals in action from an early age. So I followed him around from trial to trial, and spent a lot of time running around this place. I know this building by heart."

They turned another corner and found themselves in a more crowded hall, with two large double doors opened at the end. Above the doors, in gold letters, were the words "Hall C."

"Let's sit toward the back in case we need to get out for some reason," Gwen said, her voice cautious. She was still walking briskly toward the entrance, with Jaym and Jemma on her heels.

"I want to be in the front," Jaym answered. "Beck needs to see us."

Gwen flashed him an anxious look. "I don't think that's a good idea Jaym. Honestly Beck is probably so overwhelmed he won't be paying attention to who's in the crowd. He might even be drugged."

"Why would they drug him?" Jemma asked.

"They sedate people sometimes if they're worried about … obedience." They were almost at the room's entrance when a voice rang out, stopping Gwen dead in her tracks.

"Fancy seeing you here, Gwen." She knew immediately whose voice it was, and spun around. *I should've guessed he'd be here.* Piers stood tall, in a black suit, next to Alyx and a few other men.

"So, you come to see a lowlife criminal face the Justices, but you don't come to your own father's funeral? Interesting choices, sister." Piers's voice was strong and confident, and he sneered at Gwen as he spoke.

Jaym stepped up alongside Gwen, but she put her arm out. "It's okay, Jaym. I can handle this." She stared ahead at her brother, her eyes so sharp they looked as if they would pierce. "Don't you dare accuse me of anything, Piers. You're not fooling anyone. Not your friends, not the Justices, and certainly not me."

Piers took a few steps closer to her. "What are you doing with these people, Gwen? You don't belong with them." He cast her a grave, serious look. "Come with me. I'll forgive you for not being at the funeral. I know we're both going through a lot—"

"We're going through a lot? Piers, you killed our father!" Her voice was a loud, angry whisper.

Piers glared as he leaned in closer. Under his breath, he said, "I don't know what you're talking about. Our father was murdered."

"By *you*." Gwen clenched her fist but tried to remain calm.

"I ought to slap you right here. Put you in your place for disrespecting me and our household."

Gwen took a step closer, now just inches away from her brother. "You do anything to me or these people, Piers, and I'll go straight to Connally and tell him exactly what happened that night. I'll tell the whole city what you did."

Piers's mouth twisted into a sinister grin. "Go ahead, Gwen. The Chief Justices won't believe you. No one will." Piers moved forward, until he was in line with his sister. "We should get inside. The trial is about to start. Should be interesting, to say the least." Before entering the hall, he turned to Jaym. "Best of luck to your friend, Jaym. Justice is about all of us."

Before Jaym could respond, Piers entered the Hall.

"It's going to be okay, Gwen," Jaym said, putting his hands on her shoulders. He let out a breath. "Remember my promise."

Jemma stepped forward, from where she had been watching a few feet back. "Lovely family you've got, Gwen."

Gwen let out a snort. Her fists were still clenched, but she was already feeling calmer with Piers out of her sight.

"Let's go get this over with," she said, and led the group into the Hall.

Jaym and Jemma followed behind. "I have a bad feeling about this," Jemma whispered.

"Well, nothing we can do about it now," Jaym responded. "No matter what, we're going to save Beck. I'm not going down without a fight."

CHAPTER 24

The fall of the gavel rang out in the large hall. It reverberated throughout the room, causing everyone to stir with a tense energy. Jaym looked around Hall C, his anxiety mounting. On the walls, oil paintings of past Justices cast their judgmental gaze his way. Jaym looked up at the Chief Justice as he banged the gavel a second time. Silence settled over the room.

"They look so old and pompous," Jemma whispered to Jaym as she gazed up at the Justices. Jaym rolled his eyes and leaned over to Gwen. He wanted to hear her voice. He knew it would have a calming effect on him.

"Which Chief Justice is that?" he asked.

"Connally," Gwen answered. "He's the Chief Justice for the Tribunal of Rations and Sustenance. Silver crimes are tried under him."

"Is that a good thing or a bad thing?"

Gwen turned her head slightly, to meet Jaym's eyes. "It's not great." Jaym felt his heartbeat escalate a notch. With it, his senses became heightened. He took in the dais: Connally, the Chief Justice, sat in the middle of the semicircle ring of other Justices. There were seven in total, three flanking him on each side. They each wore their signature dark robes, sitting with strong, powerful postures looking down on the crowd. Behind them hung the seal of New Boston, with its signature Lady Justice standing proud.

Most of the Justices displayed expressionless looks, perhaps attempting to emulate the objectivity they claimed to stand for. One Justice stuck out to Jaym—the sole woman on the bench. She was smiling. She wore thick, black rimmed glasses and bright red lipstick, accentuating her smile. Jaym looked at her, confused. *Which way will she lean? I can't get a read on her.*

Connally began speaking into the microphone, his voice steady, almost deadpan.

"Order—this Tribunal is commencing. Trial number five-six-eight-three is on the docket. Bring in the defendant."

The doors on the left side of the hall opened with a loud thud. Two armed guards walked Beck into the room. He was wearing a gray prisoner's uniform, with his hands cuffed together. He stared straight ahead. His eyes were cold but alert, as he was led to the defendant's stand.

"He looks good," Gwen whispered. "Doesn't look like they drugged him."

Jaym nodded in agreement. *He looks hardened. Like he's already given up and just wants to accept his punishment. Stay strong, Beck.*

"Beck McGullan, you are being charged with one count of Silver manufacturing and one count of Silver possession and intent to distribute. How do you plead?"

Beck looked ahead silently.

"Don't be afraid, young boy." The woman justice spoke. "We Justices always appreciate candor. After all, justice is about all of us." Her voice had an upward inflection, almost in a singsong type of way. She tilted her head and expanded her smile as she asked, as if enjoying probing Beck. As if his life wasn't on the line.

A man in a dark police suit stood up, buttoning the jacket as he did so. On his lapel was a shiny silver badge, with the city's emblem glinting in the light of the hall. Jaym recognized the man from just moments ago. He had been standing next to Piers.

"That's Alyx," Gwen whispered. "He and Piers go way back."

Alyx cleared his throat and spoke loudly. "Excuse me, Justices. I, Alyx Corbin, am representing the Police Force of New Boston. "Before Mr. McGullan pleads, we have some new information to bring to light.

"And what information is that, Officer?" the woman Justice asked, still smiling. Her head shook lightly when she asked, and the beads dangling down from her thick-rimmed glasses clinked against each other.

"Well, Justice Wellington," Alyx said as he looked back up. He turned to face Beck. "We have a new charge to bring. We charge Mr. McGullan of one count of conspiracy to murder. Specifically, the murder of Chief Justice Marks."

Audible gasps were heard throughout the room. Jaym's face went white. *No—this can't be happening.* He nearly jumped up, but Gwen grabbed his arm. She looked at him, her eyes wide. She mouthed, "Don't."

Jaym's mind was reeling. He whispered, louder than he realized, to Gwen. "This has to be Piers. That bastard liar! Beck had already been arrested before Marks was killed!" Jaym clenched and unclenched his fists and took a few deep breaths. *Damnit Beck. Why did you ever go down there? I told you it was trouble.*

"Don't get us kicked out of the Hall. We need to see how this plays out." Gwen rubbed his arm, but Jaym could tell from the tone of her voice that she was just as anxious and scared as he was.

Jaym arched his neck to see if he could catch a glimpse of Beck's expression. On one of the screens hanging up front a camera angle swapped to show Beck's face. His expression hadn't changed; he maintained the same solid, alert, and intent stare.

"That's quite the accusation, Officer," a second Judge said. "Typically the Tribunal for High Crimes would be called to adjudicate an indictment." He was sitting one seat away from Connally, who was leaned back in his chair. Connally held his glasses up to his lips, looking on inquisitively. He didn't look overly surprised but did look like he was in deep thought. *Was he expecting this? Does he know something we don't?*

"I understand that, Justice Cawley," Alyx responded, "But given the empty seat on the Chief Justice Council, and that this evidence was just brought to light, we hope to proceed here. Mr. McGullan is a dangerous man who needs to be served justice immediately, and the evidence we have is irrefutable."

Jaym looked about the room until he saw where Piers was sitting. He sat further up ahead, just a few rows behind where Alyx stood. He was smiling. Satisfied. *That bastard is definitely behind this.*

"And the defendant? How do you plead, Mr. McGullan?" Connally asked, as he leaned forward in his seat to get a good look at Beck.

Beck stood tall, his hands hanging motionless in front of him, still cuffed together. "I am not a murderer, Chief Justice. I had nothing to do with Chief Justice Marks's death."

Tense silence followed. Jaym looked up at his friend with pride. *Stick it to them, Beck. They don't have anything on you.*

"And the other charges? How do you plead with regards to the drugs?" Wellington, the woman Justice asked.

Beck stared ahead for a moment, gathering his thoughts. When he looked up, his emotionless expression had devolved into one of loathing.

"Does it even matter what I say? You all have already decided."

"Oh God," Gwen whispered, and gripped Jaym's hand.

"Excuse me, Mr. McGullan?" Connally responded, his voice biting and sharp.

"Mr. McGullan," Wellington enunciated each syllable of Beck's name. "How do you plead regarding the charge of manufacturing and intent to distribute silver? It is a simple question."

Jaym held his breath.

"Guilty," Beck sneered.

Jaym let out his breath. "No!" he whispered.

"He had to tell the truth. They caught him in Heath's drug den," Jemma muttered.

A wide smirk spread across Wellington's face as she leaned back in her chair. "Thank you, Mr. McGullan. That charge is settled then. Regarding the conspiracy to murder, Officer, do you have any evidence to present to us?"

"I do, Madame Justice," Alyx answered. "The defendant has had run-ins with the Marks family before, including stealing a precious golden globe from the late Chief Justice's study. He was present and participatory in the attacks against Piers Marks, the late Chief Justice's son, just a week or so ago. He was a known beneficiary of the criminal Thaddeus Stevens. We believe all these points suggest a motive against the Marks family, and against the late Chief Justice. And we believe that Mr. McGullan conspired with the Marks's butler to plan the time, place, and method of the Chief Justice's murder."

The room was quiet as the Justices nodded and contemplated what they had just heard. Wellington spoke up first. "That does all sound compelling, Officer."

"Though it sounds just as compelling that this man would've liked to kill Piers Marks, aside from his father," Justice Cawley responded. "If I recall, Chief Justice Marks passed a fairly lenient sentence on to Mr. Marks attacker, who I presume to be an acquaintance of Mr. McGullan. Thus, Mr. McGullan may have held more sympathetic feelings toward Chief Justice Marks. Wouldn't you agree?"

"Why don't we ask the defendant himself," Connally interjected. Looking down at Beck, he asked, "Mr. McGullan, do you harbor ill feelings toward the Marks family and the late Chief Justice?"

Beck scoffed. "Nothing worse than I have for all of you." A few gasps were heard throughout the room. Beck spoke again. "But I already said, I didn't kill him."

"I never said you killed him. I said you conspired to kill him," Alyx jeered at Beck.

Beck retorted back. "How would I even know this butler? He didn't live in the Furrows. I've been above Sub1 only a handful of times my life."

Yes, Beck! Logic. Despite everything they say or do, the Justices have to listen to logic.

Silent tension again reigned throughout the hall. Gwen reached down and grabbed Jaym's hand, squeezing it tight. He turned to her, but she was still staring straight ahead. "This is insanity," she whispered. Jaym didn't react. His heart had been pounding nonstop, and his mind kept racing. *How do they intend to prove this? They barely have any evidence!* Jaym was running through scenarios in his head, trying to predict what might happen next.

"Officer, do you have any response?" Connally asked.

Alyx was quiet for a moment. *He doesn't know what to say!* "We have not yet determined how and when Mr. McGullan and the Marks's butler hatched their plan. But clearly they have experience with clandestine operations, so naturally we expect—"

"Oh please, Mr. McGullan isn't even twenty! This is a wild accusation," Justice Cawley cried, cutting Alyx off.

"I think we owe Officer Corbin a bit more respect, for all the work he does for New Boston, Justice," Connally chided. "Officer, thank you for the testimony. Is there any more evidence or witnesses to present?"

"No, sir," Alyx chirped.

"Good, good," Connally answered. "And you, Mr. McGullan, would you like to make any final closing statements before the Justices deliberate?"

Beck looked about the slew of Justices, all eagerly awaiting him to speak. "I would, *sir*. You all are tasked with guarding the peace and security of this city and its citizens. Yet all you do is punish us for trying to survive. I never wanted to be involved with Silver. But I had no choice!" Desperation was infused into Beck's soliloquy.

Play to their emotions. Come on, one of them has to crack.

"I did not conspire to kill the Chief Justice. Would I if I had the chance? I don't know. I don't think I could kill anyone. But what I do know, is that all of you are slowly killing all of *us*. You're starving us while you feast. You're arresting us for no real reason. But this city can't survive without us. We're the real lifeblood of New Boston."

The Justices looked on with stern faces. A few looked almost fearful. The audience looked on in awed silence.

"Thank you, Mr. McGullan," Connally began, about to bang his gavel.

"I'm not finished, sir," Beck interjected. "You sit up on that bench, or look on from your penthouses, or sneer from your balconies. You act as if you are better than us—like we're the only criminals in this city. But it's all of you who break the laws on a daily basis. The *officer* mentioned that I stole from the Chief Justice's study. Yes, I am guilty of this. But are none of you curious how I, a kid from the Furrows, found myself in the penthouse study of one of the most powerful men in all of New Boston?" Beck paused. Justice Cawley was on the edge of his seat, while Connally and Wellington both looked stressed. Perturbed. Connally was eyeing his gavel, clearly eager to end Beck's speech.

Jaym allowed himself a nervous smile, realizing where Beck was leading this. *He's about to bring the hammer down.*

Beck's signature smile spread across his face. "I was delivering a package—of Silver. Straight from the drug dens of the Furrows to Piers Marks."

Shouts of shock went up all around the hall. Several people in the audience stood and started yelling toward the Justices. Piers's face went white for a brief moment, before turning an irate crimson. His eyes narrowed in pure hatred. Connally was banging the gavel, screaming "Order!" The guards rushed over to Beck, who was smiling wide as they grabbed him, despite him standing still.

Connally stood up and yelled into the microphone, his voice booming throughout the hall. "This tribunal is in recess. The Justices will convene to deliberate and will return in one hour with our decision on the case of Beck McGullan."

Jaym could feel Gwen and Jemma looking to him, anxious for his reaction. He looked straight ahead, feeling subdued and numb. *Oh Beck. I'm so sorry I let you fall into this. It should've been me delivering that speech. There's no coming back from this now.*

CHAPTER 25

———

"Let's get some air." Jaym stood up, Gwen and Jemma follow-ing suit. They stuck together as the room had erupted into a frenzy. *Stay strong. Do it for Beck.* He felt dizzy as he walked out of Hall C. He ignored the looks cast his way from all the people in suits and clean, sharp clothing. Even in a plain, simple sweater, Jaym still stood out.

The hallways were busy with people, as the day was in full force at this point. It hadn't ever occurred to Jaym how many trials must be going on at any given time. Beck's trial was sure to garner a heavy dose of attention, especially after his shocking comment at the end. They were heading back toward the front of the building, through the long, ornate hall. On their right, Jaym saw a few cameras set up, and there stood Velma, whose face he had seen so many times on screens across the city. She was speaking earnestly into a microphone. He was able to overhear a bit of what she was saying.

"Things started off surprisingly when the Police Captain of the force who had arrested Mr. McGullan announced an expected third charge: conspiracy to murder. Specifically, the murder of Chief Justice Marks, whose funeral was held just yesterday. The Justices probed…"

Her voice faded as they moved out of range, and soon they were back in the main atrium, now even more bustling than before. Jaym spotted a small alcove tucked away near one of the many statues around the perimeter and led the group there. "Let's wait here. At least we can have a little peace and quiet."

Gwen nodded as Jemma and Jaym slumped down to the ground, feeling the weight of their exhaustion. "Agreed. I'll go grab us some water."

"Kid has got some nerve," Jemma said. Her expression looked bleak as she stared ahead.

"Always has," Jaym responded. "Leave it to Beck to spring something like that on all those pompous pricks." They both smiled and let out a small laugh. *I just hope it wasn't a shot in the foot.*

"How do you think they're gonna rule?" Jemma asked.

Jaym took a deep breath. "I have no clue. This limbo is definitely the worst part of it all. But hey, like I said earlier, we're getting him out either way."

* * *

Gwen crossed the atrium to where a small water fountain stood. She was filling up two paper cups when she heard someone come up behind her.

"Gwen, I…" The voice trailed off. The unmistakable voice of Keats. A few weeks ago, she would've done nearly anything for the guy. But now she wasn't too sure.

Gwen slowly turned around, facing Keats. She was silent, looking sullen. Almost disappointed.

"I wanted to help," he continued. "Really Gwen, I did. I'm sorry I didn't the other night, I just … I didn't know what to do. I still don't know what to do." He looked at her gravely. "Piers really is out of control."

"I'm nervous, Keats. Piers isn't going to take what just happened in there lightly. Whatever he's planning to do next … we have to stop him."

Keats looked back at her, quiet—afraid. Gwen had never seen him look afraid before.

"How? He has the Chief Justices on his side. He's untouchable. He—"

"No one is untouchable," Gwen shot back. "Just look at what happened to my father. You just have to be willing to *do* something. We can't just roll over and let Piers do whatever he wants, like you did the other night."

"There was nothing I could do, Gwen!" Keats cried.

Gwen's face hardened. "I can't accept that, Keats. And going forward, I won't." She pushed past him, heading back to the alcove. She then turned back and said, in a heavy voice, "We're all going to have to choose a side now, Keats. Better decide soon."

She left Keats standing on the other side of the atrium as she returned to Jaym and Jemma. Jaym had his eyes closed and his head leaned back against the stone wall, while Jemma had her head bowed between her knees.

"Here," she said, handing them each a cup of water.

"Thanks," Jaym said, absentmindedly. Gwen slumped down next to him and leaned her head on his shoulder.

"I'm sorry, Jaym," she whispered.

* * *

Jaym smiled as Gwen leaned her head on his shoulder. He reached up and stroked her hair as they sat in silence for a few more minutes. Then, a soft bell rang out in the atrium, and Gwen's head perked up. Jaym was about to say something, but she held up her hand. A woman's voice spoke evenly over the intercom. "A verdict in Trial five-six-eight-three has been reached. The Tribunal will resume shortly."

"How did they decide so soon," she muttered.

Jemma stirred, as if waking up. "Is that—"

"Beck's trial, yes," Gwen said. "Come on, we need to get back. The Justices have reached a decision."

They jumped up from their corner and began hurrying back toward Hall C. Many others were moving through the large double doors as well, and the room was filling up quick. The trial had indeed garnered attention; the room was even more crowded than before. Jaym led the way, pushing through the crowds. *I need to be able to see him. And see them, those presumptuous assholes.*

People were clambering with anticipation over what was about to unfold. Then, a hush fell over the crowd as the Justices, led by Chief Justice Connally, entered from the door behind the bench. Connally nodded to the Tribunal guards, who then went and opened the side door. Beck was led in by two armed policeman shortly thereafter. His smirk from when he finished his speech was gone. *He looks terrified. Come on, Beck. It's going to be okay.*

The gavel came down, but the crowd was already quiet. Jaym looked around for Piers, but he was nowhere to be found. Connally leaned into the microphone and began reading off the paper in front of him. His glasses sat halfway up the ridge of his nose as he peered down, not making eye contact with Beck, Alyx, or the crowd. "We, the Justices of this Tribunal, have deliberated on the case of Mr. Beck McGullan, and have come to a verdict. The defendant has already pleaded guilty to two of the counts of which he is accused—one count of Silver manufacturing and one count of Silver possession with intent to distribute. For these crimes, we have decided..." Connally paused and looked up from his paper. His voice had been monotone, emotionless. "A punishment of ten years in prison."

Gasps were let out across the room.

"Ten years!" Jemma wailed out.

Jaym held his gaze forward, not giving away any emotion. He could feel Gwen looking at him, but he ignored her. *Ten years isn't a death sentence. Harsh, yes, but conspiracy to the murder of a Chief Justice though—there is only one sentence for that.*

Jaym looked about the bench at the other Justices. Cawley sat with a pleasant expression, leaning back slightly in his chair. Moving along the bench, Jaym's eyes came to Justice Wellington. Her previous cunning, sly smile was gone. Instead, she looked out at Beck and the crowd in disgust. In the middle, Connally returned his eyes to his papers. Jaym held his breath.

"On the charge of conspiracy to the murder of Chief Justice Marks, this Tribunal has determined that there is insufficient evidence to charge Mr. McGullan at this time. The police may continue to build this case and bring forth the accusation to the Tribunal for High Crimes in the future. This Tribunal, however, is adjourned." Connally banged the gavel again, and then quickly stood and began existing the bench.

Jaym breathed out and Jemma gripped his arm. "No execution!"

Jaym didn't look over at her. Instead, he arched his neck to try and get a glimpse of Beck, but the guards had already begun escorting him back to the side door. *Don't worry, Beck. You're not going to waste away in a cell for a decade.*

"Thank goodness," Gwen said. "Jaym? Are you alright?" She looked at him expectantly, both her and Jemma waiting for a response.

Jaym stood up. "Come on, let's get going. We don't have a ton of time. We have to regroup with Heath in a few hours."

"You still want to go through with the plan?" Gwen's voice was hushed, but steady.

"Absolutely. And then we come up with a second plan: to get back at Piers." Jaym reached down and grabbed Gwen's hand. "Come on, let's go."

Jaym looked back at Gwen with a proud, confident smile. She nodded in return, and he followed her out of the hall. As they approached the main atrium, he heard her say under her breath, "What's going on?" The entrance to the Grand Tribunal Hall was packed to the brim with people. As they got closer, it was clear there was some sort of commotion going on. Jaym pushed through the throng of scared faces. People were milling about aimlessly, all muttering to each other. They soon reached the doors—nothing was stopping anyone from leaving, the doors simply stood there. He stood staring at the doors, a nervous fear building up inside.

"What's going on?" Jemma asked.

"I don't know, but we're getting the hell out of here," he said, pushing open the doors. A few cries and shouts came from the crowd behind the trio, but they pushed through anyways and emerged on the steps of the building.

It was immediately apparent why the people inside hadn't left yet. Jaym came to a standstill as he looked out, and Gwen stood next to him. "Oh my god…" she began to say, her voice trailing off.

Justice Square was filled with people. Crowds by the tens of thousands, maybe more. The police had maintained the building's perimeter, but from his vantage point, Jaym could see clashes were breaking out. Many people held signs in the crowd, others had begun chanting. "Lock Piers up!" "Free Beck!" "Give us food!"

The sheer volume of people was mind boggling. And it only seemed to be growing—more people could be seen coming through the tunnel to lower city levels.

The three of them stood there, looking out. Jaym smiled. He felt happy for the first time all day.

"They're all here for Beck?" Jemma slowly asked.

"They're all here to fight," Jaym answered, his voice loud and strong. "We're definitely not going back to the way things were—ever again."

CHAPTER 26

———

"What do we do?" Anxiety had replaced the initial jubilation in Gwen's voice.

Jaym took in the scene, already running potential routes in his head. Looking ahead, he thought out loud. "The police won't give up the main steps, so we can't go down that way. And they'll likely keep everyone up inside until things calm down, which could be a while." His eyes scanned as he swiveled around. He spotted a section of the stairs halfway down, where it looked like they might be able to jump. *That could work.*

"This way!" He began heading down a few of the steps.

"What about the guards?" Jemma yelled, but Jaym had already started moving.

The fighting had intensified, and more and more police officers had spewed into the fray. The police had started throwing tear gas canisters, which set a thin haze in the square—like a cloud hanging low over the mob.

They reached the section Jaym had spotted. He leaned over the balcony. *Only about ten feet. That'll work.* He turned to Gwen and Jemma. "We're going to jump down from here."

Jemma's jaw dropped. "You're kidding…"

"It's the best option we have. The guards are preoccupied; no one is watching from below. This is our chance. I'll go first."

Jemma nodded, and Jaym leaned over the edge. He readied himself but paused when Gwen grabbed his arm.

"Jaym, I'm not going with you."

"What?" he said, spinning around to face her. "What do you mean?"

"I'll meet you soon. There's something I have to do first."

"What?" Jaym couldn't contain his shock. "What the hell do you have to do instead?"

"I need to go home," she answered. She lifted her head and looked out at the crowds. "There are a few things I want to grab before it's too late. I have a feeling after today I'll never be returning there."

Jaym stared back at her. "What about Piers? If he sees you…" Jaym was already dreading the worst, and couldn't bring himself to say the words out loud.

"I'm going to slip in and out quietly. I know a back entrance to the Hall that'll get me close to my elevator. I'll meet you at Dante's as soon as I'm done. It'll be fast, I promise."

"Be careful." Jaym took a step closer to her. They were only inches apart as they looked into each other's eyes.

"Come on guys!" Jemma yelled, driving a stake in the moment.

Gwen leaned in and kissed Jaym on the cheek. "I will I promise." And with that, she turned and ran back up the stairs, toward the Grand Hall's entrance.

Jaym watched her go, her feet bounding up the steps as explosions rocked the square. He peeled his eyes away to survey the area once last time. The haze had turned red from fiery, makeshift bombs erupting across the square. The police had continued to hold the line in front of the steps to the

Grand Tribunal Hall, but other buildings in the square didn't seem to be faring well. The chaos was intensifying.

"Jaym, we have to go," Jemma chided. Jaym nodded in agreement. Without giving it a moment's thought, he bounded over the ledge. He rolled once he hit the ground and sprang back up on his feet. With the adrenaline coursing through his body, he didn't feel an ounce of pain.

"Come on!" he called up to Jemma. He held out his arms as she leapt, and she crashed onto him, knocking him to the ground.

Jemma smiled as she lay on top of him. "Thanks," she said sheepishly.

"We gotta go," he said, getting up. "Jemma ... I'm sorry for all of this. I wish I hadn't asked you to come today."

"It wouldn't have mattered if you asked me or not." They looked at each other for a moment longer before another blast grabbed their attention. They took off, running through the thick of the crowds, dodging brawls and tear gas.

The square was a full-on war scene as the pair bounded across toward the tunnel entrance to the Furrows. The air smelled acidic from blood and sweat, and the haze made it difficult to see. The sound of shattering glass was constant, and from his peripherals Jaym could see people throwing rocks and other objects at the windows of the skyscrapers bordering the square. Jaym carried on, with Jemma close by his side. The crowds thinned out as they neared the tunnel to the sublevels. There were a few people huddled, applying first aid to the wounded, and others trying to move people back underground where they'd be safe from the tear gas.

Jemma looked to Jaym, her eyes teary. "We have to help."

Jaym shook his head slowly. "I know, it's inhumane. But we don't have time."

They kept moving, winding their way down into the Furrows. Windows were shut and the alleys were mostly empty and quiet, save a few cries here or there. Nearly every news screen they passed was smashed, with shattered glass littering the ground, but otherwise things seemed calm.

They eventually arrived at Dante's, only to find the door locked. Jaym began banging on the old, wooden door, yelling "Dante! Let us in!" With each pound, he felt the wood buckle, as if the door may cave in any moment.

Hearing a shuffle on the other side, he stopped and waited as he heard a latch open.

"Jeez Jaym, are you trying to break the door down? What good would that do?" Dante exclaimed, opening the door. "Get inside, I'm not leaving this thing unlocked."

Jaym and Jemma hurried into the bar, whose dark and familiar musty scent instantly set them a bit at ease. Jemma slumped into a chair and laid her head back, panting from their run.

"How crazy is it up there?" Dante asked anxiously.

"The craziest I've ever seen," Jaym said. "Can I pour myself a drink?" He had already walked behind the bar and begun to rummage around for a glass.

Dante shook his head. "These people … what do they think this will do? Beck isn't going to be executed. We should all be happy. Rioting and fighting is only going to make things worse."

Jaym stopped rummaging and stared. "I won't be happy until Beck is out from whatever cell they're holding him in." Jaym slammed a glass down on the bar and began to pour himself liquor out of the nearest bottle.

"You're still going through with the plan? Jaym, you're putting his life, not to mention your own, in danger! It's like you're asking for an execution!" Dante gripped the edge of the bar as he spoke.

"Dante, this city may not be standing in ten hours, let alone ten years. Either way, I'm not leaving Beck in there to die. He's still in danger." *Especially with Piers pissed and upset ... who knows what he could manage to do in this chaos?* Jaym downed his drink, pushing off the anxious thoughts.

Just then, the door shook again as someone gave it a good, hard knock.

"We're closed!" Dante yelled.

A muffled voice yelled back. "It's Heath, let me in."

Jaym nodded to Dante, who went over and unlocked the door. Heath stood calmly outside with two large guards flanking him. The trio was in all black, and each had a massive machine gun slung over their shoulder, including Heath.

"Jaym here?" Heath asked. Dante stepped aside, gesturing for Heath to enter. Nodding, he led his two guards into the dark bar as Dante shut and locked the door again from behind.

"Good, glad you're here. You still want to do this?" Heath asked Jaym, standing to face him across the bar.

"Yes. We're a go."

"I had a feeling that would be the case." Heath turned and held out his hand to one of the guards, who pulled out a thick, folded wad of papers. Heath spread the papers out on the bar, showcasing a map and schematic.

"Behold, Lady and Gentlemen. The Grand Tribunal Hall," Heath said, flattening the map. "This shows all the rooms, hallways, and jail cells within the building. I have good intel that they'll be keeping Beck in the Tribunal holding cells for at least tonight, if not the next few days, before they move him to the main city prison. Especially given the current situation in the square, I don't expect they'd try and move any prisoners until the city calms down, which looks like it could take at least a day if not more."

"So our timing is good," Jaym responded, leaning in and peering at the blue lines tracing the building outline. The map was heavily detailed. Even the intricate architectural accents were clearly defined. "Where did you get this?"

Heath smiled. "Like I told you, Jaym, you're with the right guy for this job. Now, here are the holding cells." Heath pointed to a lower section of the building. "The building is sure to be under high surveillance given the circumstances. There is a side entrance here that we're going to break into and access the main corridors here." Jaym nodded, staring intently at the map, trying to memorize the schematics and plan. "From there, it's simple—we break him out of the cell, and we leave the same way we came in."

"You're just going to break him out? Of a heavily secured, fortified jail cell?" Jemma joined the conversation, having perked up.

Jaym nodded in agreement. "And what about security and guards inside the building? That place is sure to be crawling with them, right?"

Heath's sinister grin widened. "Good questions. Regarding the first, we break him out with this." Heath turned to the second guard, who pulled out a medium-sized handsaw. "Ever seen one of these?"

Jaym raised his eyebrows. "Oh, I've used one of those many a time on the construction site." He smiled, and spoke longingly, reminiscing on the past. *To think I was on a construction site just a few weeks ago.*

"It'll be a bit heavy to bring with us, and depending on how thick the bars are, it may take several minutes to cut through, but it should do the job. As for security, you're very right. That's why we're not going in unarmed. These are two of my best operatives, they'll be more than enough protection. We need to be a lean crew, so we don't attract undue attention. We'll move fast, find Beck, get out," Heath said as he motioned to the two men behind him.

Jaym looked at the two men. They were both tall, buff, well over six feet, and wore all black. Their biceps were bulging, looking as if they may burst out of their tight, black outfits.

"Are only four other guys enough?" he asked. *This actually could all work.*

"Any more and we may receive too much undue attention," Heath answered. "We're going to be swift. Access the building, extract Beck, leave. Whole ordeal should last under an hour. As soon as we're out, we head straight back into the Furrows and plan next steps then."

Nodding, Jaym turned to Jemma. She had sat up and had been listening intently. "Jemma, you should stay down here. Where it's safe."

"No! I want to help!" she jumped out of her seat.

Before Jaym could push back, Heath spoke up. "It would be good to have someone waiting for us at the building exit. That way we'll know what happened outside while we're on the inside."

Jemma looked defiantly at Heath, and then at Jaym. "What about Gwen? She seemed intent on joining too."

"I don't think that's a great idea," Heath cautioned. "Like I said, the more people, the more conspicuous."

Jaym nodded. *He's right. Plus, she's more recognizable.* "Okay. Jemma, that work? You'll stand guard outside the Hall?"

Jemma held her tense gaze. After a moment, she agreed. "Yes. I can do that."

"Good, it's settled," Heath said, clapping his hands together. "We'll head to the ground level at dusk. Easier to move in the shadows. In the meantime, I have more tactical outfits ready at our new safe house. Let's head there."

Jaym looked over to the barkeep. "Dante, keep an eye out for any banging on the door. Gwen is sure to come down here soon looking for us. Tell her to wait here, and we'll rendezvous as soon as we get back."

Dante nodded. He had been standing a few feet away, leaning up against the bar shelves. He had poured another drink, and stood holding it, looking weary. Jaym walked over to him and gave the old man a hug. "Thanks for everything, Dante. When this is all over, we're going to fix this place up and get back to the way things were. I promise."

With that, Jaym followed Heath out, Jemma at his side. *Hang in there, Beck. We're coming.*

CHAPTER 27

———

Gwen's heart was pounding. She had been at an all-out sprint since she left Jaym on the steps of the Grand Tribunal Hall. She took a moment to gather her breath, bending down from her knees and sucking in air. She was back in the upper levels of the city, having crisscrossed through the alleyways on the ground and leapt up staircases. She felt relieved no one had followed her. In the chaos, no one had paid her any attention.

A loud bang interrupted her momentary pause, and she turned back in the direction of the square. She had been on edge since the moment they left the hall. *Deep breaths, Gwen. Calm yourself.* She looked about the street. *Dead. Empty. This could be the last time you have a moment like this to calm yourself.* More bangs were going off in the distance, but these ones didn't bother her. She focused on the intricate gardens that decorated the street, the pink flowers that were in bloom. The discrepancy between the aristocratic, upper levels of the city and the Furrows she had recently spent so much time in were indescribably stark. *These people up here don't even realize what's going on in their own city.* More bangs. She resumed her run.

She continued on through the upper streets until she reached the familiar small square with Elevator Twenty-six. She pressed the code and elevator button and was soon flying above the city. Looking down, she could see glimpses of the crowds through the haze. The whole city seemed to glow red, like embers. With the setting sun, Gwen could see her reflection in the glass. She barely recognized herself. Jemma's dress and makeup made her feel like she was in a costume. Her hair looked dull and frayed. But she thought she looked stronger, older. More mature. *I guess cold showers and no shampoo really can take a toll.*

The elevator doors opened, and Gwen stared out across the courtyard. She didn't need to see her reflection to know her expression had immediately changed. Her confidence had melted away as the doors opened. She felt anxious and uneasy. Fearful. It felt strange as she looked at the serene bubbling fountain and the flowers. And there stood the entrance to her father's home. Her home. *This doesn't feel like home anymore.* She walked across and gently opened the front door. It wasn't locked.

Inside, the penthouse was lit up as usual, and Gwen paused as she quietly closed the front door. She heard a muffled voice speaking but kept moving. *Is that Piers? Or someone from the staff?* Gwen crept across the large foyer and ran up the stairs to her bedroom. Inside, she grabbed a bag and began stuffing some clothes into it. She went over to her dresser and grabbed some of her jewelry and a few other things that she figured might be helpful in the future. Going over to her desk, she rummaged in the top drawer. *Come on, where is it.* "Aha!" she said out loud, and then quickly covered her mouth. She delicately pulled out an old photograph from her drawer. She took a second to look longingly at the picture of her and her mother, one of the few things she had to remember her by, before gently folding it in half and placing it into the bag. Her sharp silver letter opener caught her eye. *A weapon could be useful.* She threw the thin blade into her bag as well.

She tossed the bag over her shoulder, left her room and went back down the main entrance stairs. She was at the front door, about to leave, but heard the muffled voice again. *Is it him?* She crossed the foyer and slowly moved along the main corridor wall. The doors to her father's study were slightly ajar, and she heard Piers speaking inside. She carefully peeked around the first door panel, trying to get a glimpse inside.

Piers sat in his father's chair facing the wall of windows. Gwen nudged the door open to get a better look, happy Piers's back was to her. She could see his left hand dangling off the arm of the chair, holding a glass filled with whiskey. The black phone cord wrapped around the chair. *Who is he talking to on father's government phone? Is it just us here?*

Suddenly hearing his voice, Gwen recoiled. She tripped as she fell backward. Stumbling, she caught herself. *Be careful, Gwen!*

"Jesus man, they attacked a vertical farm? How stupid are these people, don't they realize that's only going to hurt them?" Piers paused speaking. A few seconds later, he spoke up again.

"That makes more sense. If the crops are dead, they'll burn even quicker. But those idiots didn't know they were dead when they broke in. And no, I don't know where he is. Listen, Alyx, the city is clearly falling. If the Chief Justices haven't realized it yet, they're as naïve as they are stupid. Connally didn't even have the backbone to execute that bastard this morning. This is their fault. My father's fault. It's time for us to act. To take back power."

Alyx. Of course. But why were the crops dead? And does he really think he can just take over? From the Justices? Gwen never liked Alyx. Actually, Gwen didn't like nearly any of Piers's friends, other than Keats.

"You're right. Screw it, I'm going to go down there and take care of it myself. They're meeting this evening? Good, I can pay old Connally a visit shortly after. Let's put this all in motion. Don't be late." Piers spun around in the chair and slammed the glass down on the desk. He returned the phone to its holster. Gwen took a few steps back, moving away from the crack. After a second, she peered in again. Piers was now leaning over the desk, snorting something. *Silver. The hypocrite.* He took a big huff and stood up straight, then collapsed back into the chair behind the desk.

He's going to see Connally? That means he'll be at the Grand Tribunal Hall. I have to warn Jaym. Gwen jerked away from the door, but she moved too quickly. She stumbled into the bar cart that sat outside the study doors. A crystal decanter and glasses fell off, shattering on the ground.

"Who's there!" Piers shouted. She heard him jump up from the chair. *Shit. Get up, Gwen.* Before she could get back on her feet, Piers swung open the wide double doors. He was holding a handgun, up and at the ready.

"Oh. It's you," he sneered. He lowered the gun. "How nice of you to stop by, Gwen. Here, join me in father's study."

Gwen glared up at him, as she got up from the floor. She brushed her clothes off.

"I'm not getting near you," she started to say.

"Nonsense. Get in here!" Piers's tone was harsh and commanding.

Gwen's heartbeat jumped up a notch as she followed him into the study. He went back around the desk, leaned over and began cutting a new line of silver. "Can I interest you in a little extracurricular fun?"

She planted both her feet shoulder-width apart, attempting to assume a power stance. "You're a sick, disgusting hypocrite Piers."

He looked up, pausing from dolling out the drugs. "You know, I appreciate that." He turned his attention back to fixing the lines of silver. "Congrats on the ruling of your friend. It wasn't what I had advocated for, I'm sure you can guess. But hey, justice is about all of us." Gwen watched as Piers snorted the line. Exhaling, he leaned back in the chair. "So why have you come home? To gloat? Or to apologize, now that you see the chaos this city is falling into?"

"Apologize? You think I'm going to apologize?" Gwen asked, incredulously. "You murdered our father, Piers."

Piers spun the chair around and looked up at the portrait of Chief Justice Marks that hung on the adjacent wall. "Our father was weak, Gwen. We're in this predicament because of him. I'm trying to save us—save this city." He turned back to face her and picked back up his glass. "The Chief Justices have just called an emergency meeting for tonight, but we both know they don't have what it takes to save the city. If I don't step in, New Boston will fall by morning."

Gwen stared at him, shaking her head. She was experiencing a mix of emotions: anger at Piers's conclusions, rage at him killing her father, remorse at what had become of him, and disbelief at how confident he still was. "You think the people of this city will accept *you* as their new ruler? You're delusional!"

Piers eyed her suspiciously. "They won't have a choice."

"Of course they do!" Gwen yelled. "They'll kill you, Piers. They resent you. They all know that it's you who is to blame for this disaster. You are the one who put us on this path. You started picking fights with the hardworking people of this city, threatening them. Arresting them. Killing them. All this backlash, all this violence—it's because of you and your idiot friends!"

Piers's smile faded, as he glared at his sister. "You keep telling yourself that, Gwen. But tell me, what has Jaym ever done for New Boston? Or Beck? Other than selfishly take what we produce and create, and give nothing in return. Nothing but trouble. It was them who killed our mother, don't forget that."

"She died because the city erupted in violence and chaos! Because the Chief Justices didn't want to let the SubCity people handle their own crimes. We wanted to rule *over* them. Subjugate them for our own whims. Father understood that. You've brought us back to the edge of anarchy."

Piers snorted. "These fools are the ones pursuing anarchy. The people are rioting in the streets, trying to burn everything to the ground. The idiots just broke into a vertical farm and are burning the crops. How is that helping their cause? They're only hurting themselves. Not that it matters much. Half the farms have begun to fail anyways, apparently."

Gwen's eyes went wide. If the farms were really failing, it was a secret the Justices had kept close to their chests. A secret her father must've known. And it would explain why rations had been depleted the past few months. *Focus on Piers.* "And you sit here high out of your mind. Wasn't it you who once said drugs are what's ruining this city?" Gwen's tone was defiant.

"So, what if I am?" Piers yelled back, raising his voice. Piers stood and walked over to look out the windows. Gwen noticed it had been replaced since the night Piers threw her father out of it. "This city is falling, Gwen. You're right—this is anarchy. Except those scum deserve it."

He's not wrong. Burning the city down isn't the solution. But the Justices must have a plan. A plan to save the farms, return us to stability. With Piers's back to her, Gwen slowly reached around into her bag. She felt her hands grip the silver letter opener, and she slowly pulled it out, keeping it hidden.

"None of that changes what you've done, Piers. You murdered our father. You set yourself on a collision course with Jaym and Beck. You spurred this city into violence." Gwen took a step toward her brother, and whispered, "You're a monster."

"And you know, what?" Piers said as he turned around to face Gwen. "I'd do it all again."

Gwen's anger turned to rage, and her heartbeat shot up. Barely thinking, she screamed and lunged forward, with the letter opener gripped tightly in her fist. She focused on Piers's chest as she threw herself at her brother.

Piers barely had to react. He was twice Gwen's size, and merely grabbed her arm and threw it down to the side. She screamed. The letter opener flew out from her hand and clanged as it hit the ground.

Inches from her face, Piers sneered. "You've always been weak, sister." He pushed her away, and she crumpled to the floor.

Gwen looked up at Piers, her face filled with pure disgust. "If this city falls, you'll fall with it."

Piers smiled and laughed, returning to behind the desk. He began cutting up another line of Silver. "Even you don't believe that."

Gwen stood up and brushed herself off. "I do believe it. I'm going to make sure it happens." Gwen turned and began walking out of the office.

"If you leave this house right now, Gwen, I won't save you if the city does fall."

She turned slightly to give one last look at her brother. "I've never needed you to save me." And with that, Gwen left the study and ran out of the penthouse, her childhood home, for the last time.

CHAPTER 28

——

Piers's body was buzzing with energy. Between the Silver coursing through his veins and the adrenaline from his encounter with Gwen, he felt like he could lift a mountain. But then Gwen's words echoed back to him. *Is she right? Maybe they really will try to kill me.* He leaned back in the chair and rested his hands on the thick, leather arms. *If father were here, he'd know what to do.* He immediately cursed himself for this thought. Even when dead, he still felt his father's disappointment. He thought back on the countless times he had come into this office to talk to his father and seen him sitting in this chair, not willing to pay any attention to him. How all he had wanted was to hear an ounce of appreciation, or pride. Or just anything but the standard apathy with a touch of disdain. Yet Piers always saw himself one day sitting in this very chair, following in his father's footsteps. Becoming a Chief Justice, ruling over the council. "Well at least that came true," Piers said to himself, gripping the curled ends of the armchair and flexing his fingers.

The black phone rang, disrupting his reflection. Piers answered simply, "Talk."

Alyx spoke deliberately on the other end. "The emergency council meeting is convening in two hours, in the East Wing of the Grand Tribunal Hall. It is a closed-door meeting, no aides or dignitaries are permitted to attend."

"Good," Piers responded. "What is the status on the ground floor?"

"Things have deescalated a bit, but generally still violent. Much of the police force have abandoned their posts, though the crowd's attention has moved from the Grand Tribunal Hall to other city landmarks. Currently the most violence is outside the Cathedral and at Vertical Farm Three."

"Is the Grand Tribunal Hall secured?"

"Mostly. There are still police holding the steps entrance, and the blockades have deterred much of the crowds. We have several snipers and large machine guns armed and manned at the entrance and have made an example of anyone who has attempted to rush the barricades."

"Good. I'll be there shortly. I'll enter from the upper bridge connecting the Archives. Alyx, I think we may need a contingency plan. I'm starting to think that if we try to assume power tonight, it'll be difficult to convince the people. We need them to experience this anarchy for a few more days before they'll truly respect the stability of authority."

Alyx was quiet for a moment. "It's not out of the question. Depending on the size of the police force left, it'll be a close call if we'll have the firepower to ensure compliance with tensions this high."

Piers thought to himself for a few moments. "I have an idea. Stay by your phone, I'll ring you back shortly." Piers began putting the phone down but then paused, and brought it back up to his mouth. "Alyx, did you find Keats?"

"He was called into Police HQ to help monitor the forces

from the command center. I would guess he's still there."

Piers paused to think. *Where has he been?* He realized that they hadn't had a conversation in several days, since right after the raid. *Should I tell him of the plan? He must know the city is falling. And yet he hasn't tried to get in touch with me at all. If it comes to it, do I leave him behind?*

"Okay, thanks. Be in touch."

Piers hung up the phone before. His mind was still racing as he played out all the steps in his head, making sure he hadn't forgotten anything. *There isn't any room for mistakes. I need supplies in case we have to move to Plan B.* He left the office and went upstairs to his bedroom and started grabbing various things: clothes, KIP pills, a knife, and a pile of jewelry he had found in his father's bedroom. He began packing up a black duffel bag, grabbing other odds and ends around the room.

After he finished packing, Piers went back downstairs to the hallway off the foyer and opened the closet where his father had kept his coats and other private ends. He pushed aside the coats to reveal a shotgun propped up in the corner. Piers pulled the gun out and gave it a pump, testing it. "Good," he said out loud, satisfied. He threw the gun over his shoulder.

He walked back into the study and grabbed a second bag. He opened the zipper, checking its cargo. Five shiny grenades sat nestled in the bag, their thin, silver pins all loaded and ready. He thought back to what Alyx had said when he dropped the bag off earlier.

"Miniature grenades, for precise explosions. Their destruction is limited to a twenty-foot radius."

Piers smiled as he pulled one out and tossed it lightheartedly in the air. *Funny how such a small thing can cause so much destruction—hold so much power.* He placed the grenade back in the bag and headed back to the hallway. Just before he left the office, he turned back and took it in. So many times had he walked into the office, saw his father hunched over the desk, not willing to give him the time of day. So many times had he stood outside these doors, mustering the confidence and strength to enter, trying to ignore the pit in his stomach. He let out a huff and spat on the ground. "Good riddance," he said out loud and walked down the hall toward the front door.

A few moments later, Piers was on his way to the Grand Tribunal Hall. He moved quickly through the dark, empty streets. With each step, the shouts and explosions got louder. He gripped the gun tightly as he came to the first major boulevard, his eyes darting back and forth. *Here we go.* His body was still on fire from the Silver. He knew his face was one of the most recognizable in the city today, especially after the recent events. He reached into his bag and pulled out a hat. He slid it on, tilting the brim down over his eyes.

A few angry protestors, and I might not make it there. He tightened his grip around the gun and continued on.

He snaked his way through the city. Soon, he came upon the white, marble facade of the Hall of Archives. He had spent much of his studies in the Archives in recent years. Given how often Justice clerks used the texts for research, the building was connected to the Grand Tribunal Hall. He went up to open the doors, but they wouldn't budge. Leaning up to the dark glass doors, he could barely make out a nervous-looking security guard, mouthing "we're closed." Piers lifted his cap to reveal his face and rattled the doors again. Recognizing him, the guard ran over to open the door.

"I'm sorry sir, but the Archives are under lockdown, as are all government buildings. I can't let you—"

"Do you know who I am?" Piers asked, trying not to raise his voice.

"Yes, Mr. Marks. But I—"

"Go call your superior and say I request entrance."

The guard nodded and turned to head back to his desk. Piers quickly slid his foot into the gap by the door and edged himself inside. As the guard turned in protest, Piers turned the shotgun around and shoved the heavy butt into the guard's face. The guard slumped to the ground and lay motionless. Tossing the gun back around on his back, Piers relocked the doors. He then reached down, took the guard's keycard hanging from his pocket, and headed to the elevator. A few moments later, he was soaring again above the city.

The Archives stood directly behind the Grand Tribunal Hall, towering over the older building as if it were its guardian. The elevator doors opened, and Piers began weaving through the building. Hearing a few more explosions, he stopped and peered out a set of windows. The crowds ebbed in the square, with flaming fireworks shooting up from various pockets. Piers looked on in anger, his eyes narrowing on the mob. *Ungrateful, pathetic, bottom feeders. All of them. Little do they know what's about to happen. Soon they'll wish they had acted differently—had respected the system.*

Piers continued weaving through the hallways, navigating them with intuition. He soon came upon an unassuming door at the end of the hall. The door was wooden, looking similar to the entrance to his father's study. In small, gold letters were the words "Bridge to Grand Tribunal Hall." On the other side was an outdoor skywalk, ten stories above the alley below, to the roof of the Grand Tribunal Hall.

The guard's keycard opened the doors with ease. Inside the Grand Tribunal Hall, red emergency lights dimly lit the dark wooden walls. The building was desolate. All the people had been evacuated, as emergency protocols had been activated.

Piers descended to the main atrium and headed to the elevator bank. He clicked the button for two floors below ground level, the lowest level of the building. The elevator let him out in a much darker hallway, with dark black stone walls that seemed to grow narrower as one continued on. Piers didn't pay any mind to the seemingly closing-in walls— he moved along the hallway at a steady, confident pace. With each step, his heartbeat picked up, and he couldn't help but start grinning. He had been waiting for this moment all day. *Time to set things in motion.*

At the end of the hall was a solid metal door, left slightly ajar. He pushed it open and entered the Tribunal Hall prison cells. Each cell he passed was empty, as he made his way to the end of the row. There were no guards and no people. Save one man, his wrists in chains, in the final cell. Piers stopped in front of the cell, where a simple metal table and chair sat. He took a seat facing the cell and made himself comfortable.

In a cheery voice, Piers said, "Beck. Good to see you."

CHAPTER 29

Jaym began to feel more and more anxious about the night ahead of them. *It's do-or-die time. I'm coming Beck.*

Heath led Jaym and Jemma to a small apartment not too far from the bar. One of the two tall, black-clad men brought up the rear and one led in front of Heath as the group moved through the alleyways. Jaym had yet to hear either man speak. He was amazed and a bit terrified at their swift agility. Each time the group turned a new corner, the leading guard spun around with his gun at the ready, checking various vantage points before clearing it for safe passage.

At the apartment, Heath gave Jaym and Jemma black, spandex outfits. The clothes sealed in Jaym's sweat. He felt constricted, making him even more aware of his heightened blood pressure. Heath also put one on and began taking out various guns and weapons to arm themselves.

"The city has executed emergency protocols, including ordering a city-wide curfew. Things will take several hours to truly calm down though. Most government buildings are on lockdown, but the Grand Tribunal Hall is sure to still have ample security. The city won't just let it sit idly by and risk it being touched by protesters. Plus it has prisoners inside, so they can't be just leave it sitting unguarded." Heath cocked a handgun gun and handed it to Jaym. "Best be prepared."

Jaym held the gun in his hands, feeling the weight of the cold metal. Jemma nudged him.

"You okay?"

Jaym nodded. "I just … have never held a gun before." Jaym straightened his posture, trying to imbue confidence in himself. Turning to Heath, he said, "Let's go over the plan one more time."

Heath pulled out the map and they all leaned in over it. "Here is the auxiliary entrance we'll be entering through. The police use it for prisoner transport. It should be less guarded than the main entrance. From there…"

Jaym's attention drifted as he listened to Heath go over the plan again. He had already memorized it to a tee. But it eased him to hear it repeated again.

"Jaym?" Heath asked, bringing Jaym back to reality.

"Sorry, was just thinking. Are we sure we've considered every possible situation? And what about Jemma? She can't wait outside alone."

"We'll leave Finley with her," Heath said, motioning to one of the guards. "As for the plan, it's as airtight as a plan can be, with the chaos that's going on. There's no way to know exactly what's going to happen. But we're going to react quickly and effectively to whatever is thrown our way." Heath put his arm on Jaym's shoulder. "We're going to get him out, Jaym."

Jaym stared back at Heath. *He seems almost too confident.* "Okay. Let's do this."

"You heard him, boys," Heath said to the guards. "Let's roll out."

Outside, the group resumed its prior organization, with the guards leading them back through the winding alleys. Jaym saw people for the first time since leaving the square. *They look terrified—scared to death.* Most were darting to-and-fro, trying to find their way inside the apartments and stores lining the street. But others simply huddled together, trembling with fear, avoiding eye contact with the frenzied civilians who passed by.

Jaym shifted in his outfit. He was gradually growing used to the feel of the skintight suit, trying to pay less attention to the irritation it was giving him. The tense energy in the streets was seeping into his body. *Focus, Jaym.*

As the group surfaced to the ground level, the fighting became apparent. Gunfire rang out, echoing through the underground streets. At one burst, Jemma was so startled she almost tripped, jumping back. Jaym grabbed her, stopping her momentum. She mumbled her thanks, and they continued on. Soon, they emerged into Justice Square.

The city was a war zone.

Massive chunks had been blown out of the skyscrapers on the perimeter of the square, looking as if asteroids had taken scoops out of the buildings. Clearly people's makeshift bombs had gotten stronger. The vertical farm was still ablaze, and torches from the crowd could be seen down the main boulevard adjacent to it. The people had begun moving the fight upward in the city, attempting to break into more skyscrapers and confront the rest of the citizens of New Boston. *Is this a revolution? A coup? Or just anarchy?*

"This way," Heath yelled. Or whispered. Jaym couldn't tell; he had sensory overload. The air smelled burnt. It even looked burnt, with a red haze still hanging low in over the crowds. Jaym looked up at the Grand Tribunal Hall. The building stood intact; it had yet to take any blows. Yet all around it, the city looked apocalyptic. The expanse in front of him barely resembled the city he had grown up in. It had taken just a few days to fall into utter chaos.

They continued on, darting across the square with their guns at the ready. Jaym had yet to fire the weapon, but Heath's men were much more liberal. It seemed they fired off shots every few feet. The group made it across the square safely and began heading down an alley next to the Hall. They moved quickly; the alley was empty save for a few shattered windows and wandering, confused people.

Jaym was still so focused on taking in his surroundings that he almost bumped into Heath, who had stopped alongside the other two guards. One had put his hand up, motioning for them to pause.

"This is it," Heath said, his voice steady. "Get ready, there's sure to be someone guarding inside." Jaym felt his heartbeat accelerate. Out of the corner of his eye, he saw Jemma's eyes go wide and face go pale. She looked like she was about to be sick. Before they could think about it any longer, Heath yelled out: "Now!"

Jaym lifted his gun and followed Heath and the leading guard, as they turned and began firing at the glass door. A moment later, the door shattered, and the two men continued forward, bullets still flying from their guns. There was barely any return fire, and a minute later the shooting all stopped. Jaym saw three policemen lying dead in the room as he entered the building.

Heath ran over to the policemen, reaching into their pockets and vests. "Aha, got it!" he yelled, pulling up a plastic key card. He ran over to one of the closed doors, while the two guards set about checking the rest of the room for traps. Heath swiped the card next to the door, and the small light blinked green. "We're in."

Jaym stepped over the dead police officers. He couldn't help but look down. The color hadn't even left their faces yet, as a pool of crimson blood expanded outwards from their bodies. *So many unnecessary deaths.* Jaym looked around the room, realizing it was actually quite small. In the middle was a tall wooden desk, with a sign above that said, "Prisoner Processing." There were a few benches along the walls, but otherwise the processing entrance was bare. Heath had walked back over to Jaym and Jemma.

"Jemma, this is where you'll wait for us with Finley. I'd stay here behind the desk, so you have some cover in case something happens. We'll only be twenty minutes or so—thirty tops. Finley, if anyone tries to follow us ... well, don't let them." Heath looked at Jaym as he finished speaking. Jaym couldn't tell if he was looking for approval or some other reaction, so he merely nodded.

Jaym looked at Jemma. "You'll be okay. We'll be right back." He tried to smile and bestow some confidence to his friend.

Jemma took in a deep breath and shook her head in affirmation. "Go get Beck," was all she was able to muster. Jaym leaned in and gave her a tight hug. He wasn't thrilled that they were separating, but before he had time to think about it anymore, he turned and began following Heath through the previously locked door. They were in.

*　*　*

Beck glared at Piers. He was enraged to see him again, but also knew he didn't have the upper hand in the situation. *Play it cool.*

"You look good, Beck. Glad you've settled into your new

accommodations here nicely," Piers goaded, flashing a sinister smile at Beck.

Beck stared back, keeping his face hard and unyielding. He tried to take a step forward but jerked to a stop. The chains attached to his feet and wrists were now taut, and he had no more room to move. "What do you want?" he asked, his voice low.

Piers took out a handgun and placed it on the table. Then he took out a long, thin vial and began pouring its contents out next to the gun. The silvery powder glittered in the low light of the cell. While he was cutting the drug into lines, Piers started talking again. "You know, Beck. You and I are a lot alike. In fact, I think had I been born in your place, I would've made many of the same decisions you've made these past few weeks. Stealing from my father's study, fighting back against armed police. You know, causing trouble." Piers leaned over and snorted a line. As he finished, he threw his head back, and sucked in more air through his nostrils. "Thanks, by the way, for delivering this so far from the Furrows. You know, back on the day we met." As he finished the sentence, Piers lifted his head and met Beck's eyes.

"Screw you," Beck said. His voice was steady and charged with malice. "You're going to get what's coming. Your father dying isn't enough, you'll suffer even more pain. But oh, how I wish I could've seen you when you found your poor father murdered in his own house."

"Ha!" Piers let out a laugh, jumping up from the table. "You all are so stupid; you can't even see what's right in front of you." Piers walked around and got up close to the bars, gripping two on either side of his face. Beck could see he was flushed with a new wave of adrenaline from the silver. "I'm the one who killed my father, Beck. Pushed him out the window and watched him fall dozens of stories through the air."

Beck couldn't hide his reaction. His face went white, as he began to register how dangerous Piers really was. Fear and panic were settling in. "Why are you here," Beck asked, trying to keep his voice steady.

Smiling, Piers walked over to the cell's gate. He typed in the code Alyx had told him, and the door clicked open. "Oh, I have some business with the Chief Justice Council to attend to. But I figured I would come pay you a visit first." Piers entered the cell and began walking closer to Beck. Beck took a step back, almost cowering. "I wanted to tell you how much I enjoyed your little revelation today!" As he spoke, Piers threw his fist into Beck's gut, knocking the air out of him. He struck so fast Beck didn't have a chance to prepare himself. Beck doubled over, falling to the ground.

Coughing, Beck struggled to respond. "You got what you wanted; I'm going away. Ten years from now you won't even remember me. What more do you want?"

"You're so stupid," Piers said, readjusting his knuckles. "I didn't get what I wanted. I wanted you to be sentenced to death. But like everything else in this city these days, I guess I'll just have to take things into my own hands. These incompetent Justices can't be trusted for anything anymore."

Beck looked up, hate in his eyes. He spit down at Piers's feet. "Go ahead, kill me. I don't even care anymore. You saw those Justices' expressions: you'll never be in charge of this city."

"You're wrong!" Piers screamed. His pupils were dilated, and his right eye twitched a bit from the drugs in his system. "I will be in charge of this city. Maybe not today, but in due time. But you—you won't get the chance to see the new world I'll rule."

Just then, the sound of footsteps echoed from down the hall. Piers and Beck both snapped their heads up, hearing the sound. Piers moved back to the small table and picked up his handgun. He backed into the shadows.

"Who do you think—" Beck started to ask, whispering.

"Quiet!" Piers snapped back, holding up his hand. He took a few steps backward, moving into the corner of the room. Suddenly, a black-clad man stepped out from the shadows of the hall, with a massive gun held at the ready. Then came Heath, and then Jaym. Beck jumped to his feet and started yelling.

* * *

Jaym bounded ahead down the hallway of empty cells. They were in the depths of the building, and he could tell they were close. Then, suddenly, a familiar voice called out to Jaym. "Watch out, Piers is—"

"Thrilled to see you all," Piers finished the sentence, stepping out from the corner with his handgun up. "Now let's everyone take a deep breath. Jaym, what a surprise."

Jaym stepped out in front of Heath, his gun also drawn. The sound of his throbbing heartbeat was nearly deafening to him. But he managed to get words out. "What the hell are you doing here, Piers?"

Piers smiled and answered calmly. "Just paying our good friend Beck here a visit."

Beck piped up again. "Don't believe a word he says. He's high on Silver. He's out of his mind—"

"Shut up!" Piers screamed, turning to face Beck and firing the gun. The barrel was aimed up in the corner of the room, and the bullet ricocheted off the wall and bounced down the hallway.

"I think a deep breath is a good idea," Heath said. He took his hands off his own handgun, raising both palms up.

"You don't know this man, Heath. He's dangerous. He killed his own father," Jaym responded, not taking his eyes off Piers, who continued smiling.

"Oh, I know him. Known him for years," Heath responded, taking a few steps toward Piers, his gun refixed on his chest.

"What?" Jaym asked, shock and disbelief in his voice.

Heath turned back to Jaym. "Don't act so surprised, Jaym. You heard Beck at the trial. You even delivered a package to him. Piers is one of my best customers." Heath spoke calmly, with his gun still trained on Piers.

"You're still concerned about your business in a time like this?" Jaym's head was spinning. He had known that Heath knew Piers, but he couldn't shake a feeling of dread that was building up. He didn't even realize that, in the midst of his thinking, he had let the gun drop to his side. The black-clad man next to him suddenly reached down and snatched it from his hand and took a step back.

Before he could say anything, Heath began speaking. He had lowered the gun from its focus on Piers and turned to look at Jaym. "I'm sorry, Jaym. I never meant for you two to get caught up in all this, but things have a funny way of working out. The night of the raid, Piers and I ended up realizing that our interests aligned beyond just Silver."

Jaym's heartbeat was now racing. Everything had changed so quickly, and he didn't know what to do. He felt powerless, unstable. *Stay focused. Keep the conversation going, figure out their end game.*

"What interests," Jaym managed to say.

Piers paced around the room. "The Chief Justice Council does not have control over this city. You saw what it's like out there. Your *people*, the *oppressed*, they're destroying the city. Torching the vertical farms, attacking each other. That's why I'm taking over—to bring back the justice we all know we need."

"You think *you* have what it takes to run this city? Those people will never support *you*." Jaym regretted how snide he sounded.

"I agree," Beck piped up.

"I told you to shut up!" Piers raged, firing the gun again at the ceiling above Beck's head. Piers looked back at Jaym. "You know, my sister said the same thing. You and your *people* are so ungrateful—ungrateful and stupid. That's why I'm not taking control today. No. I'm leaving New Boston tonight. I'll let the city burn until the people realize that they need me. That they need the security and stability I'll bring as the ruler of New Boston. And then I'll be back."

He's leaving? Jaym glared at Piers. But then he remembered Heath. Looking to the man he had trusted, he asked, "And what the hell did you have to do with this?"

Piers continued speaking. "But before I left, I wanted to see you one last time, Jaym. So Heath and I came to a mutual agreement: I promised him a position in my new government. In return, Heath would convince you that he was your only way to break Beck out. He'd bring you here to me, for our final meeting."

Jaym's eyes were like daggers. Heath stared back, cold and emotionless.

"Why did you need to see me?" Jaym turned back to face Piers.

"I wanted to tell you one last time what I told you once before. You can't stop me." Piers's sinister grin had widened on his face. "And I wanted to see your face when I killed your friend."

Terror shook Jaym. He lunged forward, but it was too late. In a swift motion, Piers swung his arm around to point the gun square at Beck and pulled the trigger. Beck staggered backward and slumped against the wall, a red blood stain trailing behind. Jaym screamed and ran into the cell, kneeling over Beck's body. He awoke back to reality as he heard the metal door of the cell clang shut. And realized he was locked in the cell.

CHAPTER 30

———

Gwen had been running for nearly an hour. The minutes flew by as she dodged the fighting in the streets, angling through dark allies and moving toward the city center. Her mind had felt clouded when she initially left her brother, but with each step, she felt freer. Even as she dodged falling debris from explosions in the skyscrapers, she felt liberated.

Rounding a corner, she jerked to a halt. The main boulevard had become the epicenter of the fighting, with the crowd marching onward and a line of police holding a line a few dozen yards away. The mob had amassed weapons and flaming torches, brandishing them as they moved toward the police. Gwen's adrenaline fused with a renewed sense of fear and anxiety.

"My God," she whispered out loud. *How will we ever recover from this?* A loud boom and the sound of shattering glass shook her, and she moved to flush her body in line with the building on the corner. Looking up, she saw a cloud of smoke and fire a few stories above, and shards of glass come raining down.

Gwen knew she had to get going. She had lost all sense of time from how long it had been since Beck's trial and when she had left Jaym. She took a deep breath and started moving again. She was running against the flow of the crowd. She kept her head down, trying not to draw attention to herself. But she couldn't help looking up at the faces of the people passing by. They were covered in soot and ash, but each set of eyes she saw was ignited with anger.

Soon she made it past the dense crowd and was back in the open Justice Square. People huddled in small crowds, many crying and tending to each other's wounds. The entire setting seemed like a battlefield after the fighting subsided, with fires burning in isolated patches all around. Gwen wanted to stop and help but knew she didn't have the time. She felt overwhelmed, as if she were being pulled in a hundred different directions. *Stay focused, Gwen. Get to Dante's. One step at a time.* She pushed on, heading toward the gaping entrance to the main tunnel.

A few weeks ago, she had never even been to the city sublevels. Now, as she descended down, she felt safe. Safer than she had above ground. Especially the further she got from Piers. But the scene didn't change much in the lower levels. There were fewer people on the streets, but those who were out huddled together in desperation. Many were children, looking lost and alone. Gwen's heart wrenched, but she kept moving, quickening her pace. She soon found herself back in Sub3, nearly at Dante's. The door was locked when she reached the now-familiar wooden door.

"Dante! Jaym!" she yelled, pounding on the door. She banged for a solid minute, to the point that her hand began to bruise. She stepped back, gripping her right hand and readjusting her knuckles. As she did, she heard the grinding of metal as the door unlocked. Dante stood in the doorway, looking tired and weary.

"Dante, thank goodness you're okay," Gwen said, feeling relieved for the first time all day. "Where's Jaym?"

Dante stared back at her, his expression becoming confused. "You're not with him?"

Gwen's stomach dropped. She hadn't even considered the possibility that Jaym wouldn't be here.

"When did they leave? How long has it been?" she asked.

"An hour or so," Dante answered. "He left for the Grand Tribunal Hall with Heath and his men."

Gwen's adrenaline picked back up, and she bent her head as her mind began racing. She knew she was short on time and had to find Jaym. But she also knew she couldn't attempt to break into the hall on her own, especially unarmed. Then it hit her. *Keats.*

"Thanks, Dante. Stay safe," she said, and began turning away from the bar.

"Where are you going to go?" Dante asked, but Gwen had already resumed her run. She was back in a full sprint, retracing her steps up to the ground level of the city. She was running through possibilities of where Keats could be. Ultimately she decided police headquarters made the most sense. *Please, Keats. Don't be out in the clashes or hiding at home. And don't be dead.*

Gwen had a renewed focus as she ascended the city levels. Jaym having already set off spurred her back into action. She buzzed past the huddled people, her mind elsewhere rather than feeling the pity she had felt just minutes earlier. Her legs had begun to feel heavy from all the running, but she pressed on.

Her energy picked up as she saw the police headquarters building come into view. There were two heavily armed guards at the entrance. They lifted their guns as she came to a halt in front of them, panting.

"I need to talk to Keats Presley," she gasped, heaving between words.

"No civilians are allowed in the building right now," the first guard said, his gun still at the ready.

"Call him. He'll tell you to let me in," Gwen stammered. *He'd better.*

"We can't do that," the other guard said. They both wore dark helmets with black visors covering their eyes. Gwen wondered what expression they wore behind those veils. Were they scared, or just holding steadfast to their orders? She knew she only had one other card to play. She hated playing it, but she had no choice.

"Do you know who I am? I'm Gwen Marks—Chief Justices Marks's daughter, and Piers Marks's sister. I demand you let me into this building, it is an emergency."

The two guards turned and looked at each other, taking in the new information.

"You don't look like Gwen Marks," one said, tilting his head. In the dark glass of his helmet, she saw her reflection: her face covered in soot, her hair dangling unkempt. *So much for natural beauty.* Before she could respond, a group of people came out of nowhere up to the headquarters entrance.

"Down with the police!" one screamed and threw a Molotov cocktail in Gwen's direction.

"Get down!" one of the guards yelled, and gunfire began erupting.

Now, Gwen. Now's your chance. Gwen ducked down as the makeshift bomb fell a few feet away, and then made a dash for the door around the backside of the nearest guard.

"Hey! You can't go inside!" the other guard yelled, and more gunshots followed. When Gwen realized the shots weren't heading for her, she continued on and entered the building. Luckily the entrance hall was empty of other guards. Not looking back, Gwen resumed her run into the heart of the building. She remembered Keats describing central command to her before and decided to start there. *Should be a big room. Screens and surveillance machinery.*

The halls were eerily empty, and the sterile cleanliness was a stark contrast compared to the burning city outside. She ran past framed pictures of police captains in their crisp uniforms. The hallway soon opened up to a massive room, which was buzzing with people. *Central command. Just as Keats described it.*

Police officers were in a frenzy, poring over computer screens, running from desk to desk, yelling into phones. A head here or there turned to glance at Gwen, but quickly swiveled back to wherever the focus had previously been. She had slowed her pace to a walk, and began meandering between the various desk clusters, looking for Keats. At one point, she found herself near the far wall, where a massive map of the city spread out nearly twenty feet high. The map was covered in bright red dots and other bright colors. Gwen didn't need to know what each label and insignia meant, the message from the map was clear: the city was as violent right now as a volcanic eruption.

"Hey! Who are you? You can't be here!" a voice yelled from behind her. A man, who towered over her, grabbed her arm and began pulling her away from the map.

"Let go of me! Do you know who I am?" Gwen squealed. She glared back at the guard, trying to wrestle her arm away.

"How did you get in here?" the man asked. A few other policemen had stopped what they were doing and lifted their heads to the unexpected commotion.

"I'm here to see Keats. I'm Gwen Marks," Gwen fumed, attempting to calm her voice and speak with an even tone.

"I don't care who you are. Breaking into the police headquarters is a criminal offense," the officer responded, and began tugging her away from the map.

"I *need* to see Keats Presley immediately. It is an emergency, on high orders from the Chief Justice Council," Gwen said, her voice starting to unsteady. *Keats, where are you?*

"You can have the Justices call him directly."

Gwen tried to get her arm free, but the policeman easily overpowered her. She had a decision to make: allow herself to be pulled through the massive command center, hoping to see Keats along the way. Or put-up hell.

"Gwen?" a familiar voice called, and she breathed a huge sense of relief. Keats emerged from the amassing policemen. His voice distracted the policeman, and Gwen was able to pull away.

"Keats! Thank God," Gwen said, running to embrace him.

The officer didn't relent. "She does not have permission to be inside her. She needs—"

"I'll take care of her," Keats said, interrupting the other officer. "I think we can both recognize the extraordinary situation right now. Gwen Marks is a high priority person in New Boston. I'm sure she has just been nervous for her personal safety. Isn't that right, Gwen?" Keats grabbed Gwen's other arm and pulled her free.

Gwen nodded. She couldn't get out any other words. Tears had welled up in her eyes, and she was fighting to fend them off. Seeing Keats gave her a sense of security and safety that she realized she hadn't felt all day.

"Show's over gentlemen, you can all go back to your duties. The city isn't going to secure itself," Keats said, putting her arm around Gwen. He began leading her through the command center, away from the crowds. The other officers had begun to disperse, but the tall policeman stood still in the clearing, watching Keats lead Gwen away. Gwen's stared back at him, for a moment.

"Gwen," Keats said, calling her attention away from the man. She turned her head to face forward. "What's going on? You look terrified."

"Does that officer know my brother? I'm nervous he's going to call him. Piers is unhinged, Keats. If he knows I came here, he—"

"Gwen, take a deep breath. The police force is massive, not everyone knows each other. I don't even know that guy's name," Keats said, cutting her off. "Now, can you please tell me what is going on? Why are you here? The city isn't safe right now. It's mayhem out there."

"I had nowhere else to go. I need your help." Gwen looked Keats dead in the eyes, her demeanor serious. "Piers is going nuclear. He's unstable, and when I saw him, he was railing Silver like it was candy. He thinks he can take control of the city. He said the crops are dying. He's going to Connally to do something—I don't know what. We need to get to the Grand Tribunal Hall. Jaym is breaking in to save Beck."

"Whoa, whoa. Slow down. Piers is upset, sure, but Beck got handed a pretty harsh sentence from the Justices. And—"

"Keats! Look around. New Boston is imploding, and Piers isn't about to sit around and watch it burn. He's going to try and take the city into his own hands. We need to find Jaym and come up with a plan to stop him."

Keats looked off to the distance for a moment, processing all the information. "The Chief Justice Council is convening in an hour for an emergency meeting. That must be where

Piers is going to confront Connally."

Gwen's face was grave. "We need to get to the Grand Tribunal Hall ASAP. And we need to be armed. We need to stop Piers from doing whatever he's about to do."

CHAPTER 31

————

"You can't do this," Jaym said, his voice cold. He was still kneeling over Beck's body, the pool of blood continuing to spread out underneath him. Jaym could feel its warmth rising up. *No, no, no. Beck, I'm so sorry.*

"Oh, I can," Piers said. He had walked back over to the small table and picked up his gun.

Jaym stood up and went to the cell bars, trying to get as close as he could to Piers. He gripped the bars so hard that his knuckles were turning white and a vein on his forehead bulged. He cast a glance toward Heath, who still bore an emotionless face. Jaym was at a loss for understanding. Heath's demeanor was completely changed in the face of Piers.

"I'm going to kill you, Piers. And you, Heath." Jaym spoke slowly, deliberately—almost savoring the rage-tinged words. *Think, Jaym. Keep them here, talking. There has to be a way out.*

Piers laughed. "Come on, Heath. Let's go. We have business to attend to. This is goodbye, Jaym." Piers stood up and adjusted his jacket. He flashed Jaym one last smile and turned his back.

"No!" Jaym shouted, moving along the cell wall trying to keep pace with Piers. Heath was still standing a few feet from the cell door, staring ahead with cold, calculating eyes. He turned to follow Piers out. "Was this your plan the whole time? How could you, Heath? You betrayed us. You betrayed Beck!"

Heath paused and turned his head back toward the cell. "I'm sorry, Jaym. Survival has always been my end goal. Silver and the business, it's all a means to survive. Piers offered me the only way to get through this chaos, and I had to take it."

Then he continued on and faded into the shadows. Jaym's eyes went wide as he watched the two men disappear. Panic and terror began setting in. "I'm going to kill you! Don't you forget that! Beck won't have died in vain!" Jaym looked back at Beck, feeling a sense of dread coming over him. *Think, Jaym. There has to be a way out of this.* But the more he ran through his options, the more hopeless he felt. Piers had truly cornered him. He fought away tears as best he could, but after a point, the emotion became too much. He looked down at Beck again.

"I'm so sorry, Beck."

* * *

Piers glanced down at his watch, looking at the numbers glow in the dark hall. *Perfect, they'll have just convened.* He led Heath and the guard back up through from the depths of the Grand Tribunal Hall, as they headed toward the Chief Justices' Wing of the building. He had never seen the Tribunal halls so empty, and the dim lighting as a result of the emergency protocol cast strange, unfamiliar shadows all around.

"Keep up, we're on a tight schedule," Piers called to the men behind him. Piers smiled to himself. *Everything's going exactly according to plan. If only these idiots can keep up.* Heath and the black-clad guard picked up their pace, so that they were right on Piers's heels. The halls were as foreign to them as they were natural to Piers, who had essentially grown up in the sprawling building. They entered an elevator, and soon found themselves crossing back through the large atrium at the hall's entrance.

Piers spun around to face the group. He pointed at the guard. "You, wait here and ensure no one enters this building. We have a meeting to attend to, and then we'll be back. Heath, with me." Heath nodded at the guard and followed Piers out of the atrium to a staircase slightly down the hall. Hearing an explosion from the square outside, Piers quickened his pace.

"So what exactly is the plan at this meeting?" Heath asked, his voice steady as he bounded up the stairs behind Piers. *He isn't shaken at all? He just watched me kill an innocent man and is as even-keeled as one can be.*

"Oh, we don't have too much to discuss with them. More of a point of closure, I'd say." They climbed three more stories in the building and began heading down a hall lined with oil paintings of former Chief Justices. Piers slowed his pace and looked at the men's faces he passed. *Could any of you imagine what's happening to your precious system? If only your successors had had the strength to sustain it.*

At the end of the hall, they stopped in the center of a round room. Two large wooden doors were closed in the center of the room, and with the building so quiet, they could hear the murmuring of conversation from within the room beyond. A lone guard who had been sitting next to the door stood up, his machine gun gripped and at the ready.

"You can't be here. This is a private meeting of the Chief Justice Council," he began to say.

Piers cut him off. "I'm Piers Marks. Check your records. Chief Justice Connally gave me access to the meeting."

The guard looked troubled and concerned and turned to head back to the desk. As he did, Piers whipped out his gun with swift ease, and fired two bullets. The guard never had a chance. He fell to the floor with a dull thud. Piers set his bag on the table in the center of the room, next to a vase with fresh flowers. He pulled out another grenade and placed it in his jacket's pocket.

Approaching the set of double doors, he said to Heath, "You wait out here, Heath. This won't take long. When I come back, get ready to get down." His lips curled into a sinister smile at those last words, as he turned and opened the set of doors in a grand, sweeping gesture.

"Chief Justices, good evening! How good it is to see all of you gathered in one place," Piers said, as he strode into the council room, closing the double doors behind him.

The nine Chief Justices sat around a circular dough-nut-like table, with the middle missing. Piers took in the room. They all looked tired, with grave expressions on their faces. Piers's eyes moved to his father's chair. In it sat Justice Wellington.

He began walking slowly and deliberately around the table. Clearly the conversation had paused, likely a result of the gunshot they heard moments earlier. He felt satisfied with the discord he had caused by breaking into the meeting. The Justices eyed Piers with suspicion, several with fear and panic. Piers focused on Connally, seated at the farthest side from the entrance.

Connally stood up abruptly and began to shout. "You

have no business being here! This is a meeting of the Chief Justice Council, you insolent, depraved—"

"Silence!" Piers screamed. Connally's mouth shut in astonishment. He had never taken this much Silver before, and it was burning through his veins. He could feel beads of sweat collecting at the top of his forehead. "I have not given you permission to speak, Chief Justice," Piers continued, bringing his voice back to a calm tenor. Connally slowly sat back down in his chair, looking terrified. "I am commandeering this meeting. In fact, I am commandeering this council, and this city. You, my dear Chief Justices, have failed the people of New Boston."

Piers continued his steady stroll around the table, making eye contact with each of the justices. His eyes came to Justice Wellington, her signature thick-rimmed glasses framing her eyes. Despite her attempts to maintain a sly smile, Piers could see the fear permeating her face.

"Justice Wellington, I see you have been elevated to this council." Piers spoke bitingly, almost sarcastically.

"Chief Justice Connally asked me to join," Wellington replied casually.

Piers sneered back. "I'm afraid your tenure will be short." Looking back to the other Justices, Piers continued. "You all failed my father. You failed the citizens of this once great city. You have failed to maintain justice and keep peace. And you have failed me." The fear emanating from the Justices was palpable, and Piers savored it. *That's right, Justices. You're not in control now.*

"We understand your frustration, Mr. Marks," Justice Wellington continued, her tone even. "Nothing is irreparable. This commotion in the streets will be quelled, and law and order will be restored. We know what we're doing."

Piers stopped his pacing and stared at Wellington. "You've done nothing." His tone was grave. "You can barely handle simple tribunal cases, let alone a revolution. None of you understand justice or how to administer it. You're all weak—pathetic, frail geriatrics." Piers turned his attention to Connally, who was visibly trembling at this point.

"You have no idea what constitutes justice!" Connally yelled, his veins popping as he strove to control his anger. "You think executing that boy would've been justice? You arrogant, contemptuous boy! You'd sooner ruin this entire city to suit your own stupid, immature whims!"

Piers smiled at the Justice's outburst, "So you claim to have saved the city from harm, Chief Justice? Have you looked outside your ivory tower's windows recently? New Boston is *burning to the ground*. Nearly every one of the city's vertical farms has been lit on fire, devastating the city's food supply. Or what's left of it; I'm sure you're all aware the crops have begun to fail."

"How do you know that?" Another Chief Justice, Dent, asked. His was clearly shocked and surprised. "We have a plan for that. One that will hopefully work—"

Piers cut him off, continuing. "Further, police have begun abandoning their posts out of concern for their own safety. People from the Furrows are looting upper-level apartment buildings, casting residents out of their homes. And all this anarchy, it all started with *your* ruling." Piers looked directly at Connally, as he cast the blame.

"This unrest was bubbling up for weeks! It is not solely a cause of one ruling. We have experienced this before and have overcome it. You have no understanding of the balance in this city. You—"

"You're blind to what you've done!" Piers yelled, cutting

Connally off again. "You're so comfortable that you've become naïve to what's happening in your own city. So, I've taken it into my own hands to deliver the justice and swift actions that this city needs. Starting with fixing the punishment for young Beck McGullan."

"You don't mean to say—" Chief Justice Dent began to say.

"That's correct, Chief Justice. I've just come from the Tribunal Hall Cells, where I executed Beck McGullan."

The Chief Justices sat in a shocked silence around the table. Piers smiled even wider, basking in their disapproval. He was still fueled by the Silver in his bloodstream and felt nearly on fire with energy.

Connally broke the silence. "You must be stopped. You are not an official of this city's government. I don't care who your father was or who you think you are. You have no right to take justice into your own hands, boy. This city has rules. A system of law and order. And you are acting in direct violation to that system." Connally sat, his body still, as he delivered his diatribe.

"I had no choice. All of you put this city on a path to destruction. History will remember that you hid away, here in this room, while the bravest among us stepped in to save New Boston." Piers had rounded the room again and was now back in front of the double doors—the sole entrance and exit to the council chambers. "Goodbye, Chief Justices. Thank you for all that you do for New Boston. Or tried to do, I suppose I should say."

The Chief Justices all sat with confused faces, processing Piers's words. They watched as he opened the doors and began walking out of the chamber. He then turned slightly, pulled the grenade from his pocket, removed its pin, and tossed it far into the room. Piers slammed the doors shut. He heard the Chief Justices scrambling in peril, chairs toppling over as they likely hid under the table.

They never stood a chance. He yelled "Get down!" at Heath, and the two dove away from the chamber's entrance. The eruption blew the doors straight off the wall, and the entire chamber evaporated into smoke.

CHAPTER 32

———

Gwen's shirt was soaked from sweat. Her legs were tired from all the running, and she was relishing the momentary break. She and Keats were still in the small room, preparing to leave. Her mind was racing, exploring every negative scenario they could encounter when they finally made it to the Grand Tribunal Hall. At one point, she considered the possibility that Piers may have already killed Jaym and Beck. Her face went stark white, and she trembled with fear.

"Gwen. Gwen!"

Keats voice rocked her back to life.

"You look petrified. And exhausted. Here, let me carry your bag." Keats took the bag from her and slung it over his shoulder. He turned back to the shelf, continuing to pack ammunition and other necessities.

"What's on your mind?" he asked. He had started changing out of his police uniform into street clothes.

"What isn't on my mind," she answered, her voice trailing off. "I just hope we're not walking into an ambush—or worse."

He turned to face her, looking casual and unstressed. Almost laughing, he asked, "What's worse than an ambush?"

"That this is all in vain. That Jaym and Beck are already dead. And that my brother will shoot us both on site."

Keats put both his hands on her shoulders, and she felt his strength as he gave her a squeeze. "Stop it. Focus on the task at hand. Get in, save Jaym and Beck, and get out. Push aside any other thought or irrational fear. Now, here, take this." He handed her a handgun. "Always keep it pointed up, with your hand here and your other finger on the safety. And please don't point it at me!"

Gwen held the cold, metal gun in her hands. *Deep breaths, Gwen. You're going to get through this.* She cocked the gun and pointed it up, newfound confidence rushing through her. *Piers isn't going to stop me.* Gwen followed Keats as they headed out of the room. She gripped the gun tightly as they moved past the command center. No one paid them any attention. The noises outside were clamoring louder as they walked on. Soon, they came to a deserted lobby—the words "West Entrance" emblazoned above the empty desk.

"Ready?" Keats asked. Before Gwen could answer, he pushed open the door and exited the headquarters. She took another moment to compose herself, focused her energy, and followed Keats. Outside, the scene was overwhelming. It took Gwen's eyes a few moments to adjust; everything was much darker than inside the headquarters. The noises were deafening, as if bombs were going off just a stone's throw away. The clashes had come close to the building, and a line of policeman were fending off rioters. Gwen froze, feeling paralyzed. *How are we going to get through that police line?*

Keats had already started moving. He went up to a policeman clad in heavy protective gear. Gwen moved closer, hearing their increasingly heated conversation.

"...I have authorization!" Keats had started yelling at the man.

"I don't care! My orders are from the very top! No one breaks through this line!" the black-clad man yelled back.

"And who the hell is this?" Gwen couldn't see his eyes through the visor but could hear the rage in his voice.

"She's with me! I have authorization!"

Before the guard could say something else, Keats spun his gun around and whacked the man with the butt of the weapon. He staggered back but didn't crumple to the ground. Gwen flashed a look to Keats. *We'd better move quick. Now's our only shot.*

"Let's go," Keats said, and pulled Gwen behind him into the mess ahead. By the time the policeman regained his footing, the two had disappeared into the mess of people.

Gwen realized why Keats hadn't donned the usual police suit. He blended in much better than with the formal gear. Almost no one gave them any notice, and the few that did got a solid punch from Keats as the two barreled through the crowd.

The people thinned out as they made it farther from the headquarters and headed toward Justice Square. They moved through shattered glass, chunks of building, and debris, as they navigated the typically pristine streets. Nothing shocked Gwen though at this point; she had become numb to this new reality. Instead, she focused on keeping pace with Keats, who moved down the street with a nimble agility. He flicked his gun left and right as they progressed, ensuring no threats would catch them off guard.

Soon the Grand Tribunal Hall came into view. The building had always stood out, but it was even more striking against a backdrop of skyscrapers with blown out floors and gaping holes. The Hall stood completely intact, creating an austere juxtaposition. Even eerier, the square had emptied out, save for the handful of police and guards standing at the base of the Hall's steps.

"This way—I know a side entrance. It'll be easier," Keats whispered, and pulled Gwen back from the square. They weaved through the nearby alleys, the hall getting closer and closer each time they got a glimpse of the square. Keats made a sharp left and stopped in front of several closed double doors. The doors were unassuming; there were no signs or markers of what building they led to. But the furthest door was shattered.

"Someone's been here—stay alert." Keats had his gun up and pointed as he moved toward the shattered door. In one smooth movement, he spun into the building. Gwen heard a woman scream, and a few shots fired. She darted in behind, panic shooting through her bones. *Keats!*

"Don't shoot!"

Gwen immediately recognized the voice. "Jemma!" Her own voice cracked as she called out. She rounded the corner, and saw Jemma with her hands up, Keats trained on her. Next to Jemma was a black-clad guard, crumpled on the ground. A pool of blood was slowly seeping from the man.

"You know her?" He didn't turn to look at Gwen; his gun and focus remained on Jemma.

"Yes!" Gwen ran over to Jemma, and Keats lowered the gun as she crossed into the line. "Are you okay? Where's Jaym?"

"He and Heath entered the hall over an hour ago. They're supposed to be coming back this way once they save Beck." She glanced down at the dead guard. "He was one of Heath's guys." Her voice trailed off. She was clearly still processing the whole ordeal.

Keats reloaded his gun. "We should keep moving. Police could've heard the gunshots and could come to investigate this entrance soon."

"Come with us Jemma. It's not safe here." Gwen looked at the girl, who still looked pale.

Jemma nodded in agreement.

"I say we start at the jail cells. That's where Beck is surely being kept, and likely the first place Jaym went. We might find some clues there as to what has happened," Keats said.

"I agree. Let's get going." Gwen let out a breath. *We're in.*

* * *

Jaym paced around the cell. He had moved Beck's body to the corner and used his shirt to mop up the pool of blood. He had also cleaned up Beck's wound, straightened his hair, and closed his eyelids. Jaym paused mid circle, as he came around to face Beck again.

"This is all my fault." Tears welled up in his eyes as he looked down at his friend. Beck's cold, lifeless body had begun to turn pale.

Once Piers left, Jaym had run through the events that led to his current predicament over and over again, trying to determine where he went wrong. *There had to be something I missed. Did Heath slip up at any point? Were there any signs that he was lying? How long had he been planning this?* He kept pacing, filled with a mix of anxiety and fury. *Focus on the future, Jaym. Not the past. You need to get out of this cell.*

He turned away from Beck, back to face the cell's door. Going over to it, he began inspecting the computerized lock as best he could from inside. *What could the code be? Think. How many beeps did the lock make when Heath locked it?* He looked about the rest of the cell area. Next to the small table sat the black bag Heath and the guard had brought with them. *The handsaw!* Before he could keep thinking, he heard footsteps down the hall. Jaym popped to his feet and began backing up toward the wall. *Not like there's anywhere to hide. Think, Jaym. Prop up Beck's body as a shield? Hide behind it in the corner?*

He didn't have a chance to act on any crazy idea before he saw the barrel of a machine gun come into view. And then an all-too-familiar face. Before he could react, an even more familiar voice cried out.

"Jaym!" Gwen yelled, and threw herself to the cell's bars. All his feelings of dread went away as he ran to her, and they managed an awkward embrace through the cell.

"Gwen! How—"

"You were supposed to wait for me!" Gwen gave Jaym a slight push through the bars. As Jaym fell back a step, he revealed Beck's body in the corner. Jaym watched her eyes go wide. "Oh my God. What happened?"

Jaym turned back, nearly forgetting what had distracted Gwen. He was so relieved to see her that all else had faded away for a fraction of a second. Then it all came rushing back.

Jaym scowled at Keats. "What's he doing here?"

"Here to save your ass," Keats said, stepping forward.

"This is all your friend's doing." Jaym matched Keats's accusatory tone. Turning back to Gwen, he recounted the events. "Heath has been on Piers's side this whole time. He betrayed us. He betrayed Beck. Piers wanted him to bring me here, so that I could watch when Piers murdered Beck." Jaym was speaking so fast spit was flying from his lips.

Gwen listened intently, her face stark. "Jaym, I'm so sorry." She reached back through the cell to grab his hand. She held it tenderly. "We'll stop them. Keats, how do we get him out?"

Keats had already walked over to the cell door and had begun inspecting the lock. "I don't know the code. There's no way get this open without it." He tried swiping with the guard's keycard, but to no avail.

"The bag! Over there!" Jaym's voice was excited as he remembered. "There's a handsaw in the bag."

Keats went over and retrieved the device. Turning it on, the saw whirred as it began spinning. "This will work. Get back." As Keats began cutting through the cell door's bars, Gwen told Jaym what she knew about the emergency Chief Justice Council meeting.

"I bet that's where Piers went after he left here," Jaym muttered, his mind racing as to what their next move should be. "We could try and cut him off there, wherever the council meets. We'll surprise him and Heath. They won't be expecting it at all."

"No, Jaym. We have to get out of here. We need to regroup and strategize for what to do tomorrow when this is all over. The city is still reeling. It's nearly collapsing on itself. But first, let's get out of this damned building."

"We have to act now, Gwen. Piers is going to leave the city. I don't know how or to where, but he said so himself."

Both their heads jerked away from each other as they heard the clanging of metal bars falling to the floor. Jaym couldn't help but smile despite it all. He couldn't tell which he was happiest about, escaping the jail cell or the fact that Gwen was here, with him, and had come to save him.

"Well, Jaym. You're free. Now let's go get the son of a bitch who did all this," Keats said, reaching his hand out to shake Jaym's as he exited the cell.

Jaym stared at the hand. "How do I know you're not going to betray me too?"

"You don't. But she trusts me." Keats nodded toward Gwen. "I guess that'll have to do."

Jaym's face was still hardened. He stepped out of the cell and pushed beyond Keats's hand. "If you try to do anything, I'll kill you. Now let's get out of here."

Keats didn't respond. He began to head toward the hallway out. Jaym paused, before they followed, and looked back at Beck. "I can't leave him here, Gwen."

Gwen moved next to him. Softly, she said, "We'll come back for him. If we can."

Jaym finally peeled his eyes away from Beck's body. "He wouldn't have wanted us to. He would've rather had us focus on what really matters." He looked Gwen in the eyes. "Killing your brother."

CHAPTER 33

Piers's ears were ringing from the explosion. He stood and brushed off the soot from his jacket. He and Heath both turned toward where the double doors had stood. With the smoke clearing, the wreckage inside the chamber came into view.

"Are they all dead?" Heath asked slowly, as Piers began walking over to the room. He stepped over the rubble and bodies of the Chief Justices, inspecting for signs of life. He felt a chill as the wind blew through the room; the windows had all been blown out.

"It would appear so," Piers said, as he exited the chamber. He was smug and proud. "It had to be done."

Heath matched Piers's smug look. "They never saw it coming."

"Let's go. We have a few final loose ends to tie up," Piers began walking away from the debris-filled chamber.

"Where are we going?"

"I need to make a phone call."

Piers led Heath down the opulent hall. A thin veil of smoke had unfurled along it from the explosion. It seemed misplaced: smoky air in such a beautiful, mahogany hall.

Oil portraits of past Chief Justices looked on unknowingly at the man who had just murdered nine of their successors. Piers stopped in front of a single, tall door. A large plaque hung square above the handle, reading "Chief Justice Connally." As he looked at the plaque, Heath said, "You think it's unlocked?"

Piers swung the door open easily. "You think that was his biggest concern when he came tonight, amidst a revolution in the streets?" He stepped across the threshold, into the dark office. They found themselves in Connally's reception area, next to a secretary's desk. Piers entered another door which was slightly ajar. Inside was Connally's private office, as neat and orderly as he had left it. A computer screen glowed with the police central command's heat map. Connally's government telephone sat next to the screen. Piers's eyes drifted to the wall behind, where a portrait of Connally hung. He looked at it with disgust.

Piers sat down at the screen and began clicking away. After a few minutes of toiling, he smiled and let out a soft "Yes!" Connally hadn't locked any of the files on the computer with any security provisions. *Always the fool, Connally.* He picked up the landline phone and dialed a number, glancing back at the screen to ensure it was correct.

After a few seconds of ringing, a military-sounding voice answered the phone. "New Washington emergency line. Who is calling?"

Piers gripped the phone tightly. "This is Piers Marks, son of the late Chief Justice Marks, of New Boston. I request to speak with Chief Justice Morton immediately. It's an emergency."

The voice on the other end was silent for a moment. Piers's heart was thumping; he had no way around this part of the plan. New Washington was the closest functioning city to New Boston. The cities rarely engaged in formal diplomacy other than at the top levels of government. But Piers's father had always said that New Washington owed its survival to New Boston: it had been New Boston scientists who had come up with the original KIP formula and provided it to the other cities. New Washington had pledged to the New Boston government that it would always help in time of crisis. Piers planned to capitalize on that pledge.

Just a few more seconds. Come on...

"Roger that Mr. Marks. Patching you through now to the Chief Justice."

A few irregular beeps followed, and then a new man's voice spoke up. "This is Chief Justice Morton."

"Good evening Mr. Chief Justice. I apologize for calling you so late, but unfortunately, I have no choice. This is Piers Marks, son of the late Chief Justice Marks of New Boston. Our city is in meltdown. The people have revolted against the government, and just moments ago they bombed the Chief Justice Council. All nine are dead. There are a few of us still alive, and we are requesting asylum in New Washington until we can determine what next steps should be taken."

Piers hoped the sound of his heartbeat couldn't be heard through the phone. It felt like it was about to explode out of his chest. He waited for what seemed like a century for the Chief Justice on the other end to finally answer him.

"That is terrible news. I am sorry to hear that. I did hear the news about your father's murder; we have corresponded many times over the years."

The Chief Justice paused, and a tense silence ensued. Piers drummed his fingers on the desk. *What is he waiting for?*

A throat cleared on the other end. "What do you mean, asylum?"

"We cannot stay here. The people have revolted against the ruling class. We need to escape New Boston to regroup and plan our return to reclaim the city—to save the people from themselves."

More silence followed. "How many of you are requesting this asylum?"

"Just a handful, sir." Again, silence. Piers spoke up this time. "We're in dire straits, Chief Justice." Piers's heartbeat ticked up a notch. He hated pleading to this foreign man, hated saying "sir." But he had no choice. *He can't reject this. I can't let him reject us.*

"We have never engaged in such actions between our cities. It would be … complex."

Piers could feel the anger rising up in him. "What is so complex about it?"

"Well, for one, it will be difficult for you to monitor the events on the ground in New Boston from our city."

"We will make it right. Please, sir. This is a temporary precaution to ensure our safety. I promise our stay in your city will be temporary. A few weeks at the most." Piers drummed even quicker on the desk. "My father always said New Washington owed its own endurance to our people. This is the least you could do to repay us."

Finally, the Chief Justice acquiesced. "Okay. The City of New Washington will provide you and any other political refugees asylum. Do you have transport here?"

Piers covered the speaker end of the phone with his hand and let out an audible breath. Relief washed over him, and he couldn't help but smile.

"Thank you, Chief Justice. Your mercy will not be

forgotten. Yes, we have salvaged a helicopter and a pilot. We will leave at once. Please alert your city's air defenses that we will be coming in a few hours."

"We will await your arrival." And with that, the other end of the phone went dead. Piers placed the phone back down slowly, taking a moment to relish his success. Heath, who had been standing at the office's entrance listening, spoke up.

"What did he say?"

Piers stood up from the desk. He was still smiling confidently. "We've been granted asylum."

Heath matched his confident glow. "Let's get out of this hell hole."

"Yes, let's. One last call." Piers quickly dialed another number.

"Alyx … Yes, Plan B is in motion. Get the helicopter and meet us on the roof in twenty." Piers slammed the phone back down, grabbed his gun from the table, and left the office with Heath close behind. They moved through the Hall at a more urgent pace than before, back down the distinguished hall of the Chief Justices' offices, and up another staircase. They rounded a corner and paused to look over the balcony. They were in the Hall's main atrium. Piers was about to turn away when he heard footsteps. He put his fist up to motion to Heath, who joined him quietly leaning over the balcony. They were only one story up from the ground floor. Four people slowly crept into the middle of the atrium. As they came into his view, Piers couldn't help but smile. In fact, he nearly laughed.

Piers turned and whispered to Heath. "If they shoot, you shoot." Before Heath had a chance to question what Piers meant, he leaned over the balcony and shouted down below.

"Well, well, well, look who we have here!"

Keats spun around first, pointing his gun right up at Piers. Jaym and Gwen followed suit, just a moment behind Keats's instinctual response. A second girl stood by, having barely reacted. She looked exhausted and spent. Heath leaned over the balcony, pointing his gun down at the group as Piers held his hands up and continued speaking.

"Whoa, whoa. Don't even think about it, Keats." He nudged his head toward Heath. "If you shoot, Heath will shoot. And he'll shoot Gwen first." Piers smiled down at his sister, who glared back in return.

"You've gone off the deep end, Piers," Gwen said. "What is your endgame? You've single-handedly pushed the entire city of New Boston off a cliff. If there was any chance the people of this city were going to accept you as their leader before, that's long gone now."

"People have a funny way of behaving when they're pushed to the brink, sister. They will indeed accept me in time. They'll come to realize it's due to people like your friend Jaym, and the late, great Beck, that the city is in the sad state it's in."

At hearing Beck's name, Piers saw Jaym step forward, clearly tensed. His face was contorted in rage, grief, and pain. He tightly gripped his gun, pointing it upwards.

"You're going to pay for this, Piers. For all of it," Jaym yelled up at the balcony.

Piers let out a laugh. "Yeah? Who's going to stop me? The Chief Justices? They're dead. Outside, the crazy hordes have burned down every vertical farm in the city. I'm going to let the city continue to burn and watch from afar, in New Washington. And right when New Boston is at the point of no return, when anarchy has totally consumed it, when the last of the crops are gone, I'll swoop in to save it."

Keats looked up in disbelief. "You're going to New Washington?"

Piers sneered back down at his old friend. "I am. I've been granted asylum. And when I return, I'm going to kill all three of you. If you're not dead by then."

Piers watched as Keats face turned even more red. Suddenly, Keats fired his gun. Heath was just as quick and fired a shot, though the bullet bounced off the empty floor. Piers fell backward, Keats's bullet having grazed his arm. "You bastard!" he shouted, gripping the wound. Looking down, he could already see his shirt staining red. "I hope you're happy with your decision to side with them, Keats. You'll all be dead in no time." Piers yelled down to the group from the safety of a few feet back.

"I'm going to find you, brother!" he heard Gwen scream from below.

"Your arm," Heath started to say.

"It's fine." The pain had already subsided, a result of the adrenaline still in his system. "Let's get going." Piers started back down the hallway, leading Heath to another staircase. The pair began ascending, making their way to the roof of the building. He felt alive, almost euphoric, relishing the moment that just occurred. *I'm sure they both regret their decisions. Siding with that lowlife, and now being relegated to dying in this burning city.* He slammed open the final door and came out onto the roof. He moved over to the edge and peered down to see the square below. He could see Keats leading the group across the square, pointing his gun left and right as they moved away from the Hall.

Piers took a moment to take a deep breath. *All going exactly according to plan.* His moment of meditation was interrupted as the noise of a helicopter came roaring into the area. The flying vehicle swirled into view from between the nearby skyscrapers and began hovering near the dome of the Grand Tribunal Hall. The helicopter had two angular wings with thrusters shooting downwards. Piers grabbed the gun from the strap on his shoulder, getting ready. The door slid open to reveal Alyx, ready to greet Piers.

"Right on time!" Heath yelled over the machine's noise to Piers.

"Sorry, Heath. I can't have any loose ends in New Washington," Piers shouted back. Heath tilted his head, and Piers watched as the man came to the realization of what was about to happen. Before he could react, Piers fired a round of bullets. Heath staggered backward, grabbing his chest. His face contorted in a look of shock.

Piers ran toward the open helicopter door. He leapt off the roof, reaching up at Alyx's outstretched arms, who pulled him into the cabin.

"Let's go!" Piers yelled, and the helicopter pulled away from the roof. Alyx slid the door shut and handed Piers a headset.

"All good?" Alyx asked over the microphone.

Piers smiled back. "Couldn't be better." He settled down in the seat by the nearest window and looked out at the city. Smoke was rising from nearly every skyscraper, as the helicopter rose higher and higher. The pilot had steadied the helicopter, and moments later they crossed the perimeter of the city. Below them was a wasteland, with abandoned vehicles, buildings, and other debris dotting its surface.

Piers leaned back in his chair and closed his eyes. *Time to regroup. The people will welcome me when I return. New Boston hasn't seen the last of Piers Marks.*

CHAPTER 34

Jaym, Gwen, Jemma, and Keats burst through the doors of the Grand Tribunal Hall. The scene had become all-too-familiar by now. The square was littered with glowing fires and debris but was mostly devoid of people. The crowds had dispersed, moving into other areas of the city. Even the police who had been guarding the entrance were gone, likely having fled after hearing the explosion from within the Chief Justice Council room.

Jaym turned and looked at Gwen. She looked enraged, still fuming from the encounter with her brother.

"Hey, don't think about him." Jaym reached his arm out, touching her shoulder.

"I never want to think about him again," she responded. "Except about how we can find him and make him pay."

Keats chimed in. He scanned the square, his eyebrows tightening together. "The city's infrastructure is falling rapidly, veering past the point of no return. As soon as word gets out that the Chief Justices are all dead, the police will lose their sense of security."

"It's even worse. Piers told me that the crops have begun to fail. It's apparently been going on for some time now. I believe him, it explains why rations have been lowered. My father even alluded to it a few times. The food supply will destabilize rapidly. There are only so many reserves, and I'm sure the crowds will overrun them next."

Jaym's eyes grew. *It all makes sense now.* "We can't let the city devolve into pure anarchy," he said.

Gwen nodded. "Anarchy is what Piers said New Boston deserved without the Tribunal system in place. If the citizens didn't treat the system with reverence and respect."

"So, he lets the city destroy itself and then he'll come back with reinforcements from New Washington to take over." Keats perked his head up. "People will respect his authority much more after they realize that the city can't survive in this kind of state."

Just then, a helicopter went whizzing from the rooftop of the Grand Tribunal Hall. All four of them looked up, in awe of the flying machine. They weren't necessary after the wars ended and were ultimately retired from use. Seeing the small cab fly effortlessly across the crumbling city gave them all a sinking feeling in their stomachs.

"So that's how he's escaping," Jemma whispered, still looking up as the helicopter veered away. She had been quiet throughout the series of events.

Jaym pulled his eyes away. "We have to get people to stop fighting. Stop the city from burning and collapsing on itself and start ensuring our survival. We show the people that we don't need Piers or the Chief Justices to run this city."

"I agree," Keats said. "But how? We can't use the police; they aren't going to listen to us. I'm sure most of them are holed up in their apartments, just looking to protect themselves. People started looting upper-level houses."

"We don't need the police," Gwen added. "We appeal to

everyone. We tell them what Piers has done. What he's planning to do. We essentially give this city an ultimatum."

"How do we get the word out?" Jemma asked.

Jaym smiled at her, rejoicing that the paleness was leaving her face. He turned his smile to Gwen, excited to share his idea. "We use the news screens."

* * *

The group was moving quickly again, racing through the streets of the upper levels of the city. Keats led them across skywalks and up the stairs, avoiding elevators due to the potential safety issues. Jaym felt relatively safe following Keats. His confidence in Keats was growing, but he still wasn't wholly convinced. *I need to talk to Gwen about him. When Piers comes back, there's no guarantee Keats won't abandon us.*

The few armed people they came into contact with quickly moved away. Between the group's authoritative pace and the guns they brandished, they were a formidable force. But Jaym had cautioned everyone not to blindly shoot.

"We have to start acting how we want others to act," he said.

Soon, Keats slowed his run as they came to a towering skyscraper, still intact. Massive posters of Velma hung on it, as well as one of the largest news screens Jaym had ever seen.

"This must be one of the tallest buildings in the city," Jemma said, looking up in awe. At its top, the skyscraper boasted a tall, thin antenna.

"It is *the* tallest," Keats informed. "It's home to the broadcast studios. It's how Velma's news announcements are sent to the news screens across the city."

"And how we're going to get the message out," Jaym continued. He ran forward to the doors, but they were locked. "Step back," Keats said, raising his gun. He fired several shots at the dark, glass windows. They shattered, and the group all winced. Keats turned around and gestured to the now revealed lavish lobby inside. Jaym shot Keats a slight look of annoyance. Keats smiled back. "I know, I know. No more unnecessary shooting. But hey, we're inside."

Jaym let out a playful snort. He entered the building, careful not to cut himself on the jagged glass. Jaym and Keats raised their guns as they cleared the room, while Gwen and Jemma ran behind the desk.

"Looks deserted," Keats said.

"Floor fifty-two!" Gwen perked up from behind the desk. "That's the main production studio. Let's start there."

"The building looks intact enough. We should be okay using the elevators." Keats motioned toward an elevator bank beyond.

"Good. Let's go," Jaym said, leading the group beyond the lobby. They hopped over the secure turnstiles. Luckily nothing was locked beyond, and soon they were whizzing up through the building.

The doors opened to floor fifty-two, and the group exited into another plush lobby. Keats raised his gun again, clearing the room, but Jaym didn't bother. He looked about the room and spotted a sign that said "Studio One" above a hallway. Without waiting for the group, he headed toward it. At the end of the short hallway, he burst through two double doors.

On the other side was an expansive television studio. Hundreds of lights hung from the ceiling, large camera equipment littered the floor. In front was a stage and desk, all still illuminated as if filming had just ceased. Dozens of dark screens covered the far wall. The group slowly walked about the room, admiring the sophisticated machinery.

Then, something crashed in the corner. Jaym watched as Keats spun around with his impressive agility, gun raised. Jaym followed suit.

"Who's there!" Keats shouted. "We're armed. Come out with your hands up."

"Please, don't shoot!" a voice called back.

Jaym saw Gwen flash him a look. "Did that sound like…"

"Velma!" Jemma yelled. She ran over to the woman, who was crawling out from the corner. Velma wasn't covered in any of the soot and grime that was caked on the rest of the group, but she was more disheveled than her usual do up. Her signature bun had come undone and strands of hair fell on her cheeks.

"Who else is here?" Keats's tone was still forceful and authoritative.

"Just a few cameramen and me. We're not armed, I promise," Velma answered. "We've been hiding here since we heard the explosions. What's happening outside?" She sounded scared, but genuine.

Jaym lowered his weapon. "The city is in chaos, Velma. We need to tell the people to stop fighting. Do you know how to operate all this stuff? Can you help us broadcast a message out on the news screens?"

Velma slowly nodded her head. "Yes, I can help. So can they." She motioned to the corner from where she emerged. A few other men had started crawling out.

Jaym smiled triumphantly. "Good. We don't have much time. Let's go."

They helped the camera men crawl out. With the guns dropped, the tension in the room quickly dissipated. The men, led by Velma, quickly got to work. They adjusted cameras, altered the lights. The screens popped alive on the far wall, showing various camera angles of the stage. Velma walked over to Jaym, her hands full of a few small makeup brushes.

"Make up?" she asked, shrugging.

Jaym couldn't help but let out a laugh. "No, thank you. The people should see that I was out in the streets. Fighting alongside them." He made his way to the stage. When he turned around, he saw Gwen, Keats, and Jemma all standing behind the camera line.

"Get over here, guys. You're the face of this revolution too." Jaym beckoned to the group.

Gwen smiled, as she walked to the stage. "I'm not talking, but I'll stand behind you. We're all standing behind you." Keats and Jemma nodded in agreement, and the trio took up spots behind Jaym.

"One minute," a camera man called out.

Jaym turned back to Gwen. "Don't think I forgot about my promise. We're going to stop Piers. We're going to find him and make him pay."

Gwen's smile grew even larger. "Okay. Focus on your big TV debut."

Jaym grinned back and turned to face the cameras. Velma began counting down from five.

Across the entire city, news screens flashed alive. Many were cracked or shattered, but the fuzzy pixels gave no mind. Velma had activated the emergency broadcast procedures, so even on large screens hanging from skyscrapers, Jaym's face was projected.

"People of New Boston." He spoke as sincerely as he could. "Please, listen. My name is Jaym Torrey. Born and raised in the Furrows. Some of you may have seen me from my

Tribunal a week ago. But none of that matters now. Our city is at a crossroads. And a dire one at that. Our entire way of life, our society, our future—it's all on the brink of destruction. We have to lay down our weapons, stop the destruction, and focus on rebuilding. Join us in saving this place we call home."

Jaym paused and turned his head back toward Gwen. She nodded, giving him the encouragement he needed to continue.

"There are many parties responsible for what has happened here today. But the main culprit is Piers Marks, the son of the late Chief Justice. Piers murdered his father. Today, he murdered the entire Chief Justice Council. New Boston is currently without any leaders. But we are not without a future. We can save this city. All of us. We will hold those accountable who must be brought to justice for their crimes. Justice hasn't been about all of us. But it *should* be. It should work *for* us—be our salvation and our foundation. But first, we need to ensure New Boston will survive to see another day."

Jaym looked beyond the cameras. Velma and her staff all stood, captivated. Velma was even smiling. Jaym looked back to the main camera in front of him and focused directly on the lens.

"A new era is dawning. It begins today. One in which everyone will be treated fairly. Everyone will abide by the same ration laws. No longer will anyone be allowed to subvert the system for their own personal gain. We can ensure that New Boston survives beyond us—becomes a place of prosperity for future generations. Join me in ensuring our future. Together, we will ensure that New Boston will thrive. It can, and it must."

The camera man called out, "We're off!"

Jaym let out a breath, as Gwen ran over to hug him.

"That was incredible."

He smiled back. He could hear a soft chanting. "What's that noise?" Everyone followed as he walked over to the edge of the studio and peered out the dark glass windows. Fifty-two floors below, a crowd had gathered. They were cheering, all looking up at the massive news screen. Looking up at Jaym.

"This might actually work," Keats said.

"It has to work," Gwen contended, her voice strong.

Jaym turned away from the window. "We'll make it work. It's not going to be easy, but I have hope." Jaym looked Gwen straight in the eye. "But first, you and I have something to do. We're going to stop Piers once and for all. We're going to New Washington."

ACKNOWLEDGMENTS

Writing this book has been a journey, and it wouldn't have been possible without the incredible support of so many people in my life.

First, thank you to my always supportive family. Most specifically my parents. Mom and Dad, I wouldn't be who I am without either of you and all that you have done for me. I love you both to the moon and back. Dougie and Daniel, thanks for putting up with me all these years, and taking all my unsolicited advice. You both make me an insanely proud older brother. Grandmother and Grandma, you both instilled in me a love for reading from such an early age, and I owe so much of my creative energy to you both. And Grandfather, I get my logic and brainpower from you. Aunt Phyllis, Uncle Bruce, Uncle Mark, Uncle Sheldon, Aunt Shelia, JD, Judy Sue, Cousin Steven, Susan and Jake (and the whole Bernstein family), and Mara: thank you all for the constant support and for being present in my life. Mark and Brittany, thanks for being the older siblings I never had. Mom, Grandmother, and Aunt Phyllis—thanks for all reading the book in advance too (and for reading everything else I've written over the years).

The number of friends that supported me on this—it makes me tear up just thinking about the outpouring of support I've gotten from all of you. Old and new, you all mean so much to me. Starting from high school and working forward:

To my Carlisle crew who has known me literally since elementary school, I'm so happy we've remained good friends. John, Trevor, Tyler, and Cameron, when we see each other, it's like no time has passed. John and Trevor, special shout out for taking all the time to read the book in advance and give me feedback. Ali and Emily, so glad we've managed to still see each other each year and down many a bottle of wine. To Kaitlin and the rest of the Norris family, I know I can always count on you for support. Thank you all so much. And Chris, glad we've stayed friends since our days as Cub Scouts.

To all my teachers, thank you for helping me become who I am today. Dr. Jennings, your support means so much. I wish I could see from your perspective how much I've grown from the rambunctious sixth grader you first met fifteen years ago.

To my Penn friends: when our five year reunion eventually happens, first round of Copa margs on me, before we head back to Smokey Joes. Megan, thanks for being my long-time best friend and my go-to therapist. Zack and Becky, Alex and Chelsea, Danny and Caroline—you guys mean the world to me. Andy and Matias, special shout out for reading the book in advance. It was awesome to get texts of support and excitement from both of you when I sent you new chapters. Of course, the ski team fam: Tara, Dot, Andy (again), and everyone else. I love that our group chats are still thriving. Ethan and AV, I miss living with you guys. And thank you to so many friends who I miss seeing on Locust Walk (or in Smokes, more realistically), your support means so much:

James and Sam, Mike and Paul (Lucky Cat on me when I'm back in NYC), Juhanna, Chris, Shira, Marc, Emily.

To my New York and AlphaSights community: you all made my first four years as a "real adult" a blast. I miss seeing you on a daily basis and am so grateful for all the support. Neil, miss living with you and all our fun times. Scott, James, Ryan, Opp, Gromer, Jesse, Christian: I didn't expect to get a group of best friends from my first job after college, but I'm so grateful that I did. My former managers, thanks for grooming me into the young professional I am (especially you Paige, I really miss our weekly catchups). Sean, Alex, and Greg, the company is in good hands being steered by you all. And to all the other people from my Alpha days, I'm grateful to have worked with and become friends with you all: Andy, Jack, Bobby, Connor, Oren, Pete.

To my Excel friends, I love how Excel has remained a huge part of my life. Monica, Sophie, Andrew G, Andrew L, Allie; next time we're all back in Tel Aviv, we'll celebrate at the Clara together.

To my Fuqua family: it's still hard to believe I've only known you all for under two years. You all have been an incredible source of support both throughout this project and during all the other craziness pursuing an MBA during a pandemic has been. Michael and Ben, thanks for reading the book early and giving me invaluable feedback. I know it wasn't a small amount of time and effort, and it truly means so much to me. To all my amazing friends I've met here, thank you so much for supporting me in this. In alphabetical order: Adam, Alexa, Anna, Annie (honorary Fuqua), Ben, Binz, Brendan and Paige, Chris, Christian, Clay, Dana, Dent, Eddie, Emily, Farnos, Fernando, Frank, Henry, Hich, Hymanson, Jen, Kate B, Kate Z, Kirk, Kelcey, Lizzy,

Lucy, Moose, Michael G, Olivia, Ollie, Patrick, Pigott, Phong, Preetam, Rich Richards III, Ritschel, Shivani, Shyon, Taylor, Teddy, Tommy, Willa. To the third years, giving you all your own list: it means so much that you all supported me on this too, and I appreciate it so, so much. Belick, Holly, Jay, Reed, and Sravya.

Eric Koester, thanks for reaching out to me on LinkedIn and pushing me to embark on this journey. To the full New Degree Press team, thanks for all the guidance throughout this process. My editor, Sarah, you've been a fantastic guide. Sorry for all the frantic messages. Alex, Brian, Kristy, and the rest of the NDP team, thank you all for everything you did to get this book published.

Gerry, Jacob and Jay, thank you for the early praise, kind words, and advice. I didn't have many expectations reaching out to authors who I had never met, and it was incredibly kind of you both to help me. I'll be sure to pass on the good deed to any author who reaches out to me in the future, if I'm lucky enough to have a fraction of the success you both have achieved.

And to anyone else reading this who isn't listed above, thank you for buying the book and getting this far. Can't wait to hear how you liked it next time we see each other.

Made in the USA
Monee, IL
17 May 2021